I'd combed the place from one end to another and found no sign of Lissa. Where the Sam Hill could she be? Not in the showroom. Not in her office. Not in the kitchen. Not in the copier room. In the ladies' room? Abducted by aliens? Hiding in a closet? I was out of options and time. So, for giggles and squeaks, I pulled open the doors to the enormous sample closet that stretched across the back wall and peered inside. Good news. I found Lissa Charney. The question was, did she have my key?

A dozen swimsuits picture-framed Lissa's battered, bloody corpse like a museum exhibit. Ringed with matching black and purplish-blue shiners, her wide-open, sightless eyes stared into space as though surprised by her situation. No kidding. That made two of us. I was no doctor, but you didn't need a medical degree for this diagnosis. No need to take her pulse. One thing was for sure. Lissa Charney had made her last sales presentation.

Naturally, I burst out laughing.

I0693178

Praise for Susie Black

"Holly Schlivnik has attitude to spare."
~*Ellen Byerrum, author Crime of Fashion series*

"Hilarious and fun!"
~ *CeeCee James, author Flamingo Realty Mystery Series"*

"Death by Pins and Needles is a fun read."
~ *Elise Sax, author Matchmaker Mystery Series*

"Susie Black nails her latest mystery, Death by Pins and Needles."
~ *Charlotte Rains Dixon, author Emma Jean's Bad Behavior*

"Holly Schlivnik and the rest of the Yentas are back and better than ever."
~ *Kim Hunt Harris, author The Trailer Park Princess Mysteries*

Other Wild Rose Press Titles by Suzie Black:

Holly Swimsuit Mysteries Series:
Death by Sample Size, Book 1
Death by Surfboard, Book 3
Death by Cutting Table, Book 4

Death by Pins and Needles

by

Susie Black

Holly Swimsuit Mystery Series, Book Two

Death by Pins and Needles

Cover Art by *The Wild Rose Press, Inc.*

The Wild Rose Press, Inc.
PO Box 708
Adams Basin, NY 14410-0708
Visit us at www.thewildrosepress.com

Publishing History
First Edition, 2023
Trade Paperback ISBN 978-1-5092-4677-9
Digital ISBN 978-1-5092-4678-6

Holly Swimsuit Mystery Series, Book Two
Published in the United States of America

Dedication

This book is dedicated to the two most important people in my life. Thank you, Alex and Larry for your unwavering encouragement and support of my writing adventure, your remarkable patience with my incessant questions, and most of all, for making me laugh every day. You make every day a gift, an opportunity, a mystery, an adventure, and a challenge.

Chapter One

A size ten woman's foot strapped to a sexy black four-inch stiletto jammed the shoe's razor-sharp heel between the closing California Apparel Mart elevator doors. A shrill alarm rang in the car as a disembodied, nasally voice from the lobby side of the doors whined. "Can ya hold it?" Was there a choice? As if. I pressed the open button and rolled my eyes as the inconsiderate woman pushed her way into the crowded car. I checked my watch. Ten-thirty on the dot. As usual, late for work Royal Swimwear showroom manager Lissa Charney expected the rest of the industry to accommodate her lazy lifestyle.

The elevator stopped on the eleventh floor and the busty, hennaed, late -thirtyish woman with a Toucan nose and startling aquamarine eyes put her arm out the same way as a fullback going into the end zone. Rude Lissa Charney shoved aside the herd packed tight as sardines in a tin and forced her way out of the car ahead of the crowd. I followed behind her as she made her way to the Royal Swimwear showroom a few doors away from mine.

At this point, allow me to introduce myself and explain my role in this tale. I am Holly Schlivnik, one of Lissa's competitors in the Los Angeles ladies' swimwear industry and President of the junior and private label divisions of Mermaid Swimwear.

The sausage-skin-tight neon pink capris tautly stretched over Lissa's apple-shaped tush made it difficult for her to navigate the narrow aisle. She broke into a clumsy run when her telephone rang and came dangerously close to twisting an ankle in those sky-high stilettos. As though the party on the phone heard her, Lissa shouted through her door. "All right already! Hold your panties on. I'm coming."

She balanced a grease-dotted takeout paper bag with the mart deli logo printed on the front and a to-go cup of coffee in her cleavage. She slung her overstuffed hobo-style purse on her shoulder to free an arm. She scooped a gorgeous bouquet of blood-red roses nestled in a ceramic vase off the floor in front of the showroom window.

She anchored the vase in the crook of her arm while unlocking the door. She pushed the door open with a flick of her hip and ran back to her office without turning on the showroom lights or shutting the door.

Regrettably, Lissa's annoying voice carried. With her door open, no one on the entire swimwear aisle missed Lissa confirming her appointment with Sue Ellen Magee, the sharp-tongued, powerful, my time is valuable and yours isn't swimwear buyer at Bainbridge Department Stores. "Hi, Sue Ellen." Lissa's whine was a dead-ringer for Fran Fine from an old TV program, The Nanny, if Fran passed a kidney stone while answering the phone. Lissa honked out the words through her nose with the same sound of a patronizing goose with a deviated septum. "Ok. That works for me. See you soon."

****

My colleague Queenie Levine and I walked in front

of the Barely There Swimwear showroom on the way to our room. Barely There owner Annette Mason's chatty parrot Corky spied Lissa Charney seated at a workstation in the front of the Royal Swimwear showroom casually flipping through the pages of a fashion magazine. The boisterous African Gray screeched at the top of his lungs for the whole aisle to hear. "Lissa is lazy, Lissa is lazy!" Queenie and I grinned at one another. Even the bird had Lissa Charney pegged.

Lissa worked at Barely There for five years until she'd been recommended for her current position by her BFF Beverly Hills high school chum Lauren, Royal Swimwear CEO Butch Oldham's youngest daughter. Corky was the bane of Lissa's existence from her first day on the job until the minute she left the company. With a Toucan nose going for her, Lissa should have been the bird's object of affection, but it didn't turn out so.

The apple of Annette's eye, Corky freely roamed the showroom and got away with countless acts of mischief. He dive-bombed Lissa's head, pecked her nose, stole sandwiches off her plate, and embarrassed her in front of accounts with his litany of insults. Lissa left Barely There over a year ago, but from the nasty comments squawking across the aisle, her absence did not make Corky's heart grow any fonder.

As Queenie and I stopped in front of our showroom, Lissa stalked into Barely There. Professional snoops and nosy-parkers like us, we didn't rush opening our door. No love was lost between Lissa and Annette Mason. Annette blamed Lissa's departure for the steep drop in the Barely There business. No way would we miss this cinemascope and technicolor confrontation with fireworks and daggers written all over it. Corky sat perched on a credenza filled with ribbons and trophies Annette and her son Roddy won as champion water skiers. The bird made a beeline for Lissa as soon as she opened the Barely There door. Lissa batted Corky away with the rolled-up fashion magazine as he divebombed her head, aiming to peck Lissa's nose. Corky flapped his wings and squawked. "Lissa's a bad girl, Lissa's a bad girl."

"Annette," Lissa snarled. "I'm working with Sue Ellen Magee in five minutes." Lissa waved the magazine at Corky. "Please do something to keep him quiet. Can't you put him in his cage and cover it?"

Azure-blue-eyed Annette Mason's wild mop of corkscrew bleached-blonde hair billowed out below her shoulders. The tall, statuesque, fit woman in her mid-fifties resembled a human version of Big Bird.

Annette grabbed a half-empty bottle of water off a workstation table. She poured a portion of the water into a bowl for Corky and glugged the rest in one large gulp. She opened a bar-sized mini-refrigerator in the back corner, took out another bottle, and drank a third of the water. Corky lapped some of the water, hopped on Annette's shoulder, and sang. "Corky loves mommy, Corky loves mommy." Lissa rolled her eyes as Annette gave Corky a love pat on his head and cooed. "Mommy's sweet little baby boy."

Annette strode with the bird still perched on her shoulder towards the showroom entrance decorated in a parrot jungle motif. Annette stood in the center of the room and pointed to the samples hanging on a rack behind a workstation. "Sorry, no can do. Your appointment is right before ours." Annette laughed deep and throaty. "Sue Ellen adores Corky." No big surprise. Sue Ellen and Corky? A match made in heaven. The bird's nasty personality mirrored Sue Ellen's to a T. Annette glared at Lissa. "Besides, he's an important part of the presentation."

I gave Queenie the big eyes as she made the international gag sign. Is Corky presenting the line while Annette models the samples? This is one presentation I'd pay good money to see.

Annette smiled like a shark. "Corky's a lover. You're the only one he doesn't care for." Annette narrowed her eyes. "Bird's instincts warn them if someone is not a good person." Annette gave Corky another love tap and cooed." My baby boy knows who's been mean to his mommy. Right, sweetie?" On cue, Corky puffed out his chest and crooned. "Corky loves mommy. Lissa's a bad girl."

"Come on, Annette." Lissa whined crankier than a toddler who needed a nap. "Be reasonable. No one on our aisle can get anything done with Corky screeching his head off all day." Lissa held out her hands in supplication. "You're still pissed I left. It's not right for you to fault me for bettering myself."

Anger glittered in Annette's beautiful azure eyes. "Oh yeah? You did a helluva lot more. You walked out on me in the middle of the season with no warning and took my business with you."

Lissa's jaw dropped precariously close to her boobs. "You're joking, right?" Lissa snorted loud as a hog in heat. "You apparently forgot I brought *my* business with me to *your* company." Lissa's laugh took a nasty tone. "Before me, your label was appropriately named. It was *barely there* in the industry. I brought you the business.

It's not my fault you can't hold onto it." Lissa pursed her lips. "You're working with Sue Ellen, so why are you complaining?"

Annette became fascinated with the ceiling's acoustic tiles. "It's an appointment, but nothing more than a cover your ass meeting," Annette gritted her teeth. "so, I can't complain to Sue Ellen's boss her buyer hasn't shopped our line." Annette had the grace to blush. "Sue Ellen hasn't placed a single unit since you left." Annette gulped. "I'm desperate. I'll do anything. I must get back in her store."

Lissa stood in the open doorjamb and pointed at Corky. "Keep your bird quiet while I'm working or I'll shut him up myself. If you don't, one of these days you're gonna find a stuffed bird in a cage instead of a live one squawking ugly comments."

Annette put a protective left hand over Corky's head and growled. "I better not see even one feather ruffled on his head." Annette grabbed the empty water bottle with her right hand and aimed it at Lissa like a pistol. "Or I'll come gunning for you. You won't be able to hide. I. Will. Find. You. And. I. Will. Make. You. Pay. And. It. Will. Not. Be. Pretty."

Chapter Two

Annette Mason and her son Roddy walked into A Jolt of Java in the California Apparel Mart lobby as I left the barista station. I headed for the Yenta's table in the back of the store with a tray of steaming coffees. The Yentas, Joan Binder, Hope Greenberg, Queenie Levine, Sonia Wilson, and I met each workday morning for coffee at A Jolt of Java for the last two years. The now-daily event started as a once-in-a-while get-together and became the glue binding our group of colleagues together.

I distributed the beverages, and the slack-jawed Yentas stared as I retrieved my wallet from my purse and pointed to Annette and Roddy still waiting for their coffees. "I'll be right back. I have a debt to repay." I returned to the barista station and paid for Roddy and Annette's coffees.

I took my seat at the Yenta table and took a big slurp of coffee.

Vivacious, quick-witted, independent sales rep Joan Binder puckered her lips as if she'd bitten into a wedge of grapefruit. "A *debt* to repay? To who? Surely not to Roddy Mason?" Joan's reaction? Not a big shock. No one in our group relished interacting with obnoxious Roddy Mason.

I shook my head yes. "Yeah. Believe it or not, him of all people. I got to my car last night and found my right rear tire flat as a pancake. With the all-day soaker of rain yesterday, the Auto Club quoted a four-hour wait for a service call. Who's willing to wait for so many hours and maybe they never show up? Not me. I opened the trunk to change it."

Mystical Dreamer Swimwear National Sales Manager Sonia Wilson arched a brow and interrupted my story. "You can change a flat tire?"

I batted my eyes. "Can't everyone?" I grinned as sharp-tongued Mermaid division President Queenie Levine choked on her coffee. "My dad insisted all of us kids learn."

And I thank my lucky stars he did. I worked for my dad as a road rep in the deep southern states at the start of my apparel sales career. I got a flat tire several times while in the middle of the boonies. They say the Good Lord helps those who help themselves. With no mobile service or emergency roadside phones, either I waited for some Good Samaritan to come along and help me, or I changed the tire myself.

Joan tapped her index finger to the side of her head. "She's right. It's something all women ought to learn. My late husband, rest his soul, insisted I learn to do it as well. Good thing too. I've changed a few flats since I've been on the road."

Sonia looked around the table. "In high school, girls should be required to take auto shop and boys cooking."

I made the OK sign. "Absolutely. Women ought to be familiar with all the stuff under the hood of a car, and men should be capable of preparing a meal involving more than opening a can."

Queenie wrinkled her nose. "No thanks. If the Auto Club isn't an option, I'd wait for a knight in shining armor to save me." She wiggled her fingers. "No sense ruining a perfectly good manicure if it's avoidable."

Joan wrinkled her brow. "What's a flat tire got to do with Roddy Mason?"

I pointed to Roddy's backside. "I opened the trunk to get out the spare, and Roddy appears out of thin air and offers to change the tire."

Joan's squawk rivaled Corky's. "*And you let him*?"

I pursed my lips into a funnel. "The new gabardine pants I wore for the first time yesterday set me back a small fortune."

Joan narrowed her eyes. "And he actually *changed* the tire, or just acted macho?"

I whistled low. "Are you kidding? I'd put Roddy Mason against the Auto Club guys any day of the week. He changed the tire in five minutes. Mason Construction owns almost one hundred vehicles. Before he became a project foreman, Roddy said he ran the company's vehicle maintenance division."

Sonia widened her eyes. "Wow. That's an important job."

Ditzy Swimwear showroom manager Hope Greenberg asked, "Where did he learn auto repair?"

I said, "Roddy explained he always loved cars. When he was a kid, he and his dad fooled around with an old beater on weekends. Roddy took auto shop in high school. He said he's always been a physical guy and enjoyed doing things with his hands. He was never much of a student and had no interest in going to college. He went to a trade school after graduating from high school. He's a certified master mechanic."

Sonia tapped two fingers to her upper lip. "Now since you mention it, a while ago, my battery died in the mart parking lot and Roddy jump-started it for me."

Queenie slit her eyes. "Roddy offered to help you both? A major league surprise. He's normally such a jerk. He never does anything for free. Some way, this is gonna cost you." She beamed an evil grin in my direction. "Did he give you a bill? He's the type to charge."

I waved the idea away with a flick of a wrist. "Nah. I offered to pay him, but he said to buy him a cup of coffee someday. I hate being beholden to anyone, so I bought their coffee this morning."

Annette and Roddy Mason glared at each other as they sat across from one another at a table in front of ours. I jerked my chin in their direction. "When I got to the barista station, even a blind person could tell I interrupted them arguing over something. Wonder why their bloomers are in such a bunch?"

Sonia raised her hand like an eager to please school girl. "Bet I know. Yesterday I hung a bunch of new samples on the rack closest to the door. With my room across the aisle from theirs and the Mason's door open, I overheard their entire conversation. Annette told Roddy about her argument with Lissa. She finished, and Annette and Roddy duked it out in a doozy of a fight of their own."

Queenie furrowed her brow. "Fighting over…?"

Sonia's lips twitched. She was unable to contain her grin. "Lissa."

Queenie's jaw swung open wide as a gate. "And Roddy took *Lissa's* side?"

As if. A laughable idea. I snorted my coffee into a napkin. "Never happen. Those two hate each other."

Sonia smiled. "Nope. Holly's right. It's the other

way around. It sounded as if Barely There is barely there."

The four of us gave Sonia the stink eye.

Sonia tapped the side of her head and laughed. "Don't you get it? *Barely there in business*? They're in big financial trouble. Annette said since Lissa's been gone, they've lost twenty-five percent of their accounts, and the customers they still sell to are writing much smaller orders."

Joan's eyebrows rose to the middle of her forehead. "And *Lissa Charney* is the reason for their success?" Joan curled her upper lip. "Come on. Get real."

Sonia shrugged. "Yeah. That's the way Annette made it sound."

Queenie cocked a brow. "Can't be right. A few days ago, Annette accused Lissa of stealing her customers."

I snapped my fingers. "Queenie's right. Annette isn't president of Lissa's fan club"

Hope absently tapped the rim of her coffee cup with a spoon. "Lissa's been gone from Barely There for over a year. If their business is so down, why they didn't replace her?"

Sonia dipped her head. "The word on the street is they've tried, but there weren't any takers."

Joan smirked. "Maybe no one wanted to work with the bird."

Sonia gave the group the big eyes. "Annette said she made a huge mistake ever allowing Lissa to leave."

Holy Guacamole. I burst out laughing. "Oh boy. I bet Roddy pitched a fit."

Sonia laughed loud like a loon. "Roddy said if you love them lazy, Lissa is a champ. She arrived to work late, left early, and did you a favor and brought in a few accounts who owed her one."

Roddy Mason might not be the sharpest knife in the drawer, yet his take on Lissa's loosey-goosey work ethic? Accurate as a bullseye.

Sonia's eyes widened as big as the rim of her coffee cup. "Annette said, 'I don't care if she came in late, left early, or if she presented the line dressed in her bathrobe and slippers. Results are what count. And she brought the business in. She left, and the business went with her.' "

Hope gulped. "Good grief. I bet Roddy freaked."

Sonia jerked her bobblehead doll noggin up and down. "Oh, yeah. Beyond words. Annette laid out a plan to get Lissa back, and Roddy went utterly gob-smacked."

Joan slapped the table so hard that half the coffee sloshed out of her cup. "No way!"

"Yeah. Way." Sonia put her hand over her heart. "If I'm lyin', I'm dyin'."

My jaw dropped. "What did Roddy do?"

Joan muttered. "Get his mother committed?"

Sonia snorted a laugh. "Close. Roddy asked if she'd lost her mind."

No big shocker. He might be right.

Sonia said, "Roddy asked, 'How? We struggle to make payroll now.' "

Hope asked, "And Annette's response?"

Sonia widened her eyes. "She said I don't care if you and I don't eat, we're gonna find a way to pay her, even if we don't take another dime out of the business."

Queenie angled her chin towards Roddy. "With his short-fuse, I'm amazed he didn't throw a chair or something."

Sonia pursed her lips. "Annette pulled no punches. She said, 'You're not too good with numbers. Let me spell it out for you. A hundred percent of nothing is still nothing. You better put a smile on your face, keep your big mouth shut, and pray she comes back if you want us to stay in business.' "

Chapter Three

Lissa Charney, Queenie, and I got off the elevator on the eleventh floor at nine o'clock the following morning. Must be a first for Lissa. Maybe she'd finally been called out for slacking off?

Another ceramic vase with a dozen gorgeous blood-red roses stood in front of Lissa's showroom door. I inhaled the delicious fragrance and cooed sweetly as a dove. "Aren't those flowers magnificent?"

Queenie whispered. "They're incredible."

I sighed. "Such a lovely way to start a day. She gets the same delivery each morning." Jealousy tied my heartstrings into knots. I shushed Nana's lecturing voice playing inside my head. "Be careful what you wish for. Sometimes God punishes us by granting our wishes." Oh-so-wise Nana's advice would turn out to be prophetic.

Queenie clucked her tongue. "It's hard to believe a woman with such a sour personality has *anyone* in her life, let alone someone so devoted." Queenie put her hands over her ears. "And that whiny voice. A big turn-off in my book. And a *guy* finds it attractive?"

I wiggled my eyebrows. "I doubt her charming personality is responsible for those daily deliveries. Any idea who the lovesick admirer is?"

And the answer? The smart money always bets on Queenie Levine. Telephone, telegraph, tell Queenie.

Cable news has nothing on my pal, the megaphone of the mart. Remarkably, this time she proved me wrong. She shook her head no. "I've no clue. I can't wrap my head around *anyone* sending *her* flowers." Queenie grinned mischievously as an elf. "Thorns I understand. But roses? And delivered daily, no less? Come on." Queenie tapped the tip of her nose and mused out loud. "Maybe she sends them to herself."

Mental head slap. Someone as status-conscious as Lissa Charney faking having a man in her life? The possibility never occurred to me, but the scheme sounded right up her alley.

Roddy Mason held the official company title of Barely There Vice President of Production and Operations. A euphemism for chief gofer. The head foreman for his father's construction company, Roddy helped Annette out between his construction jobs.

Roddy was a big, tall man with Samson-like broad shoulders and ham-sized hands. He pulled a metal rolling rack loaded with a half-dozen gilded bird cages, an electric drill, and a nail gun down the swimwear aisle. Roddy made no attempt to slow down as Lisa bent to retrieve the flower vase. She jumped out of the way as the rolling rack brushed the backs of her knees.

"For crying out loud, Roddy." Lissa snarled. "Watch where you're going. You almost mowed me over!"

Roddy raised his left index finger, held it over his thumb, and laughed a nasty laugh. "Too bad. I missed you by thaaaat much." Roddy pointed to the roses and sneered. "Nice weeds. Does your imaginary boyfriend send them?"

Queenie gave me a *"See? I told you so."* smirk.

Lissa clucked her tongue. "Pretty rich, coming from

15

you. My boyfriend works for your father's company."

Queenie and I did a double-take. Lissa and Roddy ran in the same circles? Hard to believe.

Roddy wrinkled his nose as if he'd taken a whiff of yesterday's garbage. "A glorified flunky is the best you can do?"

Lissa sniffed. "Bobby is more man than you'll *ever* be." Rays of anger sparked from Lissa's eyes. "At least he doesn't need his *mommy's permission* for every little thing the way *you do*."

Meow. Guess they don't travel in the same circles after all.

Roddy closed his sausage-sized fingers and made a fist. He pivoted and punched a good-sized dent into one of the gilded cages. Roddy snapped. "Why throw away good money on flowers for a tramp like you?"

Lissa flicked her tongue like a snake and licked her lips. She smiled a nasty smile. "Oh, believe me, I make it worth his while."

Roddy knocked the flower vase over with the steel toe of his work boot and batted his eyes. "Oops."

Lissa patted the flowers back into the vase. "You big ape. You did that on purpose!"

Roddy bared his teeth and made a deep-throated growling sound.

Lissa pointed to the birdcages. "Annette's not bringing any more birds, is she?"

Good grief. A half-dozen cages. Imagine the racket?

Roddy adjusted the heavy tool belt slung on his wide hips and hitched his pants over his thick waist. "Nah. Don't get your panties twisted over a bunch of stuffed birds she bought at the San Diego Wild Animal Park." Roddy laughed. "Gonna drive Corky crazy. The mart office called Big Bird to remind her to check her lease. Pets are not allowed in the building." Roddy slit his eyes. "Somebody finked on her. Any idea who?"

Lissa held her hands in the air as though Roddy pointed a gun at her head. "Don't blame me. I had nothing to do with it. But it could have been anyone." She waved around the aisle. "The whole floor is ready to shoot Corky over his constant squawking."

Allison Bennett from Contemporary Casuals arrived at the Royal showroom as Roddy pulled his rack away. Roddy towered over Allison and invaded her space. He cornered her as he stopped to greet the slightly-built buyer. He smiled a toothy used car salesman's smile. "Hey Allison, good to see you. Stop by after you're done with your appointment. We added some new things to the line that are right up your alley."

I'd give a month's salary to see this performance. Godzilla presents a line of bikinis. Allison waggled a noncommittal wave as she opened the Royal door and walked towards the workstations.

Lissa cracked the door open and called, "I'll be right in. Take a seat at the work station with the samples on the grid." Lissa pulled the door closed and pushed her way in front of Roddy. She jabbed her index finger into Roddy's chest. "You've got some nerve buttonholing my account."

Roddy drew himself up to his full, imposing height. "You don't have an exclusive on her or any other customer." Roddy stood in front of the Royal door and snarled. "You better walk her to my room after your meeting is over or else. You don't wanna tick me off, or trust me, you'll be sorry."

Lissa shook her fist in Roddy's face. "You want an

appointment?" Lissa waved her mobile in the air. "Pick up the phone and dial the same way the rest of us do." Lissa turned on her heel, opened her door, and stomped to the waiting buyer.

Roddy steered the wide, packed rolling rack to the middle of the aisle and it took up most of the narrow path. I yelled, "Roddy! Look out!" He tried to avoid us, but even a strong ox-like Roddy proved unable to slow the rack's momentum.

As he passed us, the edge of Roddy's state waterskiing championship ring scratched my arm. I yelped, "Ouch!" as a thin ribbon of blood trickled out and stained my shirt sleeve. I folded the cuff and pressed my fingers onto the wound to staunch the bleeding. I yelled. "Hey, you're not the only one on the aisle!"

He didn't answer. Either he didn't hear me or he didn't care. Full steam ahead, he pushed the rolling rack into his showroom and slammed the door behind him. Guess he gave me my answer.

Chapter Four

Hope Greenberg squirmed in her seat as if a nest of fire ants was crawling around in her undies. She twitched her lips into one of those I-got-a-story-for-you-guys kind of grins. "Yesterday evening I visited my mother at the Home Sweet Home senior living facility out in the valley. You'll never guess who bumped into me in the lobby." Hope gushed the answer like a burst fire hydrant. "Lissa Charney, of all people."

Joan blew out her cheeks. "No doubt stealing their jewelry and cheating the residents out of their money."

Hope made a sour face. "No, Miss Smarty Pants. Her mother is a resident at the facility. Our mothers are both in the dementia wing and their rooms are near one another. Irene is my mother's closest friend."

Joan snarked. "Lissa Charney has a mother? You mean she's not the devil's spawn?"

Hope tsked. "I told you. My mother and Lissa's mother are friends." Hope's eyes filled. "My mother always recognizes me, but she gets confused as to who I am. Somedays I am her daughter. But mostly she lives in the past. Those days I am one of her childhood girlfriends she used to go to the movies with, and Irene Charney is the nineteen-thirties movie star, Irene Dunne. Last night Mom told me Irene left in the morning to go out on location. It always confused Mom more if I corrected her, so now I just play along."

Sonia asked, "Lissa visited her mother last night?"

Hope gave the Yentas the big eyes. "Not exactly." Hope quirked a Mona Lisa smile with a secret to reveal. "Believe it or not, Lissa has been volunteering at the home three nights a week for several years."

Joan clucked her tongue. "Volunteering for what? Teaching seniors the sneakiest way to nab an extra helping of Tapioca pudding at dinner time?"

Hope crossed her eyes. "No, of course not. Lissa said she works with the social director and teaches a memory class using music and photos."

Joan cocked a brow. "Lissa volunteers three times a week, and yet you've never run into her before last night? Sounds more like a story she pulled out of her tush to improve her lousy image."

Hope held her hands out. "No. We usually go on different nights. That's the reason I've never seen her." Hope sighed. "My mother is unable to tell one day from another. It doesn't make a difference to her which days I come. But I usually go on Mondays, Wednesdays, and Saturdays. Lissa said she goes on Tuesdays, Thursdays, and Sundays. I couldn't go this Monday. So, I went Tuesday instead."

Joan sucked in her cheeks. "She handed you a line. She's the type to ingratiate herself with the staff to get close to the residents and scam unsuspecting old people."

Hope shook her head emphatically. "Nope. She wore a striped volunteer's uniform and a security badge hung around her neck."

Sonia asked, "Where did you run into Lissa?"

Hope said, "I bumped into her in the lobby on my way out. She asked whether I'd just arrived or was I leaving. I told her I'd already visited Mom and was on my way out. She had a break between two sessions and asked if I had time for coffee. I wasn't in a hurry, so I joined her. She gave me some helpful ideas for improving Mom's memory issues. She said my mom was in her next session, and she'd give her some special attention." Hope shook her head. "Same annoying voice. But this was not the whiny pain in the tush from the mart I avoid like the plague. I discovered a nice person buried under a grating personality. We chatted a bit about nothing in particular. News, weather, and sports. But by the way she squirmed around in her seat, even a blind person could see something was on her mind." Hope surveyed the table. "Lissa and I say hello if we happen to bump into one another in the mart. Nothing more. So, her seeking me out seemed rather weird."

Sonia bit her lower lip. "Maybe telling a stranger something difficult is easier than confiding in a friend?"

I dipped my head. "Does she have any other family besides her mother? A sister or an aunt to reach out to?"

Queenie tapped the tip of her nose with her index finger. "I'm pretty sure her father is dead. And for some reason or other, I wanna say she lives with her older brother out in Van Nuys?"

Joan hooted like a barn owl. "*Van Nuys*? Are you sure?" Joan poked herself in the chest. "I'm from the valley. Van Nuys is a boring, cookie-cutter valley town. Trust me. Nothing special ever happens in Van Nuys." Joan laughed with derision. "The streets roll up at 8:00 at night. Van Nuys is a hum-drum, ordinary burg beneath the full-of-herself Lissa Charney. Lissa's waaaay too much of a snob to live in such a pedestrian town. She's always bragging that she comes from Beverly Hills and all the movie stars' kids she went to Beverly Hills high school with." Joan made a sour face. "She and Butch Oldham's daughter *Lauren* became chummy while they both attended that snooty patootie school."

Sonia patted her cheeks. "Hold the phone girls. Queenie's right. Lissa does live in the valley with her brother." Sonia toasted Queenie with her coffee cup. "I'd forgotten until you jogged my memory. Two seasons ago, Lissa was in the booth next to mine at the Miami Swimwear Market. On the last day of the trade show, the convention center was so dead, you could bowl down the main aisle and not hit a buyer. Out of either boredom or desperation, Lissa and I started chatting. I don't remember the way the subject came up, but the part of town we lived in did. Lissa said she grew up in Beverly Hills, but moved in with her brother in the valley to save enough money for a new car."

Queenie counted back on her fingers. "If she's still in the valley, she's been living at her brother's house going on for three years."

Joan snarked. "Is she saving for a Rolls?"

Hope crossed her eyes. "Lissa complained about the distance between Beverly Hills and Van Nuys." Hope squinted. "Maybe I remembered it wrong?" She wagged her index finger. "Wait a minute." Hope dug around in her purse. "We exchanged personal contact information in case we noticed something not right with the other one of our mothers. She gave me the top of a bank deposit slip." Hope pulled a crumpled paper out of her wallet. "Nope. I'm right. Lissa Charney 6747 Ventura Canyon Avenue. Van Nuys, California 91402." Hope narrowed her eyes. "I missed this before. This is odd." She pointed to the bottom of the address. "Look at this. Below the street address is a Post Office Box. PO Box 1123 Beverly

Hills, California 90210"

Joan's eyes sparkled with delight. "Miss Priss Charney might be ashamed to admit it, but she's no longer a Beverly Hills prima donna." Joan clucked her tongue. "Prancing around as though she's better than the rest of us, as if hers doesn't stink. But the reality is she's just a plain old valley girl like me."

Sonia touched Hope's arm and prompted. "The story?"

Hope fluttered her fingers. "Oh, yeah. Right. Sorry. Anyhoo, I've no idea why she picked me of all people to pour her heart out to. But wow. This turned out to be one heck of a story. Lissa starts out rambling and made no sense. It was more like she was talking to herself and not me. She said maybe she'd been wrong. Maybe Eileen Hirsch had the right idea." Hope scrunched her eyes. " It was so darned weird. Nor did I know Eileen Hirsch from a hole in the ground." Hope blinked wide-eyed. "Then out of the blue, she said something completely off the wall. She says maybe being gay *is* the right way. She asked if it's possible to turn yourself into a gay person?" Hope hiccupped a nervous laugh. "You can imagine my reaction. Stunned speechless, to say the least."

Queenie's jaw dropped to the rim of her saucer. "You're kidding, right? "Hope entwined her baby fingers and tugged. "Nope. Pinky swear. I'm telling the Gospel truth." She held out her hands. "Could I make up such a crazy story?"

Not in a million years.

Hope queried the table. "Anyone know an Eileen Hirsch?"

Queenie pointed her index finger at herself. "Eileen is a showroom manager for a junior sportswear line on the thirteenth floor."

Sonia asked, "If this Eileen's not in swimwear, how do they know one another?"

Joan shrugged. "Maybe they went to school together."

As usual, telephone, telegraph, tell Queenie Levine, AKA the mouth of the mart, was the usual go-to for answers. "No. Eileen is from back east. A small town in upstate New York. It's an odd name. And for some reason, I wanna say it has something to do with apparel." She squeezed her eyes closed trying to recall the name of the town. She snapped her fingers and announced triumphantly, "Gloversville."

Hope turned to Queenie. "She a friend of yours?"

Queenie shook her head. "No. Eileen and I went to fashion school together. We shared the same patternmaking teacher. Eileen was a whiz. She whipped them out perfectly. And me?" Queenie tapped her chest and laughed at herself. "Incapable of even tracing one properly to save my life. Our teacher asked Eileen to tutor me. If not for Eileen, I'd have failed the class and had to repeat it to graduate. Thanks to Eileen, I ended up with a B in the class. We'd meet in the patternmaking room three days a week for two hours after school. We had nothing in common besides school, so we didn't become friends. But while we worked, we shared some of the details of our lives. Eileen is the youngest of five siblings from a blue-collar family. She is the first to go to college. If I remember correctly, she said her sisters are all married with a bunch of kids, and her dad and brothers are carpenters. She never mentioned her mother. Maybe her mom is dead?"

Sonia frowned. "It's unusual for a small-town kid to

move across the country to a big city. Maybe some of her family is in L.A.?"

Queenie tapped her nose with her index finger. "Nah. Not in so many words, but she gave the impression there was a big falling out between Eileen and her family, and she came west to get away from them."

Joan asked, "And Lissa and Eileen's connection is…?"

Queenie said, "Lissa and Eileen worked together years ago for a short time as assistant buyers at Bobby Shops. I guess they stayed friends."

Hope continued with her story. "Anyway, Lissa said a month ago, she and Eileen went away on a long weekend together to New Mexico. They walked past Kit Carson's house in Taos and out of the clear blue sky, Eileen pushed Lissa against the sidewall of the museum and kissed her hard on the lips. Lissa said at first, she stood still as a statue. She was too stunned to react. Then Eileen whispered, 'I've wanted to kiss you since the first day I met you.' Lissa said she tried not to hurl and slapped Eileen across the face. Lissa said she screamed. 'Are you crazy?' She ran to the rental car and didn't care if she stranded Eileen. She drove back to the hotel, packed her bag, and took the first flight to LA. She said Eileen has been calling her nonstop for almost a month, but she hasn't taken any of the calls." Hope shivered. "Eileen's last voicemail scared her the most. This isn't over. If I can't have you, nobody will."

Chapter Five

I gulped at the highlighted specials on the menu. Abgoost? Mirza Ghassemi? Tahchin? I struggled to pronounce any of the dishes, let alone have the courage to try one. Visions of a takeaway pepperoni pizza with a pint of a Rocky Road chaser danced in my head. Blame it on a brain fart for me to have agreed to meet my friend Christine at Ali Baba's Persian restaurant in the San Fernando Valley.

Chris said she wanted to try something different, to spread her wings, and be daring. This is from a woman who wouldn't take a chance with extra spicy salsa on a chicken burrito. I fluttered the menu like an opera fan. "Which one of these exotic delicacies tickles your fancy?"

Chris blew the air out of her cheeks. "I dunno. I can't tell one from another." Fanfreakingtastic. "Miss I want to spread my wings and be daring" was as clueless as me. How do you make a selection? Close your eyes and throw a dart?

Chris waved to get the attention of a waiter standing at the bar. "Let's ask the server to make a few recommendations." Note to self: make it an extra-large pizza and a quart of Rocky Road. You owe me bigly for this little walk on the wild side. Spread her wings? Be daring? My Aunt Fanny's tush. But, since I didn't come up with a better idea, I agreed. "Ok. Sounds good." Yeah, right. I better get triple friend points for this nutty escapade. Additional note to self: don't allow Chris to pick another restaurant for at least a decade.

As the server left to put in the order of our mystery meal, Lissa Charney and a swarthy-complexioned man followed the hostess through the crowded restaurant to a table for two in front of us. Lissa had a deer in the headlight expression as I waved hello.

Chris angled her head at Lissa and her companion. "Friends of yours?"

I shook my head no. "Nah. Not even acquaintances. The woman is a competitor who works on my aisle in the mart, but I don't recognize the guy."

I'd soon learn that as an industrious Iranian immigrant, Lissa's boyfriend Reza Javadi, called by his Americanized name Bobby, worked construction during the week at a company owned by Annette Mason's husband, and sold cars at a dealership on weekends.

After the waiter left to put in their dinner orders, Bobby smiled wanly and brushed Lissa's lips with a kiss. "I'm sorry I'm late. I had an appointment with an immigration attorney, and it took a lot longer than I expected."

Lissa squawked with surprise. "Immigration attorney? Don't you carry a green card?"

Bobby dipped his head. "I do. But I received a letter from INS saying they found a problem with my status. I didn't understand the issue. A confusing letter from the INS is not something to take any chances with, so I went to a lawyer." Bobby gulped. "My paperwork has an issue they say invalidates the green card and they might deport me." Bobby's eyes filled. "It's impossible for me to go back to my country. The government will persecute me.

They're a bunch of radical religious nuts."

Lissa tsked. "Boo-Boo, that's awful." Lissa covered Bobby's hand with hers. "What can you do?"

He said, "If they rule in favor of deportation, the lawyer explained I'll be granted a hearing before they throw me out of the country. I can appeal their decision based on my length of stay here. I contribute to society. I don't take welfare and I'm not a burden on the state. I work at a full-time job and my employer will vouch for me. I've never been in trouble with the law. I pay my bills and my taxes. If they choose to deport me, of course, I'm gonna fight it. The lawyer said my case is a good one, but he offered no guarantees except for one."

Bobby's fingers brushed the small box he'd put on the table between them. Desperation and hope laced his tone. "If I marry a US citizen, they have to let me stay."

Lissa smiled, but the smile never made it to her eyes. "I'm sorry, but I can't help you."

Bobby opened the box and took out a platinum engagement ring with a tiny diamond solitaire. Lissa pulled her hand away as he tried to put the ring on her finger. "Lissa, please. Just listen before you say no. This can be a marriage of convenience if you want. Divorce me the minute the problem gets straightened out." Panic raised his voice from a baritone to the high squeak of a strangling mouse. "The lawyer said even though I had a good case, at best, it's only fifty-fifty I'd win the appeal. If I lost the appeal, I'm done. Deportation is guaranteed. You're my only chance. I'm begging you. If you say no and I get deported, my life is over. The government is run by extremist Muslim clerics. I'm an infidel to them. I'll be tried for trumped-up charges in a kangaroo court. And no matter the strength of my defense, I guarantee you that I'll be convicted. If they don't execute me, they'll jail me and throw away the key."

Lissa waved off the waiter carrying the tray with their meals. From the sound of her end of the conversation, she didn't plan on staying long enough to eat. "I'm sorry about this huge problem of yours. You don't deserve it. You're a nice guy." Lissa stood and leaned over to kiss him on the cheek. "I hope it works out ok for you. I don't blame you for hating me, but I'm not willing to be the solution to your problem. Good luck to you, but this is goodbye. Please don't contact me trying to change my mind. I won't."

Lissa grabbed her purse and walked to the restaurant's front door. No one in the restaurant missed Reza Javadi's scream. "Have you no heart? Don't you have a conscience? If I get sent back and die, this is on your head! You selfish bitch. I will get you for this."

Wow. Whoda thunk? This evening ended as quite an unexpected adventure. Delicious and exotic mystery food. And a floor show. Revised memo to self: Better let Chris pick the restaurants from now on.

Chapter Six

I waved good morning to Annette and Roddy Mason seated at two tables from the Yentas while I distributed coffees to the group anxiously waiting for their cuppa. I turned to Joan and did a double-take. She was oddly dressed in paint-splattered overalls and torn sneakers. She might have taken the Friday casual dress thing a little too far? I grinned. "Next Friday you coming to work in your bathrobe and slippers?"

Joan snorted and slapped the table. "Aren't you a riot? Such humor. Amazing. And before any coffee. For your information Miss Smarty Pants, I'm in the middle of redecorating the showroom. I've been working since the crack of dawn. I was too lazy to change back into my regular clothes to meet you girls for coffee."

Joan winced as she grabbed her coffee with a bandaged left hand. Some of the coffee sloshed onto her overalls and blended in with a large stain of dried blood.

I pointed to the blood splotched on the front of Joan's overalls. "What did you do to yourself?"

Joan held out her bandaged left hand. "I rushed cutting a piece of wood and didn't pay attention to the grainline. I overcompensated, and cut a little too close to a corner and nicked my hand." She smiled and patted the front of her stained overalls. "It's not as bad as it seems. But it took a few minutes to staunch the bleeding."

Hope said, "Tell us about the changes you're

making."

Joan proudly puffed out her chest. "Putting in two additional work-stations, re-racking all the workstation walls, building a changing room for the models, a second level in the back closet for samples, and re-painting the room."

Queenie squeaked like a mouse. "And you're doing all this *yourself*?"

Joan grinned wide as a Jack O'Lantern. "You betcha."

Hope's eyes bugged. "You're kidding. You're not hiring a contractor?"

Joan waggled her fingers. "Nope. Doing it all with my own two hands. Even if I had the money for a contractor, which I don't, hiring one is not a good option. Most of them are too slow, do slipshod work, and are unreliable. Who wants to chase a guy all over town if he doesn't finish the project and I've already paid him for most of it?"

Hope stared at Joan as though she'd been speaking Swahili. "And you're doing everything *yourself*? How?"

Joan said, "After my late husband and I married, we bought a Spanish-style fixer-upper in the Beverly Hills flats for a song. My handy Andy husband taught me to paint, carpentry, and plumbing. We both had full-time jobs, so, we worked on the house nights and weekends. It took us six months of hard work to complete, but we did all the repairs and additions on our own. Everything, that is, except for the electrical stuff or putting a new roof on."

Sonia smirked. "Afraid of heights?"

Joan blushed as she laughed. "As a matter of fact, yes. We both had a problem with heights, so forget about roofing. And with the electrical stuff? Who wants to take the risks? Any mistakes and the house burned down."

Queenie pointed a manicured finger into her cleavage. "Any time I get the urge to redo my condo, I go into Designer Depot. I wander around the aisles, look at all the strange doohickies and foreign gadgets for a few hours until the urge passes." She made an abracadabra motion and laughed. "I get home and poof, it's a miracle. The house is magically fine exactly as is."

Joan, a smart, petite single mother of two teen-aged daughters, had been the Royal Swimwear showroom manager for almost twenty years. Arnie Silverberg, the original owner, retired and sold the company to a big conglomerate and the new management hired Butch Oldham as CEO.

Butch hired David and Queenie to run design, merchandising, and sales. A few years later, Metro Mannequins modeling agency owner Lauren Oldham convinced her father to fire old school Joan Binder and replace her with Lauren's BFF from Beverly Hills high school, Lissa Charney. The talk on the Yenta hotline as to the reason for Lissa's surprising big promotion? Payback. A reward for pressuring all her garment industry friends to use Lauren's modeling agency.

After getting let go, Joan reinvented herself as a multi-line independent sales rep. I studied Joan over the rim of my cup. The dark circles under her eyes and the slouchy shoulders spoke legions. Having been a road rep myself at the start of my apparel career, I needed no convincing. Traveling for a living is one rough road. Add raising two teenage girls alone to the mix and things were a lot more complicated. My heart ached for my friend. I cocked a cautious brow. "Out on the road still tough as always?"

Joan rubbed her arms and winced. "I'm not gonna lie. Ya do whatever it takes to make it happen, but it's tough. I've been at it a while now and I've done ok. But I've paid my dues with my blood, sweat, and tears. Life on the road? The good news is I'm my own boss, but believe me, it's a hard way to earn a buck." She pinched her lips and made a sour face as though she'd bitten into a wedge of lemon. "I hate the traveling, especially the crappy motel rooms, and the greasy restaurant food."

She sighed. "Most of all, I hate being away from the girls. My mother and sister pinch hit for me. But if a girl needs to talk, a girl wants her mother, not her auntie or her nana. But now I'm not always around if they need me."

I tapped my lower lip. "When I was a rep on the road in the south, I lived in Atlanta and traveled six states. None of the states were as big as California neither in square miles nor population, so, I had to cover every part of the territory in order to sell a lot of product to enough accounts to make it worth my while. I was, of course, single with no children to worry about. But until I scheduled my appointments so that I deadheaded to the farthest point and worked my way back to Atlanta by Thursday night, I didn't have much of a life beyond my job. On Fridays I only did day trips of a hundred-mile radius of Atlanta. Once I did that, I was able to have a personal life. Maybe you can rearrange your trips and do something like that to be home a bit more."

Joan nodded. "That's a good idea, but it isn't nearly enough. I've got to change the entire way I run my business and be home most of the time, or God knows how my girls will turn out. I'm already racked with enough guilt being away so much of the time. And now with the oldest one in high school, I'm walking the floors at night worrying about a way to pay for college in three years."

Hope winced. "Joan, I don't mean to pry, but with two kids to protect, didn't you and your husband have life insurance?"

Joan squeezed her lips into a thin line. "My husband didn't plan on dying young. Who does? At thirty-five, he worked out three times a week, ate healthily, and other than an occasional beer with his golf buddies, he didn't drink, smoke, or do drugs. In other words, he was the picture of health who should have lived long enough to become a crotchety old man.

He figured he had plenty of time to plan, but he turned out to be dead wrong. He suffered a massive heart attack on the golf course and keeled over dead at the ninth hole. Unfortunately, he planned for nothing. He left me with two babies, a mountain of bills, and no life insurance."

Sonia's eyes lit. "My kids are only a little younger than yours. Have you heard of the California Scholarshare 529 Program?" Joan shook her head no. Sonia grinned and rubbed her hands together. "Do yourself a favor and go on line and read about it. This is a fantastic tax-free program. You can sock away a fortune even if you've only got a few years to save before your oldest goes to college. Your mother and sister can contribute too. You can use the money for tuition, books, even some housing. You can withdraw up to ten grand a year tax free for any state or private school in the country if you use it specifically for tuition. Check it out. It could be the answer to your college finance problem."

Joan smiled. "Holy cow. That sounds like it could save my bacon. Thank you so much. I'll look into it tonight."

She surveyed the table. "It's not as if I'm unsuccessful. I am doing well. But it's not your earnings that count. It's only what you keep that matters. Road expenses and my showroom rent are through the roof. If you're on commission, it's always feast or famine. Commissions aren't paid until the orders ship, so the income isn't steady. God forbid an emergency happens in the first half of the season, and I'm screwed. You write the orders as fast as possible, but not all accounts take goods in early. You might write the order in October, but if the store doesn't take the goods in until March, you don't get paid until five months later when the order is shipped. But your monthly bills still come due all the same. I get a small advance against commissions from two of my lines that barely cover my road expenses, but it's not enough to pay for anything else." She grinned, "Like food, the phone, and the power bill."

Joan wrinkled her forehead. "The house is free and clear, but if things don't dramatically improve income-wise pretty fast, I'll be forced to refinance the place."

Joan patted the front of her overalls. "Cutting my expenses by being home more and traveling less is the reason I'm remodeling. My goal is to get as many of my accounts as possible to work with me in the mart and not in their stores. I'm unable to control when my accounts take in goods, but I can control my expenses. I'll still go to all the regional markets, but if it goes as planned, this remodeling ought to cut my expenses and weeks on the road by forty percent by the end of the year."

Lissa Charney left the barista station and stalked to

our table. She scowled at Joan and whined. "Are you gonna be drilling and hammering much longer? I can't work with an account, much less hear myself think, with such a racket."

Joan's glare at Lissa? Strong enough to bend a steel beam. "Gee, Leesa, you don't usually stroll into the building this early. You must be under the boss's microscope."

Lissa twitched her nose and sniffed like she'd smelled a fart. "You ought to be more considerate of your neighbors and do the banging and drilling at night."

Joan snarled. "If you didn't steal my job at Royal, I wouldn't be remodeling. And then your poor sensitive ears wouldn't suffer from all the racket."

Lissa gave Joan the stink eye. "Oh, get over yourself, Joan. I didn't steal anything from you. I didn't need to." Lissa gave her gloriously hennaed hair a melodramatic toss. "You couldn't change with the times and lost the job all on your own."

She huffed. "And for the record, my name is Lissa, not Leesa. Same as Melissa, but leave off the Muh." Without giving Joan a chance to reply, Lissa, not Leesa, turned on her heel and stomped to the coffee store exit. The Yentas sat stunned into silence as their eyes followed Lissa's, not Leesa's, backside disappear into the mart lobby.

Joan spat the words out as though they were watermelon seeds. "Payback is a bitch. The word on the street is the profitability numbers for the last three quarters Butch Oldham gave to his management are as bogus as a three-dollar bill. Butch is in big trouble and getting fired any minute. The days of Butch and his daughter protecting Lissa Charney are over. The only ass

Butch Oldham is interested in saving is his own."

Joan pointed her coffee cup at Queenie. "Remember David and Butch's relationship at Royal? Tight as ticks. If Butch gets the boot, your boss David will be his first call. I bet the farm he'll finagle a job at Mermaid." Joan laughed sardonically. "The day he arrives, better update your resume."

Joan's eyes turned as hard as diamonds. "Let's see lazy Lissa Charney get along without Oldham's protection." Joan jabbed a stubby finger into the center of her chest. "She got my job on a lucky break, but she's pissed off a lot of people." Anger darkened Joan's eyes to coal. "What goes around, comes around. Don't be surprised if something bad happens to her."

Chapter Seven

Countries were formed faster than the pace of the never-ending parade of pie charts and problems at our weekly production meeting. The endurance test snore-fest began at the usual time, Friday right after lunch. But with the number of pressing issues to be dealt with, the meeting lasted a lot longer than normal. It finally ended an eternity later at four-forty-five.

I grabbed my purse and messenger bag, and ran out of the factory as if my hair caught fire. I drove like a bat out of hell to the mart. I checked my watch for the bazzillionth time while stuck behind a local DASH bus creeping along at a snail's pace on Main Street.

I finally drove past Ninth Street and made an illegal left turn into the mart. I careened around the subterranean parking structure ramp on two wheels and screeched to a halt into the first open space. The elevator Goddess smiled at me, and I miraculously got to the swimwear floor at five-fifteen.

I had fifteen minutes to prepare for my meeting with Sue Ellen Magee to present the promotional program she requested I put together. And of course, the one available time in her majesty's busy schedule to review the presentation? Five-thirty on Friday afternoon.

Good thing my social life is in a dry spell. Ok, ok, so it's non-existent, but let's not quibble over small details. If one existed, it would not be Sue Ellen's problem if I had to break a date. It begs the question. Did she ever go out on one? As if. Is Cruella de Ville's dance card full? Catty? Too bad. Meow.

I made my way down an empty swimwear aisle. Not a surprise. Fridays the whole industry gets out of Dodge early. Patti, our showroom manager, scribbled a note on the back of an old invoice and taped it on the front of the door. She left unexpectedly early to get her sick kid from preschool.

Crap on a crumpet. In my rush to get to the mart, I left the showroom key in my office desk drawer. I didn't remember it until I got halfway to the mart, but couldn't turn back to get it. But it was no biggie. Patti practically lived in the showroom. Except for today. Fanfreakingtastic.

A delivery notification was taped next to Patti's note. With no one else around, the guy left the package of fabric swatches for my meeting with Sue Ellen at Lissa Charney's showroom. My heart sank. Cripes, of all the competitors to leave it with, he chose the one who closes shop the earliest. Unless by some miracle Lissa stayed late, count me screwed.

I called Queenie but her phone rang and rang. No one at the mart office answered either. No point in calling mart security. They don't have a master key. Friday night. The whole world is in party mode except me, thanks to Sue Ellen Magee.

I scrounged in my purse for something to jimmy the lock with. Nothing but a nail file. Oh, yeah. Dandy. Not. Explaining this key thing to crabby Sue Ellen ought to be scads of fun. About the same as an appendectomy with no anesthetic.

Think, think. I strained my brain for a solution. Of

course! I snapped my fingers and relief calmed my pounding heart. Lissa had our spare key. Hot diggity dog. Most of the swimwear vendors on the eleventh floor were in the same showrooms for years. We are friendly competitors who keep an eye out for one another. We all exchanged keys with a neighbor in case of an emergency. Royal and Mermaid personnel exchanged keys years ago.

I walked to Lissa's showroom in case God made a mistake, and by some miracle, she'd hung around. The Royal showroom lights were dark, but the internal ones leading to the offices blazed bright as a beacon. For the heck of it, I pushed on Lissa's door. Remarkably, it opened. Hallelujah. Amazingly, the fabric Goddess covered my play. My envelope with the fabric swatches lay on the first workstation table. Now for the key, and I'd be all set.

"Lissa," I called out, "It's Holly from Mermaid. I came for my package. Thanks a bunch for accepting it. Listen, Patti left early, and I forgot my showroom key at the factory. Can you give me my spare?" Dead silence. Weird. Maybe she's on the phone with her office door closed?

"Lissa!" I funneled my hands around my mouth into a megaphone and yelled at the top of my lungs. "*It's Holly Schlivnik from Mermaid.*" Still a whole lotta dead air. God short-changed me in the height department at four feet nine inches tall, but the Good Lord compensated for it by blessing me with a strong set of pipes. Unless the woman was deaf as a post, there was no way she couldn't hear me.

The clock said eight minutes left. Crap. Buyers in this industry are famous for keeping vendors waiting.

My luck, I get the one who's never late. I stuck my head out in the hall. Thank God. Lady Luck smiled down on me. No Sue Ellen. If the congestion goddess loved me, the Queen of Mean sat stuck in Friday night rush hour traffic with the rest of the homebound Angelinos.

Since hollering my head off failed to get her attention, I went back to Lissa's office. The lights were on, but nobody was home. Her beige leather purse sat on the desk with her keys on top of it. I jangled the chain. Lots of keys, but none of them mine. I slid my fingers over the grainy purse to move it out of the way, and my digits got coated with dust. Weird. I opened all the drawers and rooted around her desk, but I found no key.

Her jacket lay haphazardly draped on her chair behind the desk. She obviously hadn't left for the day. But I'd combed the place from one end to another and found no sign of Lissa.

Where the Sam Hill could she be? Not in the showroom. Not in her office. Not in the kitchen. Not in the copier room. In the ladies' room? Abducted by aliens? Hiding in a closet?

I was out of options and time. So, for giggles and squeaks, I pulled open the doors to the enormous sample closet that stretched across the back wall and peered inside. Good news. I found Lissa Charney. The question was, did she have my key?

A dozen swimsuits picture -framed Lissa's battered, bloody corpse like a museum exhibit. Ringed with matching black and purplish-blue shiners, her wide-open, sightless eyes stared into space as though surprised by her situation. No kidding. That made two of us. I was no doctor, but you didn't need a medical degree for this diagnosis. No need to take her pulse. One thing was for sure. Lissa Charney had made her last sales presentation.

Naturally, I burst out laughing. Before you label me incredibly weird or stone-cold, let me just say in my defense that genetics is not all it's cracked up to be. If you're lucky, you inherit your aunt Bertha's sexy long legs or your father's ability to add a bazillion dollar order in his head and get the total correct to the last penny.

It's easy to spout millions of fabulous traits inheritable by the luck of the draw. Did I get those sexy long legs or the ability to add past two plus two without a calculator? Noooooooooo! Lucky me. I inherited my nana's fear of death we both overcompensated with the nervous habit of laughing. Think Bozo the Clown eulogizing your favorite aunt.

With her jaw broken, Lissa's mouth hung loosely open like the drawbridge to a castle. A gaping hole revealed four front teeth missing. A deep indentation from whatever the killer used to punch Lissa's lights out cratered her right cheek. Even though she faced straight ahead, she appeared as a silhouette.

Lissa's face? A catastrophe. Something else stared at me, but I had no luck putting my finger on it. What was it? I leaned in for a closer look. Her hair. Yikes. Her beautiful hennaed hair had turned an ugly dirty dishwater brown. Was that her natural color or did she dye it? Nah. A woman so vain exchanged a gorgeous hennaed shade for one so dull and lifeless? Not in a million years.

Her arms and legs were covered with ugly bruises. She'd been shot through the heart with a nail gun. The blood-drenched body was nailed by its appendages crucifixion-style and attached to the back of the closet. A swimsuit dangled from each of the nails impaled in her body, so she resembled a macabre store window display.

A thin ribbon of blood oozed out of a small puncture wound from her jugular vein and cascaded down the side of her neck in the shape of a snake. Something smaller than a nail was embedded in her neck but was buried too deeply for identification.

Considering her ghastly wounds, she probably bled out in minutes. Yet, other than on her body, there was not much blood. No blood in the hallway and not much in the closet. Either the murder took place somewhere else and the killer brought her back to the mart, or, if it occurred in the showroom, the killer cleaned the place rather thoroughly.

The blood stained her dress in a design as though it had been tie-dyed. From its configuration, it appeared as though she'd been folded in half to fit into the closet, then straightened out and hung. The heel of one of her stilettos snapped off as though she'd been running. Apparently, she hadn't run fast enough. Lissa lost the war, but she'd put up one helluva fight.

The only thing left to do for Lissa Charney? Call the cops. I closed the closet door and almost crapped my pants as I backed into a rather irate Sue Ellen Magee.

Sue Ellen snarled. "I've been standing outside your showroom like an idiot for over ten minutes waiting for you to grace me with your presence. You're a piece of work, Schlivnik. You're late for our appointment, and yet you come over here to schmooze?" Sue Ellen leaned around me and craned her neck tortoise-style. "Where is Lissa anyway?"

I resisted the urge to open the closet door. "She's had an…" I struggled to describe it and stumbled out, "a-a-accident. We need to call the police."

Sue Ellen tsked. "If she's been in an accident, call

nine-one-one and get the paramedics."

An involuntary shudder rattled my bones as the vision of Lissa's battered body nailed to the closet wall flitted across my memory. "Trust me, she's way beyond their capabilities to help."

Chapter Eight

Two LAPD uniforms arrived ten minutes later. I led the cops to the closet and identified Lissa Charney as the victim. They separated Sue Ellen and me and interviewed us to get our stories.

I pitied the rookie patrolman stuck interviewing Sue Ellen. Five minutes with her, and he'd consider leaving his law enforcement career for something less stressful. Perhaps lion-taming.

After we gave our statements, the older of the two officers called it in. LAPD homicide detective Akira Jane "AJ" Yakamura arrived twenty minutes behind the uniforms. Flat-chested, average height and pencil-thin, nearsighted, ex-tobacco fiend and gum popping Detective Yakamura surprised many with her potty mouth and sarcastic sense of humor.

Detective Yakamura raised her eyebrows as she stopped next to me seated at the front workstation. The detective and I go way back. AJ is married to Buster Schumansky, the local LA sales rep I worked with at Ditzy Swimwear.

AJ chomped a wad of gum with her pointy front teeth with the chop of a beaver and blew a bubble the size of a tennis ball. She popped the bubble and rolled her eyes. "I'm not even a bit surprised to find you in the middle of this."

I cringed as she quipped. "Around the cop shop,

you're referred to as M times three, as in the *murder magnet of the mart.*"

Fanfreakingtastic. A smart-aleck cop. But regrettably, I couldn't argue with the detective. Remarkably, finding Lissa's corpse isn't my first rodeo. Not long ago, I discovered the bodies of buyer Bunny Frank and swimwear designer Louis Chennault in the mart.

When the cops wrongfully accused my colleague Sonia Wilson of Bunny's murder, I donned my sleuthing hat, investigated on my own, and the murderer went after me. Turns out both murders were committed by the same killer. I solved the two crimes and captured the killer, but I still barely escaped with my life.

The uniforms led the detective back to the storage closet. Since no one paid me any attention, nosy parker Schlivnik followed discretely behind.

The detective let out a surprised gasp as the older of the uniforms opened the closet doors. AJ said to no one in particular, "I started my career as a beat cop on Hollywood and Vine. Believe me, I've seen my share of crazy crime scenes." AJ shuddered. "But even for LALA land, this is a bizarre one."

AJ studied the entry points of the wounds made by the nails and walked back and forth from the beginning of the hallway to the closet. She measured the distance between the hallway and the closet to calculate a trajectory, but the numbers didn't add up.

AJ addressed the uniforms. "From the amount of blood on the body, the victim was shot at close range. Considering the condition of the body, the lack of blood in the hallway says either the murder occurred someplace else and the killer hung the victim in the closet post mortem. Or, if the vic was incapacitated at the crime scene and killed here, the murderer sure cleaned the place up."

I gave myself a mental pat on the back. For an amateur detective, I hit all the right marks.

Yakamura slipped on a pair of thin surgical gloves she took out of the inside breast pocket of her blazer. She perched a pair of coke bottle-thick eyeglasses on the wide expanse of her flat nose.

She compared the nail wounds to the wound on Lissa's neck. Yakamura stood as close as possible to examine the wound. She squinted and rotated her head to the side, setting her eyes vertical to the neck wound. "Something's lodged deep inside. The puncture on the victim's jugular isn't a nail wound. The wounds differ in size and circumference. From the angle of the blow on the jaw, our perp is left-handed."

I spun my mental Rolodex. I counted at least a half-dozen southpaws on the eleventh floor of the mart, including me.

AJ took a small notebook out of her jacket pocket and scratched a few illegible lines. She closed the closet door and walked back into the showroom. Since Sue Ellen came in at the end of the movie, she couldn't offer much information.

The normally pushy buyer turned sheet white and sat meek as a lamb waiting patiently for AJ to dismiss her. When Yakamura finally allowed her to leave, Sue Ellen practically pole-vaulted out of the showroom. Guess a corpse in the closet gave the big bad bully buyer the willies. Geesh, such a first-class wimp. Who'd ever guess Attila the Hun turned out to be such a weenie? On her way out she rather politely asked me to call her

Monday to reschedule our appointment. The murder had shaken the bitch of bikinis to her foundations. Normally, the demanding Queen of Mean insisted nothing, including a police matter, interfere with one of her meetings. Instead, Sue Ellen flew out the door as though she'd been launched by a canon.

"Quite a nervous Nelly." AJ's eyes followed Sue Ellen two-stepping double-time as her backside disappeared down the hall. "You can always tell who's a newbie."

I cringed as the detective angled her head in the direction of the closet and laughed. "Not a professional murder magnet like you, kiddo." AJ took copious notes as I repeated the same story I told the uniform. She blew a bubble the size of an infant's head and popped it. She motioned to the envelope laying on the workstation table. "This the reason you're here?"

I nodded yes. "Yep. But I also needed Lissa to give me the key to our showroom."

AJ squinted her confusion. "She has your key? Why?"

I pointed my index fingers in opposite directions. "We traded keys with her for emergencies. Our production meeting ran late this afternoon. I was in a hurry to get to the mart for an appointment with Sue Ellen. Half-way here, I realized I left my key at the factory by mistake. I didn't have enough time to drive back to get it. Our showroom is always manned, so it didn't matter. But unbeknownst to me, our showroom manager left early. Fortunately, I remembered Lissa had our spare. I walked into her open room, but found no Lissa, so, I searched for the key myself. I scoured the place looking for it. The showroom, the kitchen, the copier room, and Lissa's office, but no luck." I shivered. "I looked in the sample closet as a last resort."

AJ's husky voice rose with alarm. "You touch her?"

Am I some wet-behind-the-ears-rookie? I took umbrage and tsked. "Of course not."

She asked, "Touch anything in the closet?"

A dumb newbie question. "Nothing, except the closet door handle."

She pointed to the envelope. "Handle it?"

I held out my hands. "Nope. I figured I'd get my key from Lissa and grab the envelope on the way out."

AJ put the delivery notice in an evidence bag and the envelope containing my fabric swatches into a separate bag. "Maybe we'll get lucky and the murderer touched it."

So much for the fabric swatches. Never to be seen again once they fell into the black hole of the evidence room. I made a mental note to contact the fabric supplier for a duplicate set. Hopefully, they'd rush it. They better. By Monday Sue Ellen Magee will no doubt be recovered from her traumatic experience. She won't give two hoots the fabric swatches are now evidence from a crime scene and out of my hands.

Two EMTs pushing a gurney, followed by a CSI team, and two coroner's assistants interrupted our conversation. This episode became an old home week reunion with Los Angeles County Assistant Coroner Sophie Cutler, MD anchoring the rear of the solemn conga line.

Five-foot eleven, skinny, blonde, blue-eyed brilliant but nerdy scientist Sophie Cutler and were I friends since fate put us together as lab partners in Mr. Hepburn's seventh-grade biology class. Frog dissection made me queasy, and Sophie proved incapable of composing a decent essay if her life depended on it. So, we struck a win-win deal. I wrote her compositions and she dissected my frog. It's the reason Snip is her nickname.

She gave me the once-over and snorted a laugh. "I'm not even a little surprised to find you in the middle of this"

Good grief. AJ and Snip must collaborate on their schtick. I better keep those two apart.

I sighed to mask my annoyance. "Yeah, yeah. Nice to see you too."

Sophie pointed to the closet. "I take it you found the victim?"

I smiled tightly. "Yep, lucky me."

Sophie gave me the big eyes. "You laugh?"

My reputation precedes me. No sense denying it. We'd been friends too long. "You have to ask?"

****

Funeral-somber best described the mood at the Yenta table Monday morning. Lissa Charney never won any popularity contests, but the brutal murder of a colleague discovered on the swimwear aisle hit us all a little too close to home.

Queenie sucked in her cheeks. "Bad enough Bunny Frank gets murdered in the mart parking structure." She shuddered. "But then Louis Chennault, and now Lissa Charney both murdered on the same aisle we all work on is terrifying, to say the least."

Sonia closed her eyes. "We'd be right in the middle of it."

I put out a hand like a traffic cop. "It's not clear whether the murder took place in the mart or someplace else. It's doubtful the murder happened in the showroom.

If she was killed on our floor, even on a Friday, *somebody* would hear *something*. From the body's condition, believe me, Lissa didn't go quietly." I grimaced. "I won't describe it. It's waaaay too gruesome. Suffice it to say, she lost the battle, but she put up one heck of a fight."

Queenie asked, "Has your friend the coroner given a time of death?"

I shook my head no. "I questioned her about it before I left Lissa's showroom Friday night, but Snip couldn't call the time of death yet. We're having dinner tomorrow night. I'll find out if she has more information."

I drummed the edge of the table with a teaspoon. "Maybe we can figure out a timeline on our own. I got to our aisle at five-fifteen. The eleventh floor normally empties around three on Fridays. So, if the murder took place in the mart, the killer had roughly two hours to do the deed and clean the showroom before I arrived."

Hope whispered, "Only a monster is capable of such a horrible thing." She looked around the table and shivered. "And the worst part is the killer is no stranger."

Sonia dipped her head. "I'd bet my house you're right. It must be someone in swimwear."

I held my hands out. "Hold it, girls. Maybe yes, maybe no. Lissa had problems with lots of people, but not all of them are in our industry."

Queenie tapped her index finger on the tip of her nose. "Who had the most to lose?"

I held out four fingers. "I see four worthy candidates."

The Yentas chorused like a brood of owls. "Who, who?"

I counted the suspects off one at a time on my digits. "Eileen Hirsch, Bobby Javadi, Annette Mason, and Roddy Mason."

Normally boisterous, Joan spoke so low I had to lean forward to hear her. "You forgot one."

Hope wrinkled her brow. "Who's the fifth?"

Joan laughed sardonically. "Me."

Chapter Nine

I tried my best to wait until Snip swallowed the last bite of her burger.... well, almost...before I split open my spleen with anticipation. "Call the time of death yet for Lissa Charney?"

Snip dipped her head. "It's not exact, but it's as good as it gets right now. She'd been dead between one and three hours before you found the body. She'd lost so much blood, that setting the time of death proved mighty tricky. As a result of such a huge blood loss, livor mortis was interrupted."

What was interrupted by who? "What's livor mortis and who is interrupting it?"

Doctor Death donned her professor's hat. "Livor mortis, or hypostasis, is a stage of death. It occurs within two to four hours after death. Blood pools and settles to the portions of the body closest to the ground. The condition has certain properties: Eight to twelve hours post-death, typically dark purple bruise-like marks appear on the body and determine how long a body has been dead. The blood flows into larger veins and with a lack of a heartbeat to continue its movement, it doesn't take long for the blood to drain into the small capillaries which burst."

I scratched the back of my head. "Those kinds of bruises covered her body. Maybe no livor whatsit interruption occurred?"

Snip waggled her index finger back and forth like a metronome. "No. Those bruises came from an outside force, such as blunt trauma from an assault, not created internally by the body. Livor mortis was definitely interrupted. If not, the skin normally grows pale and translucent and the blood internally is evident. Her skin hadn't turned pale or translucent. The reason is not much blood was left in the body. If livor mortis is prevented by a huge loss of blood, the time of death can't be determined by the usual markers such as body temperature. Eyes are still moist, and the blood on the body is not caked or completely dried out yet are the minor markers used to determine how long the victim has been dead. With a blood loss as severe as hers, only an estimate as to a window on the time of death is possible, mainly by her stomach contents. Her last meal had not gone completely through her intestines."

My stomach lurched. The Thai chicken pizza I'd devoured threatened a return trip. I regretted ever asking the question. Too late now. In for a penny, in for a pound.

Snip said, "Knocked unconscious by a strong blow to her face, the victim's jaw shattered and four teeth broke off."

I rubbed my thumb along my jawline. "Punched or hit with something?"

Snip made a fist and smacked it into her palm. "Punched. There were knuckle marks on the cheek, and an indentation made from a ring or a bracelet the killer wore. The extent of damage to the jaw says whoever killed her, is as strong as an ox."

I shrugged. "So, are the police focusing on a man?"

Snip wagged an index finger back and forth again. "It's too early to make a judgment. I'd say a man is the likely culprit, but a fit woman who works out is certainly capable of delivering the blow. With the power of the blow inflicted to the head, the victim was unconscious when shot."

I winced. "But how is it possible for Lissa's eyes to be wide open with her being unconscious?"

Snip replied, "It's quite common. Eyes often open after death. An involuntary muscle contraction opens the eyelid."

I willed the pizza in my tummy to stay put. "It's a horrible way to die. Thank God, the killer knocked her out. The time of death might have been difficult to determine, but I guess there's no question to the cause of death."

Snip waved an index finger back and forth a third time. "Not exactly."

I gave my favorite coroner the big eyes. "I'm certainly not a doctor, but isn't a nail driven through her heart a pretty conclusive cause of death?"

Snip poked a finger into the center of her chest. "The nail pierced the heart and served as the instrument of death, but hypovolemic shock technically killed her."

I still lacked a few definitions for a medical degree. "Hypo huh shocked who?"

Snip said, "Hypovolemic shock is a life-threatening condition resulting from a significant and sudden loss of blood due to serious wounds. It occurs if you lose more than twenty percent or one-fifth of your body's blood. With such a substantial level of blood loss, the heart is unable to pump a sufficient amount of blood to the body. And this leads to organ failure."

Snip tapped her elegant fingers between her left boob and her breastbone. "The wound to the heart proved to be the fatal one and was administered first at the murder site. It's doubtful the murder took place in the mart."

I tapped my lower lip. "I noticed some weird things." I giggled a nervous laugh. "I mean, beyond her being dead and nailed to the closet wall."

Snip leaned her elbow on the table and rested her chin in her palm. "Such as?"

I held up my right hand and counted the first issue on my thumb. "Before I found her in the closet, I rifled her office, looking for my key. Her purse laid on the desk. When I moved it, my hands were caked with the dust covering the handbag."

Snip shook her head. "Not a surprise. Dust or sand was mixed in with the victim's blood. So, the murder likely took place outdoors. Anything else?"

I smoothed my fingers over the top of my head. "Yeah. Her hair."

Snip parroted. "Her hair?"

I combed the front section of my hair with my fingers. "I ran into her earlier in the day and her hair was its normal hennaed color, but later… in the closet…" I struggled to spit out the words. "Her hair looked dyed to a dull, dishwater brown. Hard to believe she'd dye her hair such an ugly shade with her natural color so gorgeous."

Snip fingered her blonde hair. "She didn't dye it. Her hair was caked with a thick layer of either dust or sand, the same as the substance mixed in the blood. The lab is running it through the system. After the location is pinpointed, we'll know the murder site."

I hesitated to ask. "And the nails?"

Snip parroted. "The nails?"

I bent my index finger. "Seemed to be embedded in the body oddly."

Snip fanned her fingers and held her hands six inches apart. "Being shot at such close range affects the angle. But in this case, the nails shot bent from a defective nail gun. This will help narrow identifying the murder weapon. The nails to the appendages were not a contribution to her death. She'd been dead between one and three hours before being nailed to the wall."

Snip steepled her long, tapered fingers and sighed. "The swimsuits nailed to the appendages? Strictly decorative, to make a statement."

Eek. I pinched my jugular with two fingers. "The neck wound also caught my eye. I couldn't get close enough to see it clearly. But it's smaller, like a needle mark, not from a nail."

Snip touched the same point on her neck. "You're right. A nail didn't puncture the jugular. Something undetermined is deeply embedded and it appears to be organic."

I crossed my eyes. "Meaning?"

Snip said, "Meaning it's something natural, not manmade. Maybe a rock fragment, or a shell shard, or a piece of coral."

I mused. "Maybe the murder took place at the beach?"

Snip nodded. "It's the theory the detective is working on. The mystery item is embedded rather deep. Great care must be taken not to damage it or the wound while extracting it. It may be the key to solving the murder."

I ran my fingers across the front of my shirt. "The corpse is drenched in blood, but not the closet, and no sign of blood on the floor? Hard to believe the killer cleaned the showroom that good."

Snip waved off the notion. "Nah. We sprayed the place with Fluorescein and detected only a negligible amount of residual blood on the floor. The vic bled out at the murder site. There was little blood left in the body to drain out at the time the killer administered the other nails. So, there was not much blood left for he or she to clean in the showroom."

I pulled on the front of my shirt. "One other weird thing. Her clothes looked tie-dyed from the blood. The design made it seem as if she'd been folded in half and unfolded. If the murder occurred someplace else, how'd she end up in the closet?"

I grinned. "She didn't walk into the mart. Even someone as dense as a sales rep notices a bloody stiff being pushed into the elevator."

Snip said, "We found trace elements of something plastic, maybe a container of some type, in the victim's hair, skin, and clothes. Any ideas?"

I racked my brain for a few moments. I snapped my fingers when out of the left-field, it came to me. "We all use heavy gauge plastic sample crates to pack our lines in to go on the road." I stood and put my hands on my chest. "If the sample crate is upright standing on its wheels, it comes up to my boobs."

Snip eyeballed my height from head to toe. "Do you know the dimensions of the interior of the crate?"

I shook my head no. "Never been a reason to measure the inside of a crate, so I don't know. But most vendors hang their swimsuits on plastic torso forms, and they fit inside the crate. I can give you one of the torso forms and loan you a crate."

I held my left hand on my right shoulder and my right hand on my left hip. "This is the length of the torso: From the top at the shoulder to the bottom of the point the hip meets the thigh."

I arced my torso from my lower to my upper body to demonstrate. "To fit a garment, you measure from the crotch diagonally across the chest and over the shoulder to determine the torso length. If the killer bent Lissa in half and folded her hands and legs under her, at her height, it might be a tight fit. But if arranged right, a body could be crammed inside a crate."

I bunched my shoulders. "No one pays any attention to a sample crate being wheeled into the mart. If the murder occurred someplace else, and the killer stuffed Lissa's body in a crate, that explains the way she traveled from the murder site to the showroom closet."

I shuddered. "And narrows the suspect list to those in the apparel industry."

Chapter Ten

Queenie joshed, "If your friend the cop stayed on the swimwear aisle any longer, she could present our line to a buyer by now." Queenie might have been joking, but she wasn't exaggerating. AJ spent the entire work week on our floor and interviewed all the swimwear vendors. Queenie asked, "I wonder if she interviewed anyone not in the swimwear business by now?"

I held out my hands. "AJ is a good cop and as thorough as it gets. If she hasn't already, she'll get to Eileen and Bobby. She's relentless. She won't stop until she catches the killer."

The hairs on the back of my neck stood at attention when Joan said, "If I am an example, believe me, she will leave no stone unturned." Joan puffed the air out of her mouth with her cheeks. "She questioned me for over two hours. The detective questioned the reason for the remodeling. I answered to increase sales and travel less. Yakamura seemed surprised I didn't hire a contractor." Joan held out her bandaged hand. "She asked what happened. I told her not paying close enough attention during the remodeling. She asked the type of work I did before I went on the road. I explained I was a showroom manager. She asked the name of the company. I told her Royal Swimwear. She asked how long I'd been at the company. I replied for almost twenty years."

Joan's smile dimmed. "She asked if I knew Lissa

Charney. I told her the truth: A nod in the hall. The detective asked, with such a secure job, you get a sudden dose of wanderlust and a yen go on the road?"

Warning lights flashed inside my brain. AJ Yakamura doesn't ask questions she doesn't already know the answers to.

Joan funneled her lips. "I explained that the original owner sold the company to a big conglomerate and they hired Butch Oldham as CEO." Joan's laugh hollowed empty as a bottle. "Butch wanted someone with a different sales approach. They let me go and hired Lissa. The detective asks, weren't you resentful of Ms. Charney for stealing your job? I shook my head no. Lissa didn't fire me. She merely benefitted from me being fired."

Joan widened her eyes. "The detective says, 'Come on Ms. Binder. Cut the crap. Lissa Charney's main qualification is…? The BFF of your boss's daughter. Betcha wanted to make Lissa Charney pay. Did you?' "

Joan's voice cracked. "I said, 'Are you nuts? Of course not.' The cop asked about my schedule last Friday. I told her in the morning I was at two appointments in the valley. And later in the day, at the In Style Buying Office delivering some samples. She asked if Lissa delivered samples there and I nodded yes. Lissa and I walked out of the buying office together. Lissa said she took the DASH bus to the buying office. She said she had a meeting out of the office, and worried she'd be late if she missed the bus. I told her it was no problem to drop her off in front of the mart."

Queenie gave Joan the big eyes. "Lemme get this straight. You offered to do *Lissa Charney* a favor?"

Joan squeaked a nervous giggle. "Yeah. It surprised the heck out of Lissa. Truth be told, it shocked the crap out of me. Hey. It was no skin off my teeth, right? She accepted the offer, and we wheeled our crates to my van. Since I came to the buying office straight from my appointments, all my crates were still in the van. Lissa had to move several of mine around to make room for hers. I double-parked in front of the mart, opened the back panel of the van, helped her get her crate out, and went on my way. The detective asked me to account for the rest of the day."

Sonia asked, "Could you?"

I held my breath. My heart sunk to my toes when Joan shook her head no. "My girls were both busy Friday night. So, I shopped stores at the Century City mall for the rest of the day. I bought a hot dog at a stand for dinner and went to an early evening movie alone."

Queenie asked, "No ticket stub or a credit card receipt?"

Joan laughed a self-deprecating laugh. "Nah. I went window shopping. Since I didn't purchase anything, I had no store receipts. I paid cash for the dog and the flick. I threw the movie ticket stub and parking ticket away at home. The detective asked for the time I dropped Lissa off. I guessed by the time we got the crates packed in the van, got out of the parking lot, and to the mart, around one-thirty."

Joan's voice quavered with fear. "The detective said so, you're the last known person with Lissa Charney before she died."

****

I looked up surprised from my computer report when Joan walked into my showroom the following morning. "It's always nice of you to brighten my morning, but shouldn't you be halfway to San Diego by now?"

Joan twisted her lips into a scowl. "It's pretty difficult to go on the road if the police confiscate your van, your samples, and your crates."

My eyes bugged. "Seriously?"

Joan raked her fingers through her hair. "As a heart attack. I went to the showroom early this morning for a few extra samples." Joan's nervous laugh rang empty as an abandoned mineshaft. "Detective Yakamura and two uniforms met me with a search warrant."

I slit my eyes. "Why is AJ messing with you?"

Joan shrugged. "No clue. After Yakamura handed me the warrant she zipped her lips closed tight. But I've got a good set of ears. The detective told one of the uniforms they received a tip. Unfortunately, she didn't reveal who tipped them or the subject of the tip."

Joan clucked her tongue. "I don't understand this. Even if some of the answers made me look bad, I answered all her questions honestly."

Joan raised her palms. "They told me nothing. Nor would they let me stay while they searched. I've been in a back corner booth in the mart deli for the last two and a half hours on my cell phone canceling all my appointments."

Joan pursed her lips. "Believe me, I danced some fancy tapdancing steps to cancel appointments at the last minute. Most buyers understood my excuse of a sick child. But a few of them rearranged their schedules to fit me in, and were not happy campers. Detective Yakamura called twenty minutes ago and gave me the all-clear."

Joan laughed. "Good thing. If they took any longer, by now I'd be on the second floor in the bar." Joan's eyes darkened with anger. "You wouldn't believe the mess they made." Joan shuddered. "Like a tornado hit the place. It'll take me forever to put it back together."

A mess to clean should be her biggest problem. "Are they still in the showroom?"

Joan shook her head. "No. Detective Yakamura gave me a stack of receipts for everything confiscated, told me not to leave town, and they left."

"What did they confiscate?"

Joan sucked in her cheeks. "What didn't they is a better question."

Chapter Eleven

News of Joan's arrest cut through the California Apparel Mart with the speed of a buzzsaw. But the Yentas grieved as quietly as cloistered nuns. The understanding you don't realize what you've got until it's gone battered our souls and twisted our hearts into silent reflection. Each of us brought something unique to the group. Witty, wise Joan Binder's spicy zest for life gave the Yenta soup its savory flavor.

I panned the table. "I've seen livelier crowds at funerals."

Hope twitched her lips into a wry smile. "You sound like Joan."

I took a bow.

Hope asked, "Is Rose Markowitz defending Joan?"

I smiled. "Our Joan's no fool."

Sonia grinned. "These things keep happening, you'll need to put the old gal on speed dial."

Sonia didn't have a lawyer when she was wrongly arrested for buying office executive Bunny Frank's murder. I called my Uncle Barry, a personal injury attorney in Beverly Hills for help, and he highly recommended Ms. Markowitz. "If I ever found myself in trouble with the law, Rose Markowitz is the one attorney I'd ever call." With complete trust in my uncle, I put Sonia Wilson's life in Ms. Markowitz's hands. The diminutive octogenarian criminal defense attorney extraordinaire saved Sonia Wilson's tush. Hopefully, she'll do the same for Joan Binder.

Sonia asked, "You speak to Ms. Markowitz?"

I nodded yes. "We met at her office last night. Since I discovered Lissa's body, my recollections and takes on the case might impact how Ms. Markowitz plans Joan's defense."

Hope's face creased with worry. "Is Joan doing okay?"

I made a so-so motion with my hand. "As good as expected. She's more concerned for her daughters than herself."

Hope said, "At least the arrest happened during school hours."

Sonia closed her eyes and shuddered. "No kidding. Seeing their mother led away in handcuffs? Not much more could be terrifying for a kid."

Queenie asked, "Ms. Markowitz discuss the evidence against Joan?"

I grimaced. "No smoking gun, and much of the evidence is circumstantial, but it's enough to arrest her. Even though Joan denied it, AJ said Joan blamed Lissa for her getting fired at Royal. Joan admitted to AJ things were tough for her financially as a road rep. The cops say Joan eliminated the competition in the hopes of getting her old, better-paying job back. They've confiscated the nail gun with Joan's fingerprints all over it."

Sonia made a sour face. "She has a legitimate reason for the nail gun. Besides, Roddy Mason has one. And if Lissa's boyfriend works construction, he has one too."

I shrugged. "They do. But the cops found *Joan's* in her showroom, two doors from where Lissa's corpse was nailed to the wall. Ms. M. and I agreed the nail gun is the reason they arrested Joan. I told Ms. M. I'd do some nosing around and find the names of nail gun manufacturers."

Sonia gave me a puzzled look. "Why?"

I formed my index finger and thumb into the shape of a pistol. "Since the nail gun used to shoot Lissa didn't shoot the nails straight, I figure Snip is right. The nail gun must be defective. I told Ms. M if we find the manufacturer of the nail gun used in the murder, she can ask them to supply the crime lab with one nail gun shooting the nails straight and a second one shooting the nails bent like the one used to kill Lissa. She can also ask them to provide the specs, photos of the interior of the damaged nail gun, and a certified description, as well as an expert's statement of the impact on the trajectory if the nail gun fired bent nails. The lab techs then compare them to Joan's nail gun. Then Ms. M. insists the lab shoots nails from Joan's nail gun as a comparison. If the nails from Joan's nail gun shoot straight, they aren't a match for the ones embedded in Lissa. And the prime part of the case the police has against Joan falls apart." I sucked in my cheeks. "It's risky." I puckered my lips. "If the nails match, Joan's toast."

Hope said, "Maybe the cops confiscated the other nail guns. Maybe they've already been tested and eliminated. Maybe Joan's nail gun and nails are already being tested to compare to the nails in Lissa's corpse. Maybe hers matched and that's the reason she's in jail."

Sonia's eyes bugged. "You think *Joan murdered* Lissa?"

Hope waved off the idea with a flick of a wrist. "No, of course not. But would it be hard for the killer to get into Joan's showroom, steal her nail gun, kill Lissa, and return the nail gun to Joan's room? With some planning, maybe it's not as hard as we think."

Sonia winced. "Seems kind of farfetched, but I guess it's possible."

I held up my index finger. "If the crime lab ran any tests, the police are obligated to provide Ms. M. with the results. But having Ms. M. provide an expert third party like the nail gun manufacturer as the source of comparison ensures the tests on all the nail guns in question are unbiased."

Hope asked, "Any luck finding the supplier?"

I nodded yes. "I found three major nail gun manufacturers and gave Ms. M the list. Ms. M. already has the name of the supplier of Joan's nail gun. She is contacting Joan's nail gun manufacturer as well as the ones I gave her to see if any of them sold nail guns to Mason Construction. Mason is a big company and must purchase a large number of nail guns. They'd be a major account. It won't be too difficult to find which manufacturer Mason Construction bought their nail guns from."

Queenie asked, "Anything else on Joan?"

I gave Queenie the big eyes. Is all this not enough for you? "Unfortunately, plenty. They've confiscated Joan's bloody overalls and question the way she says she hurt her hand. The overalls are being tested. If Lissa's blood is on it, Joan is done."

Sonia held up a palm. "Hold on a sec. The overalls don't even matter. Joan's overalls were bloodstained before Lissa's murder." Sonia panned the table." She wore the blood-stained overalls to our morning coffee klatch the day Lissa complained to Joan about the noise from the remodeling."

I dipped my head. "True, but if Joan committed the murder, she didn't do it wearing a tuxedo. The overalls make more sense. If Lissa's blood is on the overalls, it places Joan at the scene of the crime. And don't forget about the sample crates. Joan's were covered with dust. They're being tested to see if it's the same dust on Lissa's body."

Queenie scrunched her nose. "Joan had an explanation for her dusty crates, right?"

I nodded yes. "Yeah. She did. Remember? She told us she had an appointment at the Bikini Village in Encino out in the valley Friday morning. She parked her van in a lot near some construction. The wind gusted and blew dust on the crates. She rushed to get downtown to deliver the samples to the buying office on time without stopping to wipe the crates clean." I looked around the table and sighed. "It gets worse. Joan's fingerprints are on Lissa's crate. If it's the one the killer crammed Lissa into, Joan's explanation of the way her prints got on the crate goes out the window. Lissa's fingerprints are also on Joan's crates."

I hung my head with despair. "The police collected a lot of evidence proving Joan and Lissa were together the day of the murder. Plus, Joan admitted being with Lissa the afternoon she died."

Sonia gulped. "Ms. Markowitz is as good as they come, but the old girl is no magician." Sonia's olive complexion paled white as alabaster. "Even a lawyer as sharp as Ms. M. has their limitations. With so much on Joan, the cops are gonna keep our gal in jail and throw away the key."

Hope sniffed and scrunched her nose as if somebody forgot to take out the trash. "But come on. Her explanation made perfect sense." Hope threw her hands in the air with frustration. "For crying out loud, Joan does Lissa a favor and gives her a ride back to the mart. And the thanks Joan gets for being a nice person? She's arrested for Lissa's murder."

No good deed goes unpunished. I shook my head. "The problem is, Joan can't prove any of it happened the way she explained it. Lots of witnesses to Joan and Lissa leaving the buying office together. But none to Joan dropping Lissa off at the mart. No one reported seeing Lissa on the swim aisle or in her showroom Friday afternoon. Nor can Joan account for her afternoon the murder took place."

I flexed my steepled fingers for something to do with my hands. "Joan is unable to prove she shopped the stores, or in which mall, or even in any mall. Since she didn't buy anything, she had no receipts. Joan said she paid cash for a hot dog and the movie ticket and tossed the movie stub and parking ticket in the trash when she got home. According to the police, Joan Binder is the last person seen with Lissa Charney on the day of Lissa's death. The police position is Joan spent Friday afternoon murdering Lissa, not on a window-shopping spree."

Queenie tapped her index finger to the tip of her nose. "The cops always say on TV…"

We chorused. "Follow the money."

Sonia gave a triumphant ta-da flip of her wrists. "Then Annette and Roddy go to the top of the list."

Queenie surveyed the group. "And who has the most to lose?"

I scratched the crown of my head. "The Masons certainly. But don't forget Lissa's boyfriend. If he gets deported, he'll be arrested the minute he steps off the plane. He might even lose his life. In my book, Bobby Javadi is the one with the most to lose."

Queenie drew an imaginary line on a napkin. "Ok. Cross Eileen Hirsch off the list."

Hope waggled a finger. "Hold on a minute. If money isn't the motive, love usually is. Eileen's alibi must be confirmed."

Sonia said, "Joan's not the murderer. But how do we prove it?"

I wiggled my brows and grinned. "Stick our noses where they don't belong and sniff out the real killer."

Chapter Twelve

Saturday morning Bobby Javadi stood waiting as I pulled into the customer parking lot at the Garvin auto dealership in Sepulveda, a quiet bedroom community tucked into the north-central part of the San Fernando Valley.

Mid-to-late thirties, Bobby was slim, and of average height. Bobby's sports jacket hung loosely on his narrow frame. But his bulging biceps tightened the sleeves as he raised his right arm in a greeting. White straight teeth gleamed behind thin lips. His hooked nose bent to the right and sat below wide-set, hound dog-sad milk chocolate-brown eyes. Overexposure to the sun gave his swarthy complexion a leathery texture. He was clean-shaven, but by ten o'clock in the morning, a five o'clock shadow covered his cheeks. His thick, wiry, jet-black hair was cut in an afro.

He ran the calloused fingers of his right hand appreciably over the hood of my vintage bubblegum pink sixty-five convertible. "I love working on classic cars like this." Bobby caressed the hood ornament as he would a lover's cheek. He spoke in a soft, reverent voice with a faint middle-eastern accent. "She's a beauty. They don't make 'em like this anymore."

I grinned. "You're right. She's a classic. Soon after my mother graduated from college, she drove the hottest car on the road." I patted a love tap on the hood. " Nana bought this car for my mother the day Mom landed her first big job. I inherited my mom's love of convertibles. I'm as crazy about the rag top as her." I laughed at the memory. "In high school, I volunteered to run all my mother's errands if she let me drive her pink pride and joy."

Bobby asked, "So, the car is an heirloom your mother left you?"

I shook my head no. "No. Luckily, my parents are still alive. My mother made it a family tradition. She gave me the car the day I started my first big job after college."

Bobby played a light rat-ta-tat on the hood. "Any interest in selling? A convertible top is rare for a vintage car. It jacks up the value, especially for one in mint condition. I can get you a ton for the car and put you into a new one for practically nothing."

As if. I shrank back in horror. "So, you'd sell one of your family?"

Bobby shrugged and cocked a dark, thick brow. "Since you're obviously not in the market for a new car, why are you here?"

I pursed my lips. "I'm investigating Lissa Charney's murder and I need to ask you some questions."

He tipped his head to the side like a confused cocker spaniel. "My boss Roddy at Mason construction said someone has already been arrested for the murder." Bobby's voice bristled with a combination of fear and resentment. "What makes you think I have any answers?"

I ignored his question. "Roddy's right. Someone has been arrested. She's a close friend of mine and she's innocent."

Bobby clenched and unclenched his fists and slapped them angrily against his sides. "And I'm just as innocent."

A middle-aged guy getting out of an old, dinged coupe parked in the spot on my right stared at Bobby and me. I pointed to the dealership office. "Can we go someplace more private to talk?"

Bobby batted the idea away as though swatting an annoying fly at a picnic. "Forget the offices. Too many eyes and ears. My personal life is nobody's business."

I angled my head at the nosy guy straining to listen in on our conversation. "It's a big place."

Bobby forced the words out through clenched teeth. "It's past breakfast and too early for lunch. At this time of day, the employee cafeteria is pretty empty. Follow me."

****

Bobby handed me a ceramic mug of steaming coffee from a bandaged left hand. He took a seat opposite me in a worn fifties-style booth in the back of the deserted cafeteria. He pointed to the wall clock. "Ten minutes. Get on with it."

"How long have you worked at Garvin? You aren't in construction?"

His angular face creased with a frown. "My job at Garvin has nothing to do with Lissa's murder."

I snapped. "Answer the question, ok?"

He sighed, "Fine. A year. I work here on weekends as a side gig for extra cash. My full-time job is with Mason Construction."

I pointed to his bandaged left wrist. "Are you left-handed? If you are, it must be hard to do anything with a thick bandage on your hand."

74

He stared at his left hand oddly, as though he just discovered the bandaged wound. He held out his right hand. "This hand is pretty useless." He laughed. "Its main function is to balance me out."

Bobby cradled his bandaged hand. "Too bad I'm not ambi-something or other." He cast his eyes away with embarrassment, "I'm sorry. I don't remember the word in English. It means you're able to use both hands."

I prompted. "You mean ambidextrous?"

He smiled. "Yeah. That's it." He laughed self-deprecatingly, "My English is good, but lots of words I don't get right."

I pointed to his hand. "That's a nasty injury."

He shrugged. "I'm a construction worker. Injuries come with the job. You try to be careful, but sometimes things happen beyond your control."

He still didn't say how he got hurt, but I let it go for the moment. "How did you meet Lissa? The Masons introduce you?"

"No, we met at the Falafel Palace on Ventura Boulevard in Van Nuys." He grinned and vertical smile lines indented his cheeks. "I accidentally backed into her while searching the crowded dining room for an open table and spilled iced tea all over her shirt. I insisted I pay for her meal and the cleaning bill. One thing led to another, and we started dating."

I waved around the cafeteria. "At the time you worked here?"

He shook his head no.

I guessed by process of elimination. "So, you were at Mason Construction?"

A second negative shake. "No. Lissa fronted me into the job at Mason Construction."

I tried to keep the impatience out of my tone. "Then you did what before?"

His eyes shone with pride. "I came to this country to go to school. I graduated from Cal State with an engineering degree six months before I met Lissa. With zero luck finding a job, and school loans to pay off in addition to my monthly bills, I quickly ran low on money. I was desperate for work. Lissa saved my butt by getting me in with Mason. It turned out, I enjoy being outdoors and working with my hands, so I stayed with it."

"When was the last time you saw Lissa?"

He scratched his chin. "A couple of weeks ago."

I glared my annoyance. "Be more specific."

His voice quivered with emotion. "We met one night after work."

I pushed him for details. "Which night? When? Where? A Restaurant? A Bowling Alley? Griffith Park Zoo?"

Bobby pressed his lips into a thin line. "We met at an Iranian restaurant in Northridge. I don't remember the exact date. We met around six o'clock."

I pushed him more. "Which restaurant?"

He said, "Ali Baba on Nordhoff Street a few blocks west of Balboa." His eyes sparked with recognition. He pointed his coffee mug at me. "The same night as you and your friend."

I narrowed my eyes. "You haven't seen Lissa since?"

He shook his head emphatically. "No. We broke up. Actually, she broke it off with me. I haven't seen or talked to her since." Bobby closed his eyes and sighed. "She made it clear not to contact her, so I didn't."

I channeled AJ and asked a question I already knew the answer to. "Why'd she break it off with you?"

Bobby wrinkled his forehead. "I wanted to get married and she wasn't interested."

Such a crock. "Quite a simplification, isn't it? Isn't it a fact you're having immigration problems? You might even get deported." I glowered at his attempt to jerk me around. "Isn't it true the *only* reason you wanted to marry her is to stay in this country?"

He squealed like a stuck pig. "NO! Yes. No."

I slitted my eyes. "It's a simple question. Which is it? Yes, or no?"

Bobby squirmed in his seat." I guess technically, yes. But I really cared for her. We'd been seeing each other for a while, and the relationship became serious before my immigration troubles started. I'm working two jobs to save enough money to buy a house. I planned to ask her to marry me once I bought the house, but not right now."

He might be selling, but I wasn't buying. "She refused you and you threatened her. You called her a bitch." Bobby's swarthy complexion drained of all its color. "She left you to twist in the wind. *No one* in the restaurant missed your scream that you'd get her for not helping you stay in this country. Don't try to deny it."

Bobby hung his head. He lifted his face, and his eyes filled. "I didn't mean it." He whispered. "Angry words. Nothing more."

I switched topics. "You send her flowers?"

His curious eyes studied me as though discovering a new species. "Is it strange for a guy to send his girl flowers for her birthday?"

"Just on her birthday and not every day?"

He snorted a laugh. "On my salary?"

I switched to the main event. "Do you work with a nail gun?"

He rolled his eyes. "Hammers went out with the dinosaurs." Bobby glanced at the clock on the wall facing the booth and stood. "I need to get back to work."

I held out my hands. "Please. I've only a few more questions."

He sat back and perched on the edge of the seat, as though ready to spring into action. He held up his right hand and waggled his fingers. "Five minutes, no more."

"Do you keep the nail gun in your truck or do you leave it at the Mason office?"

He explained the company procedure. "The company has dozens of different job sites. I keep all my tools in my truck so I can go straight to the job."

"Do you lock the tools or does anyone have access to them?"

He said, "They're in a locked toolbox bolted to the back of the truck bed."

"Who has the key?"

He said, "I have one and the foreman has the other. Company rules."

I tested him again. "Who's the foreman?"

Bobby's patience ran its course. "I *already* told you. Roddy Mason."

"When was the last time you used your nail gun?"

He scooted back, rested his head against the wall behind the seat, and counted back the days. "Last Thursday. Our crew prepped an old building out in Saugus for retrofitting."

"You haven't opened your toolbox since last week?"

He answered quickly. "No."

Gotcha. "So, you don't know for sure if the nail gun is in your toolbox or not."

He smirked. "It didn't open the toolbox and walk out on its own."

"Is your name on the nail gun?"

He said, "My name isn't on it, but mine has an inch-deep nick on the left side of the grip. I dropped it two months ago."

"It still works?"

He shook his head yes.

"The gun shoots the nails straight out, or do they go into the target bent?"

He replied in the same tone as if speaking to a slow-witted child. "If a gun doesn't shoot the nails straight, the gun is replaced."

"Can I see it?"

He grinned. "Considering a career change?"

Another comedian. "Funny. If you fancy a migraine."

He waved around the building. "My truck's at home. I only drive it during the week for construction jobs." He raised an eyebrow. "Why all the interest in my nail gun?"

Bobby flinched at my response. "Lissa Charney died from a shot to the heart from a nail gun shooting bent nails."

Bobby twisted a ta-da flip of his wrists. "Then she wasn't shot with a nail from my nail gun."

"The police contact you?"

He nodded yes. "Yeah. A lady detective with a funny name called me at the construction trailer and asked me some questions two days ago."

I suggested, "Detective AJ Yakamura?"

Bobby pointed an index finger. "Yeah. She's the

one."

I cocked an eyebrow. "You meet with her?"

He answered with a touch of annoyance in his voice. "No. I *already told you.* She called and asked some questions. She said she'd get back to me if she needed more information." He shrugged. "She hasn't called back, so I guess she got all the answers she needed."

I switched gears again. "Can you prove your activities last Friday?"

Bobby nodded numbly. "A meeting downtown with my immigration attorney at nine in the morning."

I tapped the face of my wristwatch. "What time did the meeting end?"

He said, "We finished at one. Call my lawyer if you want. Mr. Martino will verify our meeting. I'll give you his contact information."

I held up my watch. "Lissa Charney's murder occurred between one and four pm on Friday. Can you account for your time during those hours?"

Bobby made a sour face. "Even though he said I have a strong case, the lawyer's evaluation was still not encouraging news. My chances of not getting deported are only fifty-fifty. I left his office pretty depressed. I drove to the beach. I parked on Pacific Coast Highway south of the Malibu Pier and walked on the sand until dark."

I could hardly contain my excitement. "Sand was mixed with the blood-drenched all over Lissa's corpse. The police are working on the theory her murder happened at the beach."

Bobby gulped as if his lungs had run out of air.

"Buy anything in one of the stores on the pier?"

He shook his head no.

"Stop at one of the food stands? If you ate at one, did you keep any receipts?"

His laugh came out bitter as burnt coffee. "Food? The last thing on my mind. I walked back and forth on the beach, trying to figure a way out of the mess I am in. I bet I walked ten miles."

"And after you left Malibu?"

"Back to my apartment and straight to bed."

I cocked a brow. "Alone?"

He responded with a snickered smile.

I slit my eyes. "So, the correct answer to my question is you can't account for your time once you left the lawyer's office."

The smile disappeared from Bobby Javadi's face.

Chapter Thirteen

I stood outside her showroom as mannish, rangy-framed Eileen Hirsch took two armfuls of sportswear samples off of a rack and laid them on a workstation table. She replaced them with other samples she pulled out of a huge cardboard carton on the floor.

I eyeballed her standing around five-ten. She dressed preppy. Her eyes were wide-set hazel. She wore her light brown straight hair cut short and blunt, parted on the right side.

Eileen transferred the samples from the workstation table into the carton. She hefted the heavy-looking box with one meaty hand and shoved it in the back corner adjacent to a closet. She grabbed a dozen samples from the wall rack and hung the garments on a metal rolling rack. She grazed the head of a steamer belching a hot mist over each of the new samples in a futile effort to get some of the wrinkles out.

I walked into the Junior World showroom and late-thirtysomethingish Eileen stopped steaming and smiled a toothy smile. She had a slight hitch in her walk as she met me at the entrance.

She gave me the once-over and extended her right hand. "Hi. I'm Eileen, the Junior World showroom manager. You need immediate goods, or do you want to see the new line?" Eileen waved at the rack behind her. "We received the first three preview groups for the new season today, but the line won't be complete for another week. You wanna make an appointment and wait until the line is complete, or start with the first three groups?"

Without waiting for my answer, she pointed to an empty chair in front of a workstation table. "Either way, take a seat and hang around for a couple of minutes. My assistant Adrian will be back from lunch soon and can present the preview collection, and make a follow-up appointment for you to see the rest of the line next week."

Eileen's smile dimmed as I introduced myself and said I worked in the building. Eileen grabbed the steamer head from its cradle and resumed steaming her line. "If you're job hunting, you're out of luck. We don't have any openings."

I paid no attention to her comments and pointed to the metal racks bolted to the walls. "I'm impressed with the set-up of your racks. You can fit a lot of samples on each one, but the work areas aren't crammed too tightly. You do the work on the showroom?"

She arched a brow. "I'm a seller, not a carpenter. The owner of Junior World hired a contractor."

I aimed my thumb and index finger in the shape of a pistol. Do you own a nail gun?"

Eileen burst out laughing.

To catch her off-guard, I queried out of the blue. "When's the last time you saw Lissa Charney?"

She gave me a deer in the headlights. "A month ago."

I channeled AJ again, and asked a question I already knew the answer to. "Where?"

She said, "Taos, New Mexico."

I rapid fired another volley of questions rat-ta-ta-tat

with the burst of a machine gun. "And you haven't seen her since? Not out, not in the mart? Not at her home? Not speaking on the phone? Not even a voicemail or a text?"

She squinted and blinked rapidly, as though trying to get something irritating out of her eye. "Who are you and why do you care?"

I ignored her question. "You left Lissa some rather threatening messages on her phone." Eileen's eyes blinked with recognition as I quoted her. "Your last one said, *if I can't have you, nobody will*."

Eileen narrowed her eyes and looked me up and down. "Ok, why don't you cut the crap and tell me who you really are. You don't work in the mart. You must be the cop who left a couple of messages on my answer machine." Eileen held out her left hand and waggled her fingers. "Show me a badge before I call security." She snarled. "I can't believe the bitch called the cops. That's a joke. What's her problem?" Eileen pointed an unmanicured finger at her chest. "I'm the one with the right to be angry. She left me stranded in Taos. It took me two days to get home."

I held my palms out. "I'm not a cop. I told you, I work in the building."

Eileen clucked her tongue.

I kept my tone conversational, but the question? Anything but. "Make good on your threat?"

Her eyes bugged. "Of course not." Eileen jutted her jaw. "I had a right to be mad, but I'm over it." Eileen put the steamer head back in its cradle and crossed her arms over her chest as though warding off a blow. "She gave the signals, but I guess I read them wrong. I made a play. It didn't work out. I moved on."

I narrowed my eyes. "Why all the threats?"

She pointed to the mist puffing out of the steamer. "Letting off steam. Now I'm over it. Ya win some, ya lose some. Life goes on."

I sucked in my cheeks. "Not for Lissa Charney."

Eileen snickered. "She changed her mind and sent you to deliver the good news?"

I tsked. "You wish. Someone murdered Lissa on Friday. Can you account for your time?"

The sample she'd been holding fluttered to the carpet like an autumn leaf. Eileen turned sheet white and grabbed the back of a chair to steady herself. She gasped. "Lissa's *dead*?" She choked the word out as if a chicken bone was stuck in her throat. "How?"

Eileen retched when I replied. "Shot through the heart with a nail gun." My eyes turned as hard as one of the nails. "Let me repeat the question. Are you able to account for your time Friday?"

Eileen snapped, "You're not a cop. Why do you care?"

I jutted my chin. "A good friend of mine's been accused of the murder. She's innocent. The police stopped looking for the real killer. So, it's up to me. Once again. Can you prove where you spent the day?"

Eileen smirked. "Not anyplace near Lissa Charney."

Interesting. "And, she was...?"

Eileen waved to the hallway. "I assume the mart. If not, I don't know. But I was on an early morning flight from New York to LA."

"You landed and went...?"

Eileen waved a one-eighty around the room. "My home away from home."

I pointed to the aisle. "Anyone see you?"

Eileen shook her head no and tsked. "Nah. I

collected my luggage at baggage claim and my van from long-term parking. I hit the heavy Friday getaway weekend traffic crawling in both directions on Interstate ten. It took forever getting into downtown. I got to the mart between two-thirty and three o'clock." She laughed. "You said you worked in the building, right? Fridays, who isn't anxious to get outta Dodge early?"

I ignored her question. "See the mailman or any delivery guys?"

She shook her head no.

"Stop for lunch at the mart deli?"

Another head shake.

"Food delivered?"

Another negative head jerk.

I switched topics. "Send Lissa any flowers?"

Eileen furrowed her brow. "On her birthday, I think, last year."

"Last Friday or this week?"

She snorted. "And the occasion? A reward for stranding me a thousand miles from home?"

I tossed out a wild pitch to see if she'd take a swing. "Enticing her to bat on your team?"

She rolled her eyes. "I told you already. I made a play. She said no. Nothing more to it. Why?"

"Someone's been sending Lissa flowers and one of the cards said, "If I can't have you, nobody can." I smiled like a shark. "Sound familiar?"

She fanned her fingers and flexed them a couple of times. "Not me. I keep an account with Shoots and Blooms downstairs in the mart lobby. I'll authorize the manager to give you a printout of all my purchases for the last year. You'll see Lissa's name maybe twice. I pay by debit card. Check it out."

Do I look stupid? I rolled my eyes. "Shoots and Blooms isn't the only florist in town. Besides, maybe you paid with cash."

She made a funny face and laughed. "Who uses cash anymore? I might keep five bucks in my wallet, but I'm not sure. It's been a while since I went into my wallet for anything but a debit card."

"Why were you in the mart last Friday?"

She turned around and pointed to the carton on the floor. "I brought two cartons of samples up and unpacked them. I went through the mail, listened to messages, made a few calls, and left."

"How long were you at the mart?"

"Lemme think." She squinted with concentration and massaged her chin. "Until Five."

I couldn't keep the impatience out of my tone. "*And?*"

She shrugged. "And after an endlessly long day, I went straight home and into bed."

I smirked. "Alone?"

Eileen laughed like a hyena. "Nope. My best friends Mint Chocolate Chip and Cherry Vanilla joined me."

I crossed my arms over my chest. "So, the fact is, you're unable to account for your time Friday afternoon and evening."

Her grin melted faster than her Mint Chocolate Chip and Cherry Vanilla on a hot summer day.

Chapter Fourteen

Sonia surveyed the Yenta table. "Do you believe those roses are still being delivered to Lissa's showroom?" She grimaced. "It's so creepy."

Hope wrapped her arms around her shoulders and shivered. "No kidding. I go past that room and see them lying on the floor, and get an industrial-strength case of the willies. My God, the woman is *dead*. I can't believe they're still coming."

Sonia puckered her lips as if she'd bitten into a sour pickle. "It takes a sicko to do something so icky." She waved at the crowd in the coffee shop. "Who?"

I twisted a ta-da with my hands. "Who else? The killer."

Sonia asked, "Each delivery came with a card. Can the police identify the card writer?"

I nodded yes. "The lab brought in a handwriting expert. The writer is a left-handed male."

Hope's annoyance mirrored the group's exasperation. "Oh, come on, for crying out loud. This is the *LAPD* crime lab, not some two-bit hole in the wall town with a police force of two lazy cops. With their legion of hot and cold running experts and the latest equipment out the wazoo, you're telling me LAPD has *nothing* more specific?"

Queenie tapped her index finger on the tip of her nose. "Don't get your panties in a bunch yet. It might be enough. Both Bobby and Roddy are left-handed. Right?"

I nodded. "They both are. The lab ran the writing samples from the cards through the system, but no handwriting or fingerprint matches hit. Whoever wrote the cards doesn't have a criminal record."

Hope asked, "Can't the police get a writing sample from our two left-handed male suspects and compare it to the writing on the cards?"

I posed the same question to AJ, but she squashed the notion like a pesky bug. "Unless the two men volunteer it, the answer is regrettably, no. The police can't compel them to provide a writing sample without any probable cause."

Sonia pointed out to the lobby. "You talked to the florist in the mart?"

I gave her the thumbs up. "Yep. All the flowers delivered to Lissa at the mart came from the florist in the building. I spoke with Caroline, the owner of Shoots and Blooms. She typed Lissa's name into the computer and printed out a report of all the deliveries her shop made to Lissa Charney for the last year."

Sonia asked, "To both Lissa's house and the showroom?"

I shook my head no. "Caroline only delivers within a five-mile radius of the mart. If Lissa received any flowers at her house, they weren't from Shoots and Blooms."

Sonia asked, "Did Caroline's report indicate who ordered the flowers she delivered?"

I dipped my head. "The deliveries paid in cash had no indication of a sender name. The report corroborated everything Eileen and Bobby told me. Eileen sent Lissa flowers on her birthday in November. Bobby also sent her flowers on her birthday as well as on New Year's Eve."

Sonia asked, "How did they pay?"

"Eileen by debit card. Bobby by credit card."

Queenie scrunched her eyes. "And all the other deliveries? Who sent them and how were the bills paid?"

I furrowed my brow. "Cash sales and no name. A name is required if the sale is paid by debit, credit card, or check. Cash sales don't require any identification."

Hope said, "Eileen and Bobby can still be the ones who sent the other deliveries. People do pay in cash."

I could not argue. "Certainly possible. No way to find out if Eileen sent any other deliveries but the ones paid for by her debit card, or if she included a card."

Sonia asked, "Caroline say if a man or a woman paid for the cash sales orders?"

I shook my head no. "Nope. That was one of my questions too. But she said she couldn't recall off the top of her head. She also said she didn't handle all the sales. Shoots and Blooms is the one florist in the mart. Caroline's place is always busy. I waited quite a while for the two clerks on the floor who handled some of Lissa's orders to get free to talk. But when I questioned them, neither recalled the senders. They handle hundreds of sales and focus more on getting the order done right than noticing anything else. Besides, even if they remembered, the person placing the order isn't necessarily the sender. Lots of secretaries place orders for their bosses."

Queenie pursed her lips. "The same florist delivers the same order of flowers to the same person daily and *no one* in the store remembers a thing about the sender? I don't care if they are the busiest florist in the city. This is pretty hard to believe."

I shrugged. "Sorry, I've nothing else."

Hope asked, "And the cards?"

Huh? I parroted. "The cards?"

Hope tapped her coffee cup with a spoon. "One of the clerks should have said something to the owner or called the police about the threatening messages on some of the cards."

I sighed. "The clerks never read the messages on the cards. Whoever placed the order, wrote out the card, put it in an envelope, sealed it, wrote Lissa's name and showroom number on the envelope, and gave it to the clerk to put with the flowers."

Sonia rubbed her chin and reasoned. "Theoretically, the killer is still sending flowers to the murder victim, and the police can't identify him or her. Right?"

I bunched my shoulders. "All the flowers came with cards written by left-handed men. Eliminate Eileen unless she used a left-handed male ringer to send the flowers. But there's no way to find out. So, unless the killer leaves the flowers personally and someone sees them placing the vase in front of Lissa's door, we can't identify the murderer through the florist."

Sonia clucked her tongue. "Sucks."

I pulled a white envelope out of my purse by one corner with my fingertips as though it had cooties. "This does too."

Queenie smirked. "A fan letter?"

I tsked. "Aren't you a laugh machine?" Another comedian. Look out, Jimmy Kimmel. "I've started asking questions, and I've ruffled some feathers."

Sonia asked, "Meaning?"

I grimaced. "Meaning it's an anonymous note with

a warning."

Sonia cupped her ear." Let's hear it."

I took the note out of the envelope and read it out loud. "Don't stick your nose where it doesn't belong or you'll end up the same way as her."

Hope's hand flew to her heart. "Oh my God!"

Sonia's voice quivered. "C-came t-to t-the -s-showroom?"

I shook my head no. "Nope. My mailbox at the factory."

Hope asked, "Get it today?"

I shook my head no. "Yesterday. After lunch."

Queenie pointed to the envelope. "No idea who sent it?"

I fluttered the envelope like a fan. "It came in this plain envelope with no return address. The postmark's the same as the mart, but the zip code covers a big portion of downtown. So, whoever sent it might not work in the mart. It's impossible to identify the sender."

Sonia bent over the envelope. "This is interesting."

I leaned in closer and followed her fingers as she traced over the address, but I detected nothing out of the ordinary. "What's interesting?"

Sonia wiggled her fingers. "Whoever typed it, used a typewriter, not a computer."

Hope took a closer look. "How can you tell?"

Sonia pointed to the letters typed on the envelope. "See the way the E, H, I, and the S are deformed? Four of the keys on the typewriter are broken. If the sender typed it on a computer, the letters would not be deformed."

Queenie shook her index finger. "Not necessarily true. The issue could be in the computer's programming.

Or maybe the printer is the problem. If the printer copied it blurry it might look like a damaged typewriter key."

Hope wrinkled her forehead. "You're gonna turn this over to the police, aren't you?"

I sighed. "I will, but I'm not expecting much to come of it."

Hope did a double-take. "Why not? Joan didn't write it from jail. This is proof Joan isn't the killer, isn't it?"

I shook my head. "Not at all. The police might claim one of Joan's daughters sent this to cast doubt on their mother's guilt."

Sonia's shoulders slumped. "She's right. The police might even say one of us sent it."

I pointed to Queenie. "We both received those threatening letters from Ronnie Schwartzman and turned them over to Detective Martinez. Remember his reaction?"

Queenie scoffed. "A cross between a shrug and a yawn."

I clapped a round of applause. "Right as rain."

Hope refused to throw in the towel. "This is a different detective. She's a *friend* of yours. Don't you think it's wise to give it to her?"

I tilted my head. "Eventually."

Sonia and Hope shared a sideways glance. "Meaning?"

I squared my shoulders. "Meaning before I give it to AJ, I'm gonna confront the people I question with it and see the kind of response I get." I jerked my chin in Sonia's direction. "You made a good point. I'll snoop around and see if any of our suspects own a typewriter."

Queenie gave me the big eyes. "Who still uses a

typewriter?'

Hope frowned. "Do they even make them anymore?"

I gave her the stink eye. "Of course they are still made. Lots of people aren't computer literate. My razor-sharp Nana typed one hundred and twenty words per minute with no errors until the day she died, but she never caught on to using the computer."

Hope asked, "Which older people are suspects?"

Good grief. Internally, I rolled my eyes. "*None.* I'm giving you an example." I counted the ways on my fingers. "But if someone had been educated in another country, or had no access to a computer, or lacked the skills, or is unable to afford one, they might still use a typewriter." I surveyed the table. "Someone like Bobby Javadi. So far, I've interviewed two of our four suspects. Neither one can account for their time Friday afternoon. One is in the clear and the other one looks good for it."

Sonia asked, "Which one is which?"

"Eileen Hirsch is in the clear. She took an early morning flight from JFK to LAX, but she went to the mart from the airport. She claims she was alone in her showroom from two-thirty to five, but can't offer any witnesses to corroborate her story."

Sonia huffed. "If she's unable to account for her time, she should not be off the suspect list."

I patted my midsection. "My gut says she's not the killer."

Hope leaned forward in her seat. "But those threats she left on Lissa's phone were pretty scary." Hope shuddered. "Especially, the last one."

I bent my arms like a Venice Beach bodybuilder. "Physically, Eileen is certainly capable. She tossed a heavy carton around as if it was a feather. She's strong as an ox. No sweat for her to pack Lissa into a sample crate and hang her in the showroom closet."

Queenie clucked her tongue. "I dunno why you'd eliminate Eileen at all. She's my first choice."

Hope joined the Eileen fan club. "She sure makes a darn good candidate in my book."

I dipped my head. "If she'd denied it, I might not be convinced of her innocence, but she *admitted* making the threats. She was angry with Lissa for stranding her in Taos, and according to Eileen, the threats were her way of just letting off steam. Eileen's knees buckled when I told her about Lissa's murder. Unless she's one heck of an actress, her reaction is a hard one to fake."

Sonia said, "See a nail gun in her showroom?"

I shook my head. "Nope. Tons of samples, boxes, and crates, but no nail gun."

Queenie made a moue with her lips. "Doesn't mean she doesn't own one."

I agreed. "She could kill Lissa and dump the nail gun, but I don't see Eileen doing the deed. Being rejected after sneaking a kiss as the motive doesn't pass the sniff test. I'm pretty sure we can cross Eileen Hirsch off the list."

Sonia asked, "The other one you interrogated?"

"Lissa's boyfriend. Bobby Javadi."

Sonia asked, "Get anything useful out of him?"

I bit my lower lip. "It took some arm-twisting, but he answered my questions. He says the day of the murder he had a meeting with an immigration attorney downtown Friday until one o'clock. The meeting went poorly. He said he drove out to the beach to figure things out. He claims he walked on the sand until dark and went straight home alone."

I ticked off the points against him. "Escaping deportation doesn't look too good for Bobby. Lissa refused to help him stay in this country by marrying him. Furious, he threatened to get back at her in front of a crowd of witnesses, including me and my friend Chris, in a packed restaurant. He's got motive and the means out the wazoo. He's in construction and owns a nail gun. He's strong enough to pick Lissa up and pack her into a sample crate. He drives a full-sized pickup truck with enough room to haul a crate with a body in it. The lawyer's so-so at best evaluation of his case freaked Bobby out. After the meeting, Bobby says he went to the beach to calm down and consider his options. Maybe there's sand in his truck matching the stuff on Lissa's body? He has no receipts for food, gas, or anything else to prove he spent the afternoon alone at the beach. He can't account for his time Friday afternoon or evening."

I glanced around the table. "Try this scenario on for size: Maybe he went to the mart first before the beach and confronted Lissa, hoping to change her mind? Maybe he convinced Lissa to go with him to the beach? She goes, but still refuses to marry him. Suppose he goes nuts? Maybe he kills her in a rage and goes back to the mart? What if he gets a crate from Lissa's showroom, goes to some obscure location, say one of Mason's construction sites, and stuffs Lissa in the crate? Then he takes her back to the showroom and nails her to the wall." I turned a ta-da motion with my hands.

Queenie tapped her nose with her finger. "An awful lot of what-ifs and maybes in your scenario."

I held my hands out in supplication. "Granted, but also enough questions to push AJ to take another pass at this guy. Bobby says AJ interviewed him over the phone, but not in person. Maybe AJ needs to get a warrant and test Bobby's nail gun. His truck and apartment might be hiding a smoking gun." I smacked my palm on the edge of the table. "I'm tellin' ya girls, he's good for it."

Queenie said, "Don't discuss Bobby with the detective until you've spoken to the Masons."

I sighed. "No luck so far getting in touch with them." I billowed my cheeks and blew out my frustration. "Neither one has been in the mart since AJ interviewed them. I've tried getting a hold of them, but big surprise. Neither of them has returned any of my calls. If I don't hear back from them by tomorrow, I'm gonna take a ride out to their factory." I drummed a beat on the table. "Maybe we're doing this backwards?"

Queenie gave me a wary look. "M-meaning?"

I grinned. "You ready for another Schlivnik adventure?"

Queenie smacked her forehead and groaned.

Chapter Fifteen

I shined the flashlight app on my phone so I could fit the key into the door the night Queenie and I snuck into Lissa's showroom. Queenie squeaked like a rubber ducky as the entire dark-as-a-cave swimwear aisle lit up as bright as if I'd used a klieg light. Three ceramic vases with wilted red roses stood in a row as fallen sentries on the floor in front of the Royal Swimwear showroom.

I shuddered. "Good grief! That's so ghoulish."

Queenie slit her eyes. "What is?"

I pointed the toe of my shoe at the vases. "It's creepy."

Queenie stared as though conversing with a Martian. "What's so creepy about it?"

Must you ask? "She's *dead* and her boyfriend is still sending flowers?"

Queenie twisted the corners of her mouth. "Don't people send flowers after a person dies? My Great Aunt Tilly passed away last year and all her canasta friends sent a huge bouquet of gorgeous flowers to my grandmother."

I needed Queenie's help looking for clues so, I tamped back the snarky comment sitting on the tip of my tongue. "Ok, yes, people do. But they send the flowers to the *mourners, not the dead person.*"

Queenie made a sour face. "Not true. Flowers are sent to funerals all the time."

I gritted my teeth. "Yes. You made my point. Flowers are sent to a *memorial*, not to the dead person's office."

Queenie tapped her index finger on the tip of her nose. "Maybe it's not the way it seems."

I could hardly wait for this explanation. "Really?"

Queenie touched the nearest vase with the toe of her shoe. "Let's say the boyfriend sent the flowers as his way of mourning. You know, like a tribute. The way fans put flowers on an actor's star in front of Grauman's Chinese Theater in Hollywood after the actor dies."

Rather farfetched, but it's always good to consider any conceivable scenarios. "Fair enough. Let's find out."

She gave me a strange look. "How?"

I pointed to the vases. "Any cards?"

Queenie bent at her knees. "Yeah." She took two envelopes and handed me the third.

Queenie read the first one out loud. "I will love you forever." She took the second one out of the envelope. "You will be mine forever."

I made a sour face. "A tad controlling for my taste. But ok, some women prefer a take-charge kind of man."

Queenie pointed to the card in my hand. "Read yours."

I read the card and gulped. "If I can't have you, nobody can."

Queenie held her two cards out. "Put these in your messenger bag. The cards and flowers need to get to your friend the cop."

I crossed my eyes. "Are you crazy?"

Queenie furrowed her brows. "Why? It's evidence. The first two cards, ok, controlling, and creepy. The third card? It's either a threat or somebody confessed to a murder. Isn't it our duty to give it to the detective?"

Good grief. Imagine AJ's reaction as I handed over the stuff? The vision alone gave me the heebie-jeebies. "It's bad enough we already messed with the chain of possession by touching the cards. If we destroyed all the value of the evidence by moving it, she'd string us up by our toes."

Queenie waved the two cards back and forth. "Well, if we don't turn them over to her, leaving them out *here* isn't an option. Someone might help themselves to the flowers and throw away the cards."

I scoffed. "Who wants wilted flowers almost as dead as Lissa?" I beamed the flashlight app around and searched the length of the pitch-black aisle dark as a witch's cauldron. "We're the only ones on the floor. Who'd help themselves to the flowers? I'm not about to call AJ in the *middle of the night* to tell her several floral bouquets and cards are lying in front of a dead woman's showroom. I'd scare the crap out of her if I called now. And if I told her the *reason* for my call, she'd be furious." I smiled. "And explaining *our* being in the mart in the first place?" I laughed. "Dedicated employees getting a project completed on time? Ok, maybe a few hours ago. But now? It's the middle of the night, for crying out loud. Who's gonna believe we're working *this* late? No one. Nothing is gonna happen to the flowers between now and morning. The cleaning crew has come and gone and left three days- worth of flowers sitting in front of the door. I guarantee you the cleaning crew hasn't been inside the Royal showroom since the murder. They've been instructed by the police not to breech the crime scene tape on the door. Security doesn't make the morning rounds on our floor until ten-thirty. I'll get in early and call AJ. I'll tell her I noticed the flowers and cards as I walked past Royal on my way to our showroom and say she ought to check them out. I'll offer to stand guard over them until she sends a uniform to bag them and take them to the lab. She won't suspect we've been nosing around."

Queenie pointed to Lissa's door and clucked her tongue "The way we're going to now?"

I grinned. "Exactly."

Queenie sighed with resignation. "Ok, Nancy Drew. Let's get this little misadventure of yours over with." She twisted the key and pushed the door open a crack. We stepped over the flowers and ducked under the yellow crime scene tape X-ed across the threshold.

Queenie muttered, "I'm amazed I let you talk me into another burglary."

I tsked. "What's your problem? Lissa's dead, remember? She's not gonna walk in on us like Ronnie Schwartzman. It's the middle of the night. The building is empty. Relax. No one's gonna interrupt us. But to be on the safe side, lock the door from the inside and turn off the lights." I sniffed. "Besides, technically, it's not a burglary." I pointed to the key in her hand. "As long as we use that, we're not breaking in…"

Queenie clucked her tongue. "Let me remind you, Miss Smarty Pants, we used a key the last time, and still almost ended up as dead as Lissa."

I gave her the stink eye.

Queenie asked, "And we're looking for…?"

I lifted a shoulder. "I dunno. We'll know it when we see it."

Queenie said, "Don't you think the police already took anything important by now?"

I shrugged. "Maybe yes, maybe no. Maybe the cops

focused on the closet and chose not to go through the offices too thoroughly. The police aren't familiar with the players or the industry the way we are. Maybe they missed something important in plain sight, but they didn't realize it." I turned a three-sixty and looked around the room. "Something to connect Lissa to whoever killed her is in this complex. I can feel it in my bones."

Queenie smirked. "By any chance, can you feel the *location* of this mysterious thing in your bones?"

I headed to the back. "Let's go through Lissa's office and see if anything jumps out. If we don't find anything useful, we'll search the rest of the place."

Queenie stopped walking and put her hands on her hips. "Pay attention, as I want this to be crystal clear." She crossed her heart and twisted her fingers into a pinky swear. "Let me assure you if Lissa's office is a bust, under *no circumstances*, am I going near the creepy closet."

Yikes. Somebody, alert the media. Queenie Levine is an Olympic gold medal champion weenie. If an empty closet gives her the willies, imagine her finding Lissa nailed to the wall? If she didn't die of fright, think of a lifetime of therapy three times a week. I cuffed her shoulder. "For crying out loud, will you relax? Don't get your bloomers in a bunch yet." I tipped my head towards Lissa's office. "Let's get going. We don't wanna take all night to do this."

Queenie announced with a flick of her wrist. "I can't speak for you, but trust me. *I* won't be in the mart all night."

Thirty minutes later Queenie closed the bottom drawer of the file cabinet. She winced as she stood and massaged the small of her back. "I've gone through all the files in all four drawers, and all I got for my trouble is a ginormous crick in my lower back. Nothing out of the ordinary in all those files. Either the police or the killer already took everything from the files related to Lissa's murder." She motioned to Lissa's desk. "You find anything?"

I gave her the thumbs-down sign. "So far, the desk is a big nothing burger. The top drawer has more cosmetics in it than the Bon Belle counter at Bainbridge Department Store. The center drawer has Lissa's major account files. I went through them all. Same as you. Nothing but orders and invoices. I've one more drawer to go through. If it's a bust, we go through the rest of the place."

Queenie folded her arms on her chest. "Correction. *You'll* be going through the rest of the place. *I'll* be on my way home."

I ignored her and pulled the handle on the bottom drawer, but it stuck. I leaned over to see the problem. Off the track. As if someone forced it open. I tried jiggling it back into place, but nothing doing. So far, this escapade was not going the way I'd planned. Out of frustration, I smacked the drawer hard with the heel of my hand. To my astonishment, it slipped back on track. I pulled the drawer open. More files, but all shoved haphazardly in the back, not stacked neatly in alphabetical order like the ones in the other drawer. Impossible to tell if they were rifled through or jostled as I yanked open the drawer. I pulled out a handful of files from the back and flipped through the first four. Major accounts, but nothing unusual. This adventure was a major waste. If the rest of the complex is more of the same, then it's time to admit defeat and boogie. Two documents fell out of the fifth folder and my eyes bugged. I fought the urge to shout out loud. Miraculously, I kept it somewhere between a war-whoop and a whisper. "Come over here. You're not gonna believe this."

Queenie leaned over my shoulder and gasped as I fluttered the first document under her nose. A letter from Annette Mason to Lissa. It was dated a week before the murder with a request for a meeting to discuss Lissa returning to Barely There. The meeting date was for last Friday, the final day of Lissa Charney's life. The second document detailed a contract making Lissa a forty-nine percent partner in the company with an eye-popping salary and benefits.

Queenie slapped her cheek. "And the police missed those papers?"

I shrugged. "Maybe no one looked."

Queenie asked, "Better yet, how did the killer miss them?"

I rolled my eyes. "Possibly, the killer was too busy nailing Lissa to the back of the closet to look around?"

Queenie's eyes ran the length of the contract and she whistled loud as a longshoreman. "Boy, Annette said she'd do *anything* to get Lissa back, and she meant it. The offer is astounding. We should be so lucky. No buy-in. No requirement to even cough up a dime." Queenie batted her eyes. "Unreal. No exclusions, no thresholds of any kind to be met. An almost equal equity position gift-wrapped. And all Lissa has to do? Go to the meeting and sign on the bottom line."

I gave her the stink eye. "Don't get too excited. The salary is impressive *only* if Annette has the money, which, as we gathered, she'd be hard-pressed to scrape together. But even if she could? As to the partnership? Big freaking deal. Nothing but a wing and prayer full of hot air."

Queenie crossed her eyes. "So, lemme get this straight. Somebody makes *you* an offer this big and you'd say no to such a great opportunity?"

I scoffed. "Some great opportunity. Minority ownership of the Titanic as it's going down. This one's a double whammy. It sounds great in theory. But at the end of the day, all a minority partnership means is you're responsible for your share of the liabilities, but with no benefits, since you don't have a controlling interest." I circled the date of the meeting with my finger. "I bet this was the meeting Lissa told Joan about."

Queenie pointed to the last page of the agreement. "The documents are unsigned. She passed on the offer."

I pursed my lips. "Not necessarily. Maybe she wanted to hear more before she signed. Or, Lissa goes to the meeting, the deal doesn't ring her chimes, and she says no. Desperate Annette goes nuts and kills her. Either way is possible." Queenie gave me the big eyes as I put the documents in my purse. I waved her off with a don't lecture me swat of a hand. "Yeah, yeah. I got the message about AJ and her evidence chain of possession crap. Yep, she's gonna be super pissed. Too bad. I'll deal with her later. Right now, I've bigger fish to fry and another drive out to the valley. If we take the lead from the cops on television and follow the money, Annette Mason just jumped to the top of our suspect list."

Chapter Sixteen

The weather goddess rewarded me with one of those Chamber of Commerce-gorgeous kinds of days. A light breeze to tickle your fancy, and not a cloud blemished the baby blue sky. A sunny eighty-five in the middle of winter. No wonder all those Rose Bowl fans never make it back to the frigid Mid-west.

I dropped the top of the convertible, turned the radio dial to the oldies station, and blasted the Beach Boys loud enough to wake the dead. My friends call my choice of music old-fashioned, but I prefer to say I am an old soul. The surfing culture born in the 1960s took my parent's generation by storm. Whether you lived in Bakersfield or Birmingham, every bikini-clad girl or a boy sporting baggies coveted a Woodie with a surfboard strapped to the roof. My parents raised their kids listening to the Beach Boys, Dick Dale's Deltones, and the Ventures, and watching all the "beach blanket" surf movies with Annette Funicello and Frankie Avalon.

The traffic Goddess smiled down at me as I headed north on the Hollywood Freeway to the San Fernando Valley. Miraculously, it didn't take all day to get over the hill. I pulled up to a jungle-green Quonset hut with a mural of the Amazon painted on the front. The quirky headquarters of Barely There Swimwear sat on a dirt-scrabbled side street between Lankershim and Magnolia Boulevards, at the intersection of the old industrial area of North Hollywood and the hip new No Ho Arts District.

The lobby continued the jungle décor with live palm trees and lush tropical plants. Photos and posters of exotic birds and models frolicking at the beach wearing skimpy bikinis adorned the green walls. A taped audio played background jungle sounds relaxing enough, I could have taken a nap.

A ditzy blonde sat behind a bamboo counter with a headset on. She bopped and swayed in her seat as she greeted me. A few minutes later, I followed Annette through the maze of production line cutting tables and sewing stations to her office in the back of the factory.

Annette closed her office door and sat behind an antique French Provincial desk completely out of place in the jungle décor and ornate enough to belong to Marie Antoinette.

Huge potted jungle-like plants, a riot of colorful exotic flowers, and a waterfall filled the large room, making the office as tropical as a rainforest. A four-foot-tall birdcage covered with a dark canvass cloth sat in the far corner across from Annette's desk.

The tinkling of the waterfall was the only sound in the office. No jungle sounds, music, or chatty birds squawking nasty comments interrupted the start of our meeting. Curious. Normally, the bird and Annette are attached. "Corky take a day off?"

Annette pointed to the covered cage. "He's usually out and active, but since this past Friday, he hasn't been himself. The tip of his beak is chipped. Normally he'd fight being confined, but the last few days he's stayed in his cage and kept to himself. He's not hungry or too chatty." Annette's eyes darkened with concern. "I'm getting worried. If he isn't back to his squawking self in a day or two, I'm gonna take him back to the vet, even though he just had his annual checkup this past Friday. He's not gonna be talking your ear off today."

Annette steepled her long, elegant fingers and smiled, but the smile never reached her eyes. "You didn't drive all the way out to the valley to discuss my bird. So, what brings you to my neck of the woods?" She grabbed a half-empty water bottle off her desk with her right hand, glugged a long gulp, and smiled a hopeful smile. "Considering a job change?"

As if. "No. To discuss Lissa Charney."

Annette's smile faded. "What about her?"

"I'm looking into her murder."

Anette blinked her surprise. "Nothing to look into. The killer's been caught."

I shook my head. "Someone's been arrested, but not the right person. Joan Binder isn't the killer. I'm gonna find out who is."

Annette tipped her head with confusion. "And you want from me…?"

"I've got questions."

Annette folded her arms across her chest. "Don't come to me for any answers."

I clucked my tongue. "Humor me."

Annette swept an arm. "Ask away."

"How long did Lissa work for you?"

Annette cast her eyes to the ceiling as though it held the answer. "Five years."

"How would you characterize your relationship with her?"

Annette busied herself refilling the water bottle and avoided looking me in the eye. "She worked for me. If you're asking if we had a close personal relationship or if we socialized, the answer is no. I didn't see her too often. She came to the factory if she needed to. And I went to the mart for market weeks, or to work with a major account." Annette swilled a third of the water in the bottle and gave me an expectant look.

Before I could ask my next question, Annette wriggled around in her chair and said, "Excuse me a minute." She stood and laughed. "I've gotta tinkle." Without waiting for my answer, she opened a door behind the watercooler and ran into a girlie-looking pink powder room. She came back a few minutes later and giggled. "Ah, much better." She gulped more water and batted her eyes as though lost and asking a stranger for directions. "Now, we left off…?"

I finished her sentence for her. "Discussing Lissa's job performance. You happy with hers?"

Annette took another slug of water and tipped her head to the side as though trying to shake the excess out of her ear. "Yeah, sure."

I baited the hook and cast the line out, looking for a bite. "Bet you were pretty pissed she quit."

Annette's face clouded over. "I didn't do a happy dance." She twisted her lips into a tight smile. "But you can't blame a person for wanting to better themselves."

Right. She must be kidding. I cocked a brow. "Cut the crap. The word on the street is you were furious. It's no secret you and Roddy harassed her. I've personally seen a few of those nasty confrontations. Are you ok with Lissa bettering herself? Ha. Not a chance."

Annette jutted her jaw. "No one is indispensable. We've managed to do fine without Lissa Charney."

I dismissed her with a wave. "Oh, come on, it's not

exactly a state secret. Barely There is barely hanging on."

Annette lunged over her desk and barked. "Who said such a filthy lie?" She took a legal pad out of the top drawer and slapped it on her desk. "Rumors can put you out of business if you don't squash them." She poised a pen over the legal pad, ready to write. "Gimme their names. I'm gonna sue them."

I pointed my index finger at her. "You. You told it to Roddy last week."

Her red as a radish blush betrayed her as she falsely claimed with a straight face. "I did no such thing."

The conversation had become rather tedious. I don't cotton to liars or fools. "Listen, Annette, don't bother to deny it. Half the aisle says you complained Lissa took a lot of your business with her."

Annette held out her hands and backpedaled fast as a circus clown on a unicycle. "Yeah ok. We've lost some ground since Lissa left."

Yeah, right. "The fact is, you can't get through the season without her. You were desperate to get Lissa back. You told Roddy even if the two of you don't eat, you'd find a way to pay her."

Annette's mop of wild curls whipped around to cover her face. "It's too bad she left. But, since she made her choice, we'll find somebody else."

I cocked a brow. "She's been gone over a year. Yet the position is still open."

Annette turned up her nose. "We've interviewed a half-dozen candidates, but none of them met our criteria." She huffed. "We're not gonna settle for just any warm body."

I gave her the stink eye. "For crying out loud, stop

already. You're embarrassing yourself. Swimwear suppliers are a close-knit group. We all talk to one another. If anyone has a job interview, the whole floor hears about it."

Annette smiled tightly, but had the grace to blush. "It doesn't take much for the word to get out if you're in trouble. Who wants to board a sinking ship?"

Who indeed?

Annette glugged more water. Good grief. The woman takes in as much liquid as a sponge. Somebody ought to give her the heads up to keep her fingers off the salt shaker.

"Are you able to account for your day last Friday afternoon?"

She drummed a rat-a-tat-tat on the desk with her fingernails. "Chained to my desk."

"Is anyone in the building able to verify it?"

She squinted in concentration. "The sewers leave at three o'clock. but my cutter Seguro stays until four-thirty."

"Did he see you?"

She leaned back in her chair and scrunched her eyes closed. "He probably saw me with the sewers on the production line at some point in the day." She pointed to her door. "Be my guest. Go and ask him. He's the big, burly guy with the bushy handlebar mustache laying out fabric on the cutting table."

I passed on the offer but filed the suggestion away for future reference. "Roddy in the office last Friday?"

Annette jerked her head no and the corkscrew curls curtained her eyes. "No. He was on a construction job with his crew."

"Not in the factory at all?"

She pursed her lips with annoyance. Was her irritation with the question or her answer? Toss a coin. "He was scheduled for a meeting, but he called to say there was some sort of problem with retrofitting a building out in Saugus that needed to be dealt with."

I sat on the edge of the chair and leaned forward. "Neither of you can account for yourselves last Friday, right?"

She tightened her lips into a thin line and glared.

I put Annette's letter to Lissa and the contract on the desk and pushed them in front of her. "I doubt you'd make this kind of offer to any other salespeople."

Annette's face turned the shade of eggplant. "Who gave you these?"

I snapped. "None of your business." I treated Annette to my world-famous death ray glare. "Or maybe you lured her to the meeting with a bogus partnership offer to kill her. She passed on your offer. You make her pay for ruining your business?" Annette's water bottle tottered and almost tipped over when I slammed my palm on the desk. *"Did you Annette? Did you make her pay?"*

Annette reared back as if she'd been branded. "Who do you think you are coming to my shop and insulting me?"

I waited for her to throw me out. If the tables were turned, and she made such an outrageous accusation, I would drop-kick her out the door so fast she'd be dizzy from the flight. Curious. But since I still sat in front of her, I ignored her self-righteous speech and clucked my tongue. "Your husband's construction company is only a few miles north. Gives you easy access to a nail gun."

"You're barking up the wrong tree." Annette

laughed sardonically. "I never even got the opportunity to convince her, let alone see the offer rejected. She said she'd come and hear me out. I waited all day, but she never showed up."

"The same meeting as Roddy?"

Annette's lips moved open and closed as a parched guppy, but nothing came out. She cleared her throat as if she had trouble pushing out a word too big to get past her lips. "Yes."

Annette stood and walked ten paces to a bar-sized mini-refrigerator on the other side of Corky's cage. Her right hand trembled as she traded an empty water bottle for a full one. She glugged three-quarters of the bottle in three swigs. She returned to her seat and Annette gulped as she glanced at the threatening letter I laid on her desk. She swiped her wrist over a thin line of perspiration beading her forehead. She stammered, "W-what's t-this?"

I threw out another line and went fishing. "Don't you recognize it?"

She wiped a crumpled tissue across her damp forehead and dabbed it on the beads of perspiration dotting her upper lip. "No. Should I?" Her eyes traveled over the letter again. "What is it?"

"A threatening letter sent anonymously telling me to stop sticking my nose where it doesn't belong or I'd end up the same as Lissa."

She snarled. "If you're implying I sent it, you're wrong. But maybe you ought to take the advice and quit asking all those questions before something bad does happen to you."

I slit my eyes. "You threatening me?"

She squeaked loud as a rusty gate. "No! I'm just

sayin'."

I put out my hands in supplication. "I've ruffled a few feathers. The question is, which feathers? Yours? Roddy's?" I tsked. "Joan Binder isn't the killer. She wouldn't send the letter. It doesn't benefit her. Better yet, how could she send it while locked behind bars? Either the killer or someone protecting the killer sent this."

I smiled like a shark. "Even a murderer has a mother. Is Roddy around? I need to ask him a few questions."

Corky screeched from across the room. "Roddy's a bad boy! Corky's a bad boy! Roddy's a bad boy! Corky's a bad boy!"

I jumped as if I'd been goosed. Annette stood to indicate the end of the meeting. She walked to the office door and opened it. "You'd better leave." She pointed to the covered cage. "You're upsetting my bird."

Chapter Seventeen

I spent the rest of the day preparing for the rescheduled meeting with Sue Ellen Magee. But I'd left Annette Mason's building with more questions than answers, and the inconclusive meeting kept breaking my concentration. I cut the wrong swatches and started over.... twice. Merde. I finally cut the right ones, inches before I ran out of fabric. The presentation was far from complete, but I needed a break. A pain in the patootie like Sue Ellen Magee would devour me for lunch if I wasn't on top of my game. I packed the Bainbridge Department Store file into my laptop case and wished Patti a good night. Visions of a restorative takeaway Thai chicken pizza with a Rocky Road chaser to clear the cobwebs filled my head.

As I opened the driver's side door of the car, Roddy Mason's baseball mitt-sized hand slammed the door shut. Guess Annette gave her baby boy my message. He stood close enough that I smelled his sweat mixed with the cloying cologne drenched in his shirt. I dazzled him with a dose of my finely honed snark. "I guess your mommy gave you my message, Lurch."

Roddy growled from deep in his throat. "You stay away from my mother and my crewmen or…"

I challenged him. "Or what? You gonna do the same thing to me as you did to Lissa Charney?"

Roddy narrowed his eyes, baffled. Regrettably,

sarcasm appeared lost on such a dim bulb. "Are you nuts? The cops arrested Joan whatshername. Your big mouth friend took out the lazy bitch, not me."

I waved an index finger back and forth in the air. "The cops are wrong. Joan is innocent, and I'm gonna prove it. You're pretty good for Lissa's murder. You own a nail gun, and you've got one helluva motive."

Roddy huffed. "You're crazy."

I dismissed the comment with a cluck of my tongue. "Frankly, I don't blame you. I'd be pretty pissed too if *my mother* pulled such a stunt. Imagine, her giving away your partnership. To a stranger no less. Your partnership, your future. The one you worked hard for. And Lissa Charney waltzes in and snatches it right out of your hands. Your mother said Lissa wasn't at the meeting, and neither were you."

Roddy spat. "A problem at a job site took all day to fix."

I poo-pooed it with a roll of my eyes. "Says you. I say you killed Lissa before she could sign on the dotted line."

Roddy flexed the fingers of his right hand under my nose. "Prove it."

I poked my finger into an open wound to see if it bled. "By the way, the letter you sent anonymously? Nice touch." I cut the big bruiser in half with my scorn. "Some big man you are. You write a threatening letter and don't have the guts to sign your name to it."

Roddy stared as though I spoke in tongues. "Huh?"

A moron or a great actor? Time to find out. "Do you need it spelled out?"

He held up his right hand the same as a courtroom witness swearing on a Bible. "I'm telling the truth. I swear. It isn't from me."

He might be telling the truth. He fanned his fingers and winced. He put his left hand over his heart and my eyes bugged. A bandaged wrist and swollen knuckles turned ugly shades of black and blue. His signet ring? Missing from his left finger. Oh boy.

My eyes glanced surreptitiously around the parking level. Crap on a crumpet. All alone. I bit my lip to tamp back the urge to yell, "You killed her!" I pointed to his hand. In a remarkably calm tone, I deadpanned. " Pretty nasty."

He brushed it off with a shrug. "Construction accident. Comes with the territory. No big deal. You get used to it."

Roddy and Bobby either practice the same canned speech or echo a company policy on defending against a dangerous work environment. Or, maybe while I've been so busy sniffing around, I missed the answer right under my nose? Say Bobby and Roddy murdered Lissa together? They both had the means and motive out the wazoo.

I glanced around the parking lot again. Counting my convertible, four cars, and no one else on the level. Fanfreakingtastic. Alone with a pissed-off King Kong. Now what? Nothing to do but keep going. "Can you account for your activities Friday?"

Roddy snapped. "None of your business."

I put out my hands. "So, I assume you've something to hide."

He sighed as though the weight of the world rested on his broad shoulders. "Out in Saugus on a retrofitting job with my crew."

Roddy spun the same story as Bobby Javadi, except

off by a day. One of them lied. One of them told the truth. Which one was which? "Who can confirm your story?"

He smirked. "My father."

I gave him the stink eye. "Besides the man who brought you into the world."

As though doing me a gigantic favor, he groused. "Fine. The assistant foreman, Bobby Javadi."

I slit my eyes. "I don't believe you."

Roddy backed me into the door of my car and snarled. "I don't give a crap if you believe me or not. Stay away from my mother, my crew, and me, or you're gonna be sorry."

Dad's voice played on a continuous tape inside my head. '*You might be quaking in your shoes, but never let 'em see you shaking.*' My pounding heart jackhammered against my ribs as I jutted my jaw. "If you killed Lissa Charney, you're the one who's gonna be sorry."

Roddy's eyes glittered. "For a squirt, you've got some mouth on you."

I took a mental bow. But only an idiot eggs a big goon like Roddy Mason on. Color the idiot me. "If you killed her, I'll see to it you pay for the rest of your life."

Roddy made a fist with his right hand and waved it in front of my nose. "Somebody ought to teach you some manners." He flexed his fist and sneered. "Guess it's gonna be me."

I tightened my hold on the strap of the laptop case. "So, it makes you a big he-man hitting a woman half your size?"

Roddy growled like a cornered dog.

I've never been too good at controlling my tongue. Smooth move, Schlivnik. Piss off Godzilla with no one else around.

He lunged and I ducked. He made another fist and wound up tight as a baseball pitcher. Roddy knocking Lissa unconscious and shooting her with a nail gun? Absolutely. Roddy stopping Lissa forever is a big stretch? Not anymore. And the big ape's encore? My lifeless body crammed into another sample crate? Not in this girl's plans, bucko. Twice my size? Too freaking bad. Gotta play the cards you're dealt. Bring it on, King Kong.

Roddy's knuckles only grazed my cheek, but he'd hit his mark if I gave him another opportunity. He came at me again, but I squared my shoulders, ready for bear.

Now or never. I aimed for his gut but he stood too tall and my angle slanted off-kilter, so, I'd miss my prime target. I lowered the arc and swung the laptop case into his family jewels with all my might.

He crumpled with the squeeze of an accordion and collapsed with all the grace of a sack of potatoes. I stepped over his writhing body and jumped into the car. I opened the window and leaned over. "Next time, pick on someone your own size."

Chapter Eighteen

Bobby Javadi stalked into the customer service waiting room at Garvin Auto early Saturday morning inexplicably dressed in grease-stained mechanics overalls. His greeting? Not exactly warm and fuzzy. He snapped. "Are you back to finish the job and get me fired?"

Huh? Either the guy's no morning person, or he needed more coffee.

He spat. "After your last visit, I caught it big from my sales manager. He made it painfully clear I'm paid to sell cars, not to sit around and shoot the breeze with some broad. Thanks to you, I'm on probation. One more mark against me and I'm gone."

Bobby's glare radiated his displeasure. "And as if you weren't already helpful enough, I went to the construction job on Monday, and got an earful from Roddy Mason for talking to you." Bobby narrowed his eyes. "What do you want from me now?"

Frustration peppered my tone. "I'm sorry if you're in hot water with your bosses. You asked me not to call you at either job, and I honored your request." I tapped the face of my mobile. "I'd make an appointment to meet with you at your home if you'd ever bother answering your cell phone."

He sighed. "I've torn my apartment and my truck apart, but I can't find the phone. I guess I lost it on one of the jobs last week. I've been too busy to replace it."

I looked at him funny. "Don't you use a landline?"

He shook his head. "I'm not home enough to need one, so it's pointless to spend extra money on something I'd hardly use."

I pointed to his strange attire. "Demoted?"

He patted the front of his overalls and laughed. "I wish. Mechanics make a lot more money than salesmen. I enjoy getting my hands under the hoods of old cars. The head mechanic is a friend of mine. He calls me if they get a classic car in the shop. Last night a fifty-seven vintage beauty came in."

He took a greasy rag out of his back pocket and wiped a patch of oil off his calloused hands. "We're in the middle of replacing the carburetor. I need to get back before they finish without me. You've got five minutes." He glanced at the wall clock. "Better talk fast, the clock is ticking."

I laughed. "Five minutes? Not enough time. Tell them to finish without you." I put the threatening letter in front of him. "Your story has more holes in it than Swiss cheese."

Bobby read the letter and gave me an expectant look. "This has nothing to do with me."

I paid no attention to his reply. "Do you own a typewriter?"

He screwed up his face. "Who uses a typewriter anymore?"

My tone became insistent. "*Do you*?"

Sparks of resentment radiated from his angry eyes. "Since I'm an immigrant from some backward country, I'm incapable of using a computer?"

Fair enough. "Ok, if not you, are you aware of

anyone who does own a typewriter?"

He furrowed his brows. "Garvin is completely computerized, and the Mason accounting department uses an electric adding machine."

I narrowed my eyes. "So, I'm supposed to believe you're not responsible for this?"

He picked the letter up, glanced at the two lines, and handed it back. "I've never seen this before."

I changed directions to throw him off. "You can account for yourself the morning of Lissa's murder, right?"

He clucked his tongue with annoyance. "Consider taking notes since you can't remember. *Yes.* I already told you. I had a meeting at my lawyer's office on the morning of Lissa's murder."

I smirked. "Care to revise your answer?"

He snapped. "Nothing's changed since the last time."

I gave him the stink eye. "According to Roddy Mason, you were in Saugus on a construction job."

Bobby relaxed the fists clamped to his sides. "He mixed the days up. We've got a lot of jobs all over the place, and they often overlap. If the schedule's not in front of you, it's easy to get the days confused. I told you. Thursday my crew and I went to Saugus. Thursday, *not* Friday. I took Friday off to go to the lawyer."

He might be selling, but I didn't buy a single word. "Roddy specifically said *you* were on the job with the crew on Friday. He used you as his alibi for the day of the murder."

Bobby snapped. "He lied."

Not so fast, bucko. "Maybe you're the one lying. Maybe you and Roddy killed Lissa together. You both own nail guns and a big motive to take her out."

He burst out laughing. "I don't give a flying pig about Roddy's motive. But my motive? I've got no motive. She does me no good dead." He smirked. "INS won't accept marriage to a U.S.-born corpse as a means to avoid deportation. Friday morning, I met with my lawyer. You don't believe me? I'll give you my lawyer's number. Call him, and check it out for yourself."

I tsked. "Nice try, but it doesn't clear you. The morning is not your problem, it's the afternoon between one and five. You said you left your lawyer and went to the beach. But you can't account for your time Friday afternoon. Lissa said no way to the marriage and made it clear she wouldn't change her mind. Your lawyer said deportation is a real possibility. Lissa refused to help. You wanted revenge. Say you leave the lawyer's office, go to the mart, and convince Lissa to spend the day with you and try to work something out. Instead of an afternoon at the beach, you meet Roddy. You take Lissa out to say, the building in Saugus, and kill her? The two of you pack her in a sample crate, bring her back to the mart, and nail her to the closet wall."

Bobby spat. "Prove it." He stood and faced the exit. "Now if you'll excuse me, I've got a carburetor to install."

Bobby turned about-face and headed for the door. "If you're interested in buying a car, give me a call. We have a big inventory to move and we're dealing. If not, don't bother coming back. I've nothing else to say to you."

Chapter Nineteen

The convertible started handling funny on the way to work Monday morning. My mechanic Johnny put her up on the rack and said my baby needed new shoes. He put on a new set of tires setting me back a bundle. The car drove fine on surface streets, but she rode mushy on the freeway. Merde. Another problem? I called Johnny and asked. Nah. No biggie. New tires drive differently depending on the road conditions until they're broken in. Whew. I almost collapsed with relief.

My father's younger brother Barry and I made it our business to meet for dinner twice a month. After work, I parked in the Beverly Hills city lot nearest to my uncle's office building and walked the short distance to the Noshorium deli on Beverly Drive.

We closed our menus and my uncle asked, "Is the investigation going okay? Close to figuring out whodunit?"

I batted my eyes and quirked a Mona Lisa smile. "Investigation?"

He slapped the table and laughed. "Cute you'd even try to lie."

If I closed my eyes and listened to the flat Midwest twang and deep bass laugh rumbling like a distant clap of thunder, I couldn't guess if it was my uncle or my dad. The two brothers were blessed with sharp minds, shared a common sense of decency, and a wicked sense of humor, but little else. Not many ever guess my tall, thin, pale-skinned, athletic Uncle Barry and my olive-complexioned, on the short side of average, chunky dad came from the same set of parents.

Uncle Barry gave me the big eyes." You might get away with your Miss Innocent stunt with a stranger. But with your uncle who has been part of your life from before birth? Give me a break."

I gave him the stink eye. "You have a mighty suspicious mind."

He burst out laughing. "I'm a lawyer. They pay me the big bucks to be suspicious." His eyes twinkled with glee. "Besides, I eat lunch with Rose Markowitz once a week. From the way Rose told it, the cops don't have a smoking gun, but her client still needs all the help she can get. So, are you getting anyplace with your snooping? Got a long list of suspects?"

I threw in the towel. So much for subterfuge. "Four. I've eliminated one and am on the fence with another. But the other two have the means and motive out the wazoo."

He examined me like a courtroom witness. "Any proof, or is it all circumstantial?"

I smiled sweetly. "Right now, door number two. But I've ruffled a few feathers."

My uncle the lawyer never misses a thing. "Define ruffling a few feathers. We talking somebody annoyed by you asking questions, or you do something worse to piss them off?"

I squirmed in my seat and took a few beats to consider my reply. The phrasing of my answer better be uber selective. One peep from my uncle to Mike Schlivnik about the threatening letter or an ugly confrontation in a parking garage, and my overly protective father and a posse of his fellow sales reps would be booking seats on the early LA flight tomorrow morning from Miami.

And before I say mind your own business, I'm an adult capable of taking care of myself, my houseboat is on the market, and my mother moved me lock, stock, and barrel into my old room back home. An exaggeration? With the Great God of Guilt and his blushing bride as parents? Not even close.

But, saying nothing is not an option. Silence in this family is not golden. I took a risk and went with an evasive answer giving nothing critical away. I inwardly cringed, expecting some pushback. "Let's say I've pushed the envelope pretty far."

To my utter shock, Uncle Barry inexplicably let me off the hook. "The cop and the ME are acquaintances of yours, right?"

I hurried my reply before he grilled me on everything I'd left out. "The ME and I are old school friends. And I have a history with the detective. She's married to my LA sales rep when I was at Ditzy Swimwear."

I beamed my most engaging smile. "AJ is a good cop. Once I've got all my ducks in a row, I'll turn over everything to her. No smoking gun yet, but I've got enough for her to give two of these guys a second look."

Uncle Barry studied me over the rim of his eyeglasses. "And if she doesn't? Are you willing to go much further?"

An excellent question. As I struggled for a truthful answer that wouldn't put my father on the morning flight, the server arrived and delivered two steaming plates of the brisket special and me from digging myself into a deeper hole. Fortunately, hunger trumped conversation. We dug into our meals and ate in companionable silence.

The server brought the check, and miraculously, my uncle allowed me to leave the tip. He paid the bill and insisted on walking me to my car.

We said our goodbyes, I dropped the top, and took Olympic Boulevard west to the 405 south. I got to the crest of the on-ramp and hot diggity dog. For once, the 405 traffic was remarkably light.

Never one to squander an opportunity, I opened the V-8 full throttle and let all two hundred eighty-nine horses run their hearts out. I shivered as the cold wind blasted through my thin jacket, but I couldn't care less. I tooled along in the zone, singing off-key with the Beach Boys.

And then thirteen miles later, all hell broke loose. The car vibrated violently on the transition to the Marina freeway. The right rear tire exploded and two big chunks of rubber flew over the hood as I came around the sharp curve on the backside of the ramp. The frame shimmied as the car veered sharply to the right. Instinct said to slam on the brakes and yank the wheel to the left.

Miraculously, I remembered the high school driver's ed teacher warning this specific move is a sure way to flip the car and roll. I kept my foot on the accelerator and steered in the direction of the skid and managed to regain control of the car and not crash into another vehicle. I eased up on the gas and steered into the emergency lane as the car decelerated. The car bumped and lurched sloppy as a floundering, fall-down drunk, and finally rolled to a fitful stop. I killed the engine, flipped the emergency flashers on, and called the Auto Club.

The adrenalin rush kept me alive, but with the emergency now over, exhaustion took its place. I laid my head back and closed my eyes. Had I been out long? No clue. But a guy wearing a sweat-rimmed UCLA ball cap and a grease-stained Auto Club uniform tapped my arm with a clipboard to wake me. "Miss, miss. Are you alright?"

He whistled sharply through the gap in his crooked front teeth. "This is one nasty blowout. You're lucky to be alive. From the shred of the tire, you were going pretty fast." He tsked, "It's a good thing one of the back tires blew. A blowout in the front? Even Dale Earnhardt's car is uncontrollable. Just flips and rolls." He widened his eyes. "Somebody upstairs must be looking out for you. With the top-down? No one survives a flip and roll."

I got out and followed him as he walked around the car. He fiddled with the valves on the other three tires and whistled again. "These are brand new tires, right?"

I just spent a king's ransom on them. Johnny would have some 'splaining' to do if they were defective. "Yeah. Brand new. Why do you ask? Are they defective?"

He waved the question away. "No, the tires themselves are fine."

I gave him the stink eye. "What's the problem?"

He tapped the rim of the driver's side front tire with the steel toe of his work boot. "Whoever put them on doesn't know spit about tires." He squatted in front of the tire, took the valve between his thumb and index finger, and wiggled it. "See this loose valve? *This* is your problem. Valves are supposed to be nice and tight.

Betcha the car's been driving squishy, right?"

My eyelids snapped wide open to full attention. "How does the loose valve determine the way the car drives?"

He puffed out his cheeks. "Loose valves? Screws up your air pressure. Slow leaks. If your air pressure's too low, the car drives squishy." He tapped the tire with a pen. "That's the reason the tires are sitting so low. They're all way too low on air. You're lucky all four tires didn't blow. One loose valve, ok the mechanic's lazy, or in a hurry and doesn't check all of them thoroughly."

He took the ball cap off and scratched the crown of his head. "All four valves *this* loose? Either someone allowed an untrained mechanic to install the tires or someone wanted you dead."

Chapter Twenty

Queenie grinned. "Guess the second set of tires is on Johnny."

I wish. "Guess again. Somebody monkeyed with the tires. The tow truck guy said it's the reason the valves were so loose."

Hope's hands flew to her cheeks. "My God! You were almost killed."

I pinched my cheeks and grinned. "Yeah, but this time Lady Luck smiled on me."

Sonia blew out a breath. "My advice is don't push the envelope any further."

Queenie waggled her finger. "She's right. Maybe you ought to quit before Lady Luck changes her mind and she gives you the middle finger salute next time."

I might have been thrown, but nobody's keeping me down. I'm too close and stubborn to quit now. Bucking broncos be damned. "Are you guys nuts? This is just starting to get interesting."

Queenie gave me the stink eye. "You are aware dead is forever, right?"

And? "If I don't stand up for myself, who will? Bobby Javadi enjoys messing around with classic cars. Maybe he messed with mine. The only way to find out is to get in his face."

We finished our coffee and Queenie dropped me off at Johnny's station. I followed him into the garage. My convertible sat suspended on the rack. Johnny pressed the lever and lowered the car to eye level. He squeezed the valve stem of the front right tire and wiggled it around. "I've got good news and bad news. Whaddya want first?"

I quaked at the paltry sum of my checking account balance. "Definitely, the good news."

He said, "Ok. The good news is we only replaced the two rear tires. The front two are undamaged. We only replaced their valve stems."

Hot diggity dog. Waaaay better than I expected. "Maybe the insurance company won't cancel me." I held my breath. "And the bad news?"

His face clouded over. "The tow truck guy was right. These tires were tampered with. The valve stems were purposely fouled. How all four tires didn't blow is amazing. You've no idea how lucky you are. You pissed someone off. Somebody worked awfully hard trying to make you dead." He took an oil-stained rag out of the back pocket of his uniform. He wiped his greasy fingers clean and fondly cuffed my chin. "Whatever you're doing, stop doing it." He grinned a toothy smile. "I've got two kids you're helping put through college."

I live to serve.

****

Sonia asked, "You and Bobby discuss your tires?"

I sighed. "Not yet."

Hope gave me the stink eye. "Come to your senses yet?"

I snapped like a cranky croc. "Meaning?"

Hope snapped back. "Tell Buster's wife and let the cops deal with it."

As if. "No way. I called Bobby at Garvin Auto, but the receptionist said he didn't come in. I inquired about his work schedule. She said she had no information, and passed me along to Bobby's boss. He said Bobby got injured at his other job and is on medical leave. I pushed him for an answer, but the boss wouldn't say when he'd be back."

Sonia clucked her tongue. "Geez, that's awful. Any idea what happened?"

I held my hands out. "No clue. No one at the dealership is talking." I widened my eyes. "And it gets weirder."

Queenie repeated. "Weirder?"

I batted my eyes. "I called Mason Construction, but they sealed their lips with industrial-strength glue. Not even an admission he'd been injured. All they said is Bobby took time off for personal leave."

Hope tapped her cheeks. "Maybe he got deported?"

I shook my head. "No, then they'd say he no longer works at Mason Construction."

Sonia said, "So, Bobby is a dead-end, at least for now."

I sighed with relief. "Yeah. If he tampered with my tires, at least he's out of commission and won't be messing with me." I sent up a silent prayer to be right.

Chapter Twenty-One

This had been one gold medal rip-snorter of a day. Nothing but problems. Late deliveries, impatient buyers, cranky sales reps. Even the postman's boxers were in a bunch. I'm not normally a clock-watcher, but I counted the minutes for the day to end. I practically pole-vaulted out of the mart at five o'clock. The best thing about this lousy day? In the history books.

I dropped the top on the convertible and headed west. An involuntary shudder crept along my spine as I transitioned from the 405 to the Marina freeway. My stomach growled as I exited west off the freeway and headed north on Lincoln Boulevard. My normal go-to? A takeaway pizza. Screw the pizza. The best remedy for this stinker kind of day? Rocky Road and Chardonnay.

I arrived at the basin security gate at the same time as salty Muriel Lobowsky, the prickly, independent octogenarian sailor extraordinaire who lived aboard the thirty-six-foot ketch at the end of the dock. The white-haired old coot sailed solo around the world in her mid-seventies. I'd be lucky to be as plucky as her if I lived as long.

We got to my houseboat and Muriel asked, "If you don't mind me asking, any particular reason you stopped using Below the Waterline Diving Service to clean the bottom of your boat? Kinda surprised, but I figured you changed divers for some reason. You unhappy with them?" Muriel clacked her dentures together and they shifted when she smiled. "You're certainly free to change divers, but since all of us on the dock use the same service to get a better price, the right thing to do would have been to give us a heads up. With you gone to another diver, Below the Waterline will raise the price for the rest of us for sure."

I gave Muriel a closer look. She was a woman of a certain age. Maybe dementia set in? "Who told you that? I made no change in diving services."

Muriel squinted. "You sure?"

I gave her the big eyes. "Yeah, of course, I'm sure. Below the Waterline serviced my boat and all the other boats on the dock two days ago." I narrowed my eyes. "Why do you think I changed divers?"

Muriel scratched a thatch of thinning, stick-straight white hair on the back of her head. "After lunch, a sportfishing boat dropped anchor behind your houseboat. A guy in a wetsuit and tanks disappeared under your boat for twenty minutes."

Holy guacamole. "You get a look at the guy? Tall, short, black, white, old, young?"

Muriel had the grace to blush. "Sorry, no clue. I swabbed the aft deck and wasn't paying much attention to anything but my bucket and mop. Midday, the marina is normally quiet. I'm usually the only one on the dock since most folks are working. The engine noise got my attention. The diver had his back to me when he splashed into the water, so, even if I paid him some mind, wetsuits, and masks hide distinctive features. For all I know, he was a Martian with green hair and blue skin."

I tamped back the panic rising from the pit of my stomach. "Maybe Below the Waterline left a tool or weren't finished, and went back to complete the job."

Muriel squinted. "Nah. Their boats are distinctive. Navy blue canvass overhang. Hull painted royal blue below and red above with a bright yellow stripe in the middle with their logo painted on it. My eyes might not be as sharp as they used to be, but I'd recognize one of their boats. The boat anchored behind yours? All white, no canvass overhang, and smaller."

I pointed to a power boat docked in the first slip next to the security gate. "Any markings on the boat?"

She nodded. "Yeah. Curiosity got the best of me, so I walked over to your slip and went to the end of your dock for a closer look. A hand-painted sign: B J's Diving Service draped over the port side of the boat."

The blood froze in my veins.

Muriel and I spent two hours examining my boat from stem to stern. We put extensions on our scrubbers and scraped the skeleton of the hull. We went as far below the waterline as the scrubbers reached, but other than a thin layer of slimy algae, the hull passed muster. No ticking bombs, no sticks of dynamite. Nothing more than a bunch of pesky mollusks who made the hull their home.

Muriel went back to her boat and I tried to settle in for the night. But I spent a restless one worrying about anything going on below the waterline. I finally fell into a fitful sleep. But the normal squeaks and creaks I'd usually sleep through woke me, and the slightest shift in the slip made me crazy. Exhausted from the lack of a good night's sleep, I gave up and left groggy early the following morning with my boat still afloat.

Charlie Hammond, the Dockmaster, called after lunch and said I better get to the marina ASAP to deal with a huge problem. It must be pretty bad. In all the years I've moored my boat in Porto Paloma Marina, the only time I speak with the Dockmaster is if I pay my slip fees in person at the office, instead of dropping the check into the rent mailbox. Now in the blink of an eye, I've gone from being a problem-free tenant to I have a huge problem.

I ran out of the showroom as if I had fire ants in my pants. I broke several dozen traffic laws and arrived at the marina in less than thirty minutes. My heart seized as I ran down the gangplank and stopped at my slip. A harbor patrol boat, a marine tug, a Below the Waterline dive boat, and almost all my dock neighbors surrounded my half-sunk, listing houseboat. The worry lines of the Dockmaster's face creased grimly as the harbor patrolman angled his head toward my disabled boat. "You're the owner of the vessel?"

I nodded. "I am." I leaned over the dock to examine my sinking yacht. "I left her this morning in shipshape condition. Eight hours later, she's underwater. What happened to her between those hours?"

The diver standing on the other side of the patrolman said, "She's got two-five-meter-long gashes three centimeters deep at the juncture of the keel attached to the hull."

I pointed to the tip of the bow of my half-submerged yacht sticking out of the water. "I understand the fiberglass outer layer can be ripped open, but the hull is made of steel."

The diver tapped the metal dock box with his toe. "True, but even steel isn't completely impervious." He barked a brittle laugh. "Looks like somebody took a can opener and peeled back your hull. From the depth and angle of the gashes, a grappling hook is the likely culprit. We also found a cluster of nails embedded in the keel. Not sure about the nail lengths or how deeply they're embedded. The keel might not be salvageable, but eyeballing it, it's hard to say. Can't tell the extent of the damage until she's out of the water and in drydock for a complete inspection. This is the work of no amateur." He frowned, and a deep V cratered the center of his forehead. "Someone worked pretty darned hard to sink your boat and came mighty close to succeeding. You're lucky this happened at low tide or your slip would be empty by now. Good thing it happened during the day and not in the middle of the night with you aboard. She'd sink faster than the Titanic and you'd drown in your sleep."

The patrolman pointed to Muriel. "If not for your neighbor calling the dockmaster, your boat would be sitting on the bottom of the channel."

I gingerly tapped my fingers onto the houseboat's forward guard rail. "Is it safe for me to board her and pack a bag?"

The patrolman deferred to the diver. "Not the best idea, but I guess if you're cautious, it's ok." The diver waggled the fingers on his right hand and warned. "Five minutes. Not a second more. And walk lightly."

****

I met the marine tug at the guest dock of The Boat Doctor. I signed a ton of papers, gave them my insurance information, took another week's worth of clothes, and left the houseboat in their capable hands. The Boat Doctor couldn't say how long my poor girl will be out of commission, let alone if saving her is possible. I invited myself for an extended stay at the hotel Queenie Levine.

I'm deathly allergic to cats so, Samson and Delilah, her incredibly spoiled Persians, must be good and miffed being relegated to sleeping in the garage.

Food was the last thing on my mind, but Queenie insisted we go out for a bite at Pasta at the Pier, a cozy locals trattoria located on the north side of Washington Street two blocks east of the beach and a few minutes-walk from Queenie's condo. I pushed the squares of lobster ravioli around my plate and nibbled on a sesame breadstick. Mario, the owner, overheard about my troubles, and sent a bottle of Chianti to the table, on the house. Does anyone mind if I chug it?

Queenie studied me over the rim of her wineglass. "Counting the letter, this makes three threats on your life in a week. Even for you, this must be some kind of a record. Face it, Nancy Drew, you're in over your head. You better bring in the pros and pronto. The next one might be more than a threat. The next one might get you dead."

****

I played a losing game of tug of war with AJ's King German Shepard Peso while the detective thumbed through the documents. AJ waved Annette's partnership agreement in the air like guiding a plane in for a landing. "How you got this, how long you've had it, or who you've shown it to is gonna piss me off, right?"

I snapped, "Don't look a gift horse in the mouth."

She jutted her chin and fired back. "Are you familiar with the term obstruction of justice? You're two steps away from landing in a cell next to your buddy Joan." AJ blew a bubble the size of a paperweight. "Planning to give me all this before or after Joan Binder's trial? If you wanted to help her, this might do the trick."

I smiled sweetly. "Does this mean you're dropping the charges against her?"

AJ favored me with one of her patented "boy, are you stupid" looks. And any hope of springing Joan deflated flat as a leaky balloon.

I threw my hands in the air. "See? This is *exactly* the reason not to come to you." I pointed to the documents. "Who sent the threatening letter? Joan?" I waggled my index finger in the air. "Oh, maybe the *real* killer? In case you don't remember, you put Joan behind bars, and she *remained* incarcerated while my car and boat were messed with. Does it mean anything to you? Do you even consider looking at anyone else? Nosiree, not you. Your mind is already cast in stone. Joan Binder is guilty. Lock her up and throw away the key. You say you're an open-minded cop. Not in my book." I ran my fingers through my hair. "No wonder I went it alone. Joan Binder isn't the only one with a nail gun. Bobby Javadi and Roddy Mason own them too. Maybe their nail guns shoot bent nails? Bobby said he dropped his nail gun and the handle got nicked. He denied his shot bent nails, but gee whiz, maybe he's lying? Why don't you test their nail guns while you're testing Joan's? Bobby and Roddy have much stronger motives than Joan. Especially Bobby Javadi. Roddy might be angry enough to kill her *if* Lissa signed the deal. Murdering her killed the partnership. But with Lissa refusing to marry Bobby, his life is in danger if he's deported back to Iran. And let's not forget Annette Mason. She's furious with Lissa for jumping ship. Annette blames Lissa for the loss of her company's sales. If Lissa said no to Annette's offer, maybe desperate Annette was angry enough to kill? Those three are far better suspects."

One glance at AJ's impassive expression said it all. I'd be better off making my case to Peso. AJ pursed her lips. "Putting your withholding of evidence and obstruction of justice aside for the moment, let's focus on your problems. Lemme see if I have this right. You received a threatening letter. You don't stop doing whatever the sender wanted you to stop doing and you piss them off even more. They monkeyed with your tires to send you a clearer sign, and you ignored it too. And now, your houseboat almost sunk. The ante has raised the stakes even higher. That covered everything? Right?" AJ shoved another board of pink bubblegum into her mouth and blew a bubble the size of a boxing glove.

I hung my head. "Yes. Everything."

AJ popped the bubble with her front teeth. "*And,*" her voice dripped sarcasm. "Your first move, of course, is to call me?" She wagged an index finger in my face. "Oh, no, not you, Miss Independent. Your brilliant game plan? Confront the person behind the two attacks. Right?"

Fearing arrest, I resisted the urge to throttle her. Instead, I put out my hands in supplication. "AJ..."

Fury sparked from her eyes. "Don't AJ me. It's a simple question. Yes, or no?"

"Yes, but..."

She scoffed. "No buts, except for the butthead standing in front of me. He didn't succeed the first two times, so you magnanimously gave him a third chance? Do you have a death wish, or are you merely dumb?"

I flexed my steepled fingers to do something other than strangle the detective with my bare hands. "The only thing I could come to you with were guesses. Once I had proof, I promise, I planned to give it to you. Bobby didn't answer the phone, so I went to his apartment. He wasn't exactly too kicked in the butt to see me, but I barged my way in. Bobby said his injury happened before someone monkeyed with my car, so physically, he claims not capable of doing it. He's a desperate man and I don't believe him." I jutted my jaw. "If you won't get the truth out of him, I will."

Chapter Twenty-Two

I handed Joan her coffee and gave her the once over. "For a woman who spent almost a week in jail, you look pretty good."

Joan finger-poofed her hair and laughed. "Oh yeah. I highly recommend it. A Caribbean cruise, but without those pesky high waves making you too seasick to leave your cabin. The accommodations? Luxurious. The gourmet cuisine? To die for. And the entertainment? First-rate." She slapped her cheek. "Oh, and don't let me forget the relaxing massages and facials."

Queenie's eyes shone with admiration. "Which brand of hocus-pocus did Ms. Markowitz pull out of her magic bag of tricks to get you sprung?"

Joan said, "Nothing too fancy. Her usual pushy, insistent self, but luck smiled on us, and she had help."

Sonia parroted. "Help?"

Joan held out her palms. "The evidence."

Hope repeated. "The evidence?"

Joan pointed to me and grinned. "Thanks to Holly's idea, theirs fell apart. Ms. Markowitz followed up on your suggestion. She contacted the nail gun manufacturer and received a detailed description of the interior damage to the nail gun if it shot bent nails. Ms. Markowitz asked the manufacturer to send a certified letter of authenticity along with a damaged nail gun and a new one to the crime lab. The lab techs compared them to my nail gun. The nails from my nail gun? No match for the ones embedded in Lissa. Ms. Markowitz insisted they shoot the nails from my gun. My nails shot straight."

I muttered. "It's a wonder they didn't say you owned a second nail gun."

Joan grinned as wide as a Jack O'Lantern. "Don't worry, they did. They tore the showroom apart again but found nothing. They ransacked my house, scoured the garage, practically dismantled my van, and found nothing but samples."

Sonia wiggled her fingers. "Your prints were not on Lissa's crate?"

Joan said, "Oh yeah, they are, and the police tried to make it a big deal. But it meant nothing since the crate Lissa put in my van isn't the one her body was stuffed into. No traces of blood inside or out. And the fingerprints inside the crate? All Lissa's, none of them mine. No dander flakes, no hair, or skin. Nothing to indicate a human body was ever inside the crate. The only bodies inside the crate? A bunch of plastic sample forms."

Hope asked, "So, did they confiscate the other crate?"

Joan smiled. "No one shared any information with me, but it doesn't seem so."

Queenie asked, "Anything else?"

Joan said, "A few other things."

We were hanging on Joan's every word by then. Hope twirled her hands with an *out with it already* spin. "Such as?"

Joan said, "They demanded proof I'd been at the mall, like a receipt with a date and time stamp. I told the truth and said I threw them away when I got home from the mall." Joan rolled her eyes. "I was so freaked out getting arrested, I forgot I returned a pair of jeans at Bobby Shops for my older daughter before I went to the movies. Lucky for me, my daughter remembered and told Ms. Markowitz. Ms. M. found the return receipt with my credit card imprint, signature, date, and time stamp in my wallet. And the lab report confirmed all the blood on the overalls was mine."

I tapped a teaspoon against my cup to get Joan's attention. "You said a few other things."

Joan pointed her coffee cup at me. "You."

I poked my index finger into my cleavage. "Me?"

Joan's eyes shone with unshed tears. "Your nail gun manufacturer idea sprung me." Joan covered her hand over mine and squeezed. "But more important, you put your life on the line for me."

I snorted a laugh. "Don't be too fast to pin a medal on me. I just nosed around."

Joan fondly tweaked the tip of my nose. "Don't sell yourself short. Your nosiness got me out."

I motioned across the table to Ms. Levine. "If you're gonna thank anyone, thank Queenie. She's the one who insisted I talk to AJ."

Sonia pointed a teaspoon at me. "Since Joan is in the clear, are you done sleuthing?"

I rolled my eyes. "Not even close."

Hope smacked her coffee cup onto the saucer with a loud thwack. "Why the heck not?"

Queenie snarked. "Maybe she has a death wish."

I made a sour face. "Funny as passing a kidney stone. No, Miss Smarty Pants. Don't forget the little matter of somebody screwed with my car and my house and tried their best to kill me. No one threatens Holly

Schlivnik and gets away with it. I've still got a score to settle and a killer to catch."

Chapter Twenty-Three

Snip rapped my knuckles with a spoon as I tried to sneak a forkful of the gargantuan slice of peanut butter and chocolate cheesecake occupying three-quarters of her plate. I rubbed my sore hand and whined. "Your mommy not teach you the importance of sharing?" My favorite coroner answered by shoveling a quarter of the slice into her mouth. She grinned and gave me the middle finger salute. "Ok, since you're unwilling to share your dessert, any updates on Lissa Charney you're willing to share?"

Doctor Death glugged a gulp of coffee after devouring another quarter of the cheesecake and smirked. "Yeah. She's dead as a doornail."

Who says coroners lack a sense of humor? "Nothing gets past you, Doc Death. Anything else?"

Snip said, "We've made some progress on how to extract the object embedded in the victim's neck."

Good grief. How long does it take to extract one small object? "So, if it's not out, it means it isn't identified yet?"

Snip said, "As of right now, no on both counts, but we'll have the answer in a couple of days."

Patience has never been one of my strong points. "Don't you pull small objects out of bodies all the time? It can't possibly be that hard to get this one thing out."

Snip pinched her index finger to her thumb. "Harder

than you think. The standard tweezers we'd normally use are too thick. The risk of damaging the point of entry as well as the object is too high to take a chance on using it for extraction. I've found a tweezer with a longer, thinner, and narrower head that can be inserted without disturbing the surrounding tissue. I've ordered a set and it will arrive in a day or two."

****

You can't get from the mart parking structure elevator to the main lobby without passing the newsstand in front of the mart deli. The headline above the fold on the *West Coast Apparel News* front page caught my eye. "Swimwear Manufacturer Questioned in Charney Murder"

I bought a paper and called AJ for the inside scoop on the article. But the call went to voicemail and I left no message. Instead, I went into A Jolt of Java to share the big news. I served the Yentas their coffees and laid the paper in the center of the table.

Hope quirked a sad smile. "Maybe now Lissa's poor mother will get some closure. My mom says Irene roams the halls looking for Lissa and keeps asking what she did that made her daughter stop coming to see her."

Sonia scanned the newspaper headline and widened her eyes. "Boy, you never can tell a book by its cover."

Queenie grinned. "No kidding. Whoda thunk Big Bird is a stone-cold killer?"

I stretched my arms in front of me and held out my hands. "Hold your horses, ladies. I hate to be a Debbie downer, but much of this doesn't pass the sniff test."

Queenie gave me the big eyes. "Are you kidding? Annette has been one of our big four on the suspect list. Now that she rose to the top, you have a problem with her?"

Sonia said, "Queenie's right. Lissa said no to the deal and Annette went crazy. Desperate people don't think clearly. They do knee-jerk, stupid things that end up as murder. A spur-of-the-moment thing. Like a crime of passion?"

Hope asked, "Did Buster's wife tell you she received an anonymous call to look for a crate in Annette's car?"

I rattled the newspaper. "Not directly to me, but the article implied it."

Sonia asked, "The nail gun inside the crate?"

I pursed my lips. "I called AJ to worm the details out of her after I read the paper, but she's not answering my calls. But if they brought in Annette for questioning, it stands to reason, yes."

Queenie counted the points with her fingers. "The guilty nail gun must be in the crate. Annette's husband owns a construction company. She has access to a nail gun, and I imagine she knows how to operate one. Ask me, Annette Mason looks pretty darned guilty."

I squirmed in my seat. "It all seems waaaay too pat. Nothing is ever this neatly packaged. Annette is being framed."

Hope wrinkled her brow. "Annette framed? By who?"

Sonia counted the suspects with the tap of a spoon on her coffee cup. "You already eliminated Eileen. If Annette's off the list, who's left?"

Bobby and Roddy.

Queenie pushed the end of her nose up with her fingertip. "Who has the most to lose?"

I rubbed my index finger and thumb together. "My

money's on Bobby Javadi, and I'm gonna prove it."

Queenie asked, "How?"

I sucked in my cheeks. "Good question. I'll get back to you."

Chapter Twenty-Four

Queenie and I supervised the photoshoot for our spring catalog on location at the Olympic-sized pool of The Marina Bay Club. Twelve models, each one more exquisite than the last. In what parallel universe is a size six considered overweight? After a day surrounded by these beauties, Queenie and I will be headed for therapy. We walked to the balcony overlooking the mighty blue Pacific and took a break while the models changed.

Queenie said, "I ate lunch with my friend Jennifer yesterday. Do you remember her? I introduced you to her a few months ago in the mart bakery. She's an old friend from fashion school. She sells junior sportswear up on the thirteenth floor, near Eileen Hirsch." I nodded my recognition and Queenie continued. "Anyway, before we went to the mart deli, I wanted to send a birthday bouquet to my sister, so we stopped at the florist. We ran into Eileen and her assistant."

She piqued my curiosity. "What's she like? She must be a pretty strong personality to work with someone as overpowering as Eileen."

Queenie said, "*He, not she*, and it seems as though he and Eileen work well together. They were chatting and laughing while waiting in line."

Wait. Huh? I looked at Queenie kinda wonky. "You're saying Adrian is a he, not a she?"

Queenie laughed. "Yep. She's not a she. She is a he.

A man. A male. A guy. A bloke. A fella. How many more ways do you need me to say it? About twenty years old, dressed kinda preppy. Blunt cut brown hair, hazel eyes, around five-ten, rangy frame."

Queenie pointed to my open mouth inches from hitting the guard rail and laughed. "I guess I had the same odd look on my face when Eileen introduced me to Adrian. He burst out laughing and said his name confuses lots of people. He joked that it's too bad his girlie name wouldn't exclude him from having to register with the selective service board. We chatted for a few minutes after they finished at the register, and then they said goodbye. Nice, polite guy. He extended his right hand and I noticed he wore his watch on his right wrist the way you do."

Queenie held her left wrist up with a watch strapped to it. "Why don't you wear your watch on your left wrist, the way most people do?"

I held up my right wrist. "Lefties always wear theirs on the right wrist."

Queenie furrowed her brow. "Why?"

"Our right hands are otherwise pretty useless." I laughed. "Gives the right arm something to do and balances us out."

Queenie crossed her arms over her chest. "Since you insist on continuing with the investigation, let's hear the game plan."

I swept an arm around the endless ocean. "I'm gonna start here."

She looked at me oddly. "As in the Marina Bay Club?"

I crossed my eyes. "No. As on the coast."

She parroted. "The coast."

I repeated. "Yeah. The coast." I leaned over the guard rail and pointed to the crowded beach below. "The end of the land and the ocean begins. The coast."

She swatted my arm with the model roster she'd unconsciously folded into a tube. "Planning to take a relaxing cruise?"

"Queenster, quit your day job and take your comedy routine on the road. No cruise, Miss Smarty Pants. But you're close. I'm gonna find out who owns the boat that was moored behind my houseboat."

She gave me the stink eye. "And your game plan is…?"

I wiggled my digits in the air. "I let my fingers do the walking."

She favored me with another weird look. "Meaning?"

"Meaning I went through the phone books at the library and made a list of all the marinas from Long Beach to Ventura. I'm gonna contact them all and see if the boat is moored with one of them."

She asked, "Your neighbor get the registration number?"

I shook my head no. "She figured I'd changed divers to clean the bottom of my boat, so it didn't occur to her to write the CF numbers down."

Queenie pinched her lips together as though she had gas. "You can't do much without a CF number."

I dipped a shoulder. "You're right. All I can do is give them Bobby Javadi's name and see if I get a hit. I will check with the other diving services and see if any of them are familiar with the B J Diving company. Maybe I'll get lucky."

She bit her bottom lip. "I betcha my condo B J

Diving company doesn't exist. Contacting the marinas is a long shot at best, but I guess it's worth a try. But don't hold your breath. How many marinas are we talking about?"

I sighed at the ridiculousness of the answer. "I stopped counting at a hundred."

Her eyebrows rose to form a deep V. "You're kidding. It'll take you forever to talk to them all."

I gulped. "You're right, I'll never get it done on my own." I quirked a sly smile. "But if you and the Yentas pitch in, it will take a few days less than forever. Whaddya say?"

Hey, what's the point of having friends if you can't take advantage of them?

Queenie rolled her eyes. "I say you're whizzing in the wind. But yeah, we'll help you."

****

The Yentas reported back in the morning. Not a group of happy campers.

Sonia rubbed her right ear. "My ear is still numb."

Queenie pulled on her left earlobe. "I switched ears. My right one hurt too much to keep the phone against it."

Hope pulled her right earlobe. "Two hours into it, my ear started ringing."

Joan said, "I've never been on hold so much." She laughed. "I won't complain if a buyer keeps me waiting ever again."

I surveyed the table. "With all those earaches, any luck?"

Four heads shook no.

I surveyed the table "You guys tried all the names? Reza Javadi, Bobby Javadi, Robert Javadi?"

Four heads nodded yes.

Queenie said, "I even tried Roberto Javadi."

I gave her the stink eye.

Queenie struck an indignant pose. "What's with the look? This is California. Land of loosey-goosey love. Lots of inter-faith and inter-cultural marriages. Why not one between a Hispanic woman and an Iranian man who produced a son with a Hispanic first name and an Iranian surname?"

My tone dripped sarcasm. "Find one?"

Queenie managed to keep a straight face. "They might, Miss Smarty Pants, but no one with those two names moored a boat in any of the marinas I called."

Hope tipped her head to me. "And you?"

I formed an O with my thumb and index finger. "The big, fat, Zippity doo dah."

Hope asked, "And this tells us what…?"

I shrugged. "Either Bobby Javadi doesn't own a boat, or if he does, he doesn't moor it in a marina. At least not in one from Long Beach to Ventura County."

Joan asked, "You contact the DMV?"

I twisted my shoulders to loosen the kinks. "Yes, but without a CF number, the DMV couldn't identify the boat registrant. I gave them Bobby's name and address, but no vessel registered in his name was in their system. If he has a boat, it's drydocked, and isn't registered with the DMV."

Queenie asked, "I take it none of the boatyards has a line on B J Diving Service?"

I sighed. "Nope. I even contacted the State Franchise Tax Board. No corporation is listed under the name either."

Joan scratched an imaginary line in the air. "I guess we cross Mr. Javadi off the list."

I pursed my lips. "You guessed wrong." I paid the groans emanating from the peanut gallery no never mind and jutted my chin. "I'm not ready to eliminate him yet."

Sonia said, "I ran into Annette coming out of A Jolt of Java yesterday. So, she's off the hook."

Hope clucked her tongue. "I was convinced Annette did the deed."

I shook my head "AJ kept it close to the vest and I learned nothing from her. But in a moment of weakness and after some arm-twisting, I got Snip to admit there were lots of fingerprints all over the bloody crate in Annette's trunk, but none of them are Annette's. The identifiable prints all belonged to Lissa Charney." I wrinkled my brow. "Besides, Annette's accountant gave her an alibi for the day of the murder. They waited together at Annette's office all day for Lissa, but she never arrived. I told you guys. This one failed the sniff test."

Queenie scratched the back of her head. "We're running out of suspects."

Joan threw her hands in the air. "Well, Lissa didn't shoot herself in the heart with a nail gun, stuff herself into a sample crate, drive herself back to the mart, and nail herself to a closet wall, but somebody did."

Hope asked, "Maybe we should revisit Eileen Hirsch? Remember those threats? Pretty telling, don't you think?"

I shook my head no. "Nah. Someone set Annette up. But trust me, it wasn't Eileen Hirsch. They both have showrooms in the mart, but it doesn't mean they've ever met. Their showrooms are on different floors, in different buildings, and they sell in two completely different markets. I bet Eileen wouldn't know Annette Mason from Perry Mason. Besides, Eileen's threats? A lot of angry hot air. If you want the person with it all on the line, Bobby Javadi is the one. I'm tellin' ya, he's our guy. Now we've gotta prove it. Whoever tampered with my car and my boat also murdered Lissa Charney. Those three things are connected. The same person is responsible for it all." I warned, "A murderer is still on the loose. Until he's caught, all of us are in danger."

Joan asked, "And now?"

I smacked my hand on the table. "Now, no more Mr. Nice Guy."

Queenie pointed a teaspoon at Hope." Hold on a sec. Let's not be so quick to dismiss Eileen." Queenie turned and pointed the teaspoon at me. "Eileen will clam up if you go back with more questions, but she has no idea you and I work together. My friend Jennifer is having a big sample sale in a couple of days. Her showroom is close to Eileen's. Let me go up and pick Jennifer's brain first. Then afterward, I'll go see Eileen. I bet I get more out of Eileen than you. Whaddaya say?"

I smiled indulgently. "If you see any samples for me, put them aside and call me. But until I see a nail gun in Eileen Hirsch's hand, my money is still on Bobby Javadi."

****

Peso stuck his big, wet snout into the back pocket of my jeans and fished out the dog biscuit I stashed for him to find. AJ pointed to the huge King German Shepard wolfing the treat in two bites. "No more of those, please. Thanks to you, the vet put Peso on a diet. He's gained five pounds from all those biscuits."

I gave Peso's hind quarters a couple of love taps. "Walk him more and he'll get back his boyish figure."

AJ maturely stuck her tongue out and brushed the chicken quarters with a tangy-scented barbeque sauce. They sizzled as she laid them on the grill, and my mouth watered. I poured two glasses of the Chardonnay I'd brought as my dinner contribution and handed one to AJ. She took a glug of wine and narrowed her eyes. "To what do we owe the honor of your inviting yourself over for dinner?" She barked an ex-smoker's husky laugh. "Gee, let me guess…"

I tsked. "You and my uncle Barry both have such suspicious minds."

She grinned an evil grin. "News flash. Suspicion is the first thing they teach you in detective school."

No sense beating a dead horse. "Fine. Busted. Since you released Annette Mason, update me on the latest with the Charney case."

The mask of her cop face shadowed her eyes. "Come on. You know the drill. I don't discuss an ongoing investigation."

I put my hands on my hips. "My house and car were tampered with. Somebody threatened my life."

Her harsh tone cut through my heart with the sharpness of a knife blade. "And whose fault is that? Look in the mirror."

Undaunted, I kept at it. "The nail gun?"

She rolled her eyes. "What about it?"

I wiggled my digits. "Fingerprints. You released her, so, none belonged to Annette. Any others?"

AJ jerked her head no. "No matches in the system."

I aimed my fingers like a pistol. "Nail gun shoot the nails straight or bent?"

She gritted her teeth. "Straight."

Remarkably, she kept answering, so I kept

questioning. "Did the handle of the nail gun have a nick?"

She snapped. "No."

I counted off on my fingers. "You have a bloody crate, unidentified fingerprints, and a nail gun shooting nails straight. You're back to square one and the clock is ticking."

She groused. "I don't need you to remind me."

I'm in sales so, naturally, persistence is my middle name. "Bobby Javadi or Roddy Mason? Bobby's nail gun is easily identified. He claims the handle has a nick on it. He says his nail gun shoots straight nails, but maybe he's lying? Roddy also has a nail gun. He's used it in redecorating his showroom. Can't you get a warrant and test their nail guns?"

She spoke in the same slow, patronizing tone as though addressing someone who spoke English as a second language. "We found no *physical* evidence linking either of them with the crime scene. Since we have no probable cause, my Captain refused to let me try." She waved the barbeque fork in the air. "No judge will sign a search warrant. All you accomplish is to piss them off for wasting their time."

Not so fast, sister. "Bobby Javadi is fighting it, but if he's deported to Iran, he faces prison or death upon arrival in Teheran. Lissa Charney refused to save Bobby Javadi by marrying him. I'd say Bobby Javadi has a pretty strong motive."

AJ sighed with resignation. "You're gonna keep at this, no matter the consequences, aren't you?"

I struck a defiant pose. "You've got to ask?"

Chapter Twenty-Five

Queenie went to Jennifer's sample sale on her lunch hour. The other Yentas had plans, so I ordered the Mart Deli daily special delivered. My cell phone rang as I took the first bite into my turkey on rye. Dang. I'd missed breakfast and my stomach complained loud and clear. I eyed my sandwich and almost let the call go to voicemail, but a sixth sense said I better answer. Caller ID said Queenie and my pulse spiked. She was only gone maybe ten minutes, max. I depressed the call button and Queenie barked, "You'd better get up here and fast." Before I had a chance to ask what's the big hurry, the line went dead.

Geesh, the samples must be smoking hot. Maybe somebody else wants them? I took a ginormous bite of my sandwich to tide me over. I re-wrapped the rest of it, put it in the mini-frig, and ran up the two flights of the escalator to the thirteenth floor.

No lights in Eileen's showroom two doors down from Jennifer's. No one manning the showroom in the middle of the day? Curious. I peered inside and the place looked torn apart. Bare walls. No racks or samples. Paint buckets sat on drop cloths and lined up on the side of a wall. No sign in the window indicating the time she'd re-open. Maybe the contractor didn't give Eileen a completion date yet. Crap. So much for Queenie's great idea.

A huge sign painted in giant red letters in Jennifer's window screamed *Cash only, no checks or debit cards! Must make room for the new spring line. Sample sale at seventy-five off wholesale prices. All sales final. No exchanges or returns.* Certainly explained the empty racks behind all the workstations. Jennifer looked up from counting a huge wad of cash and grinned as I walked in. I took a visual spin around the empty room. "Why the big rush? Unless you hid samples, I'm a day late and a dollar short. Story of my life."

Queenie waved me off. "Forget the samples. Not a thing was left by the time I arrived."

I gave Queenie the stink eye and turned my attention to Jennifer. "Well, it's nice to see you again, Jennifer, but I'm going back downstairs. I missed breakfast this morning, and I'm starving. A turkey on rye is in the fridge waiting for me."

Queenie pulled out a chair and patted the seat. "Let the turkey sandwich wait. Jennifer's story about Eileen Hirsch can't."

I sat and Queenie gave Jennifer a take-it-away sign. "Queenie said you questioned Eileen about Lissa Charney's murder." Jennifer stuffed the wad of cash in her purse and smiled tightly. "Eileen wasn't exactly truthful about her flight from JFK to LAX. She did fly from New York to Los Angeles, but not on the Friday of Lissa Charney's murder."

I gave her the big eyes. "If you don't mind me asking, how are you so sure?"

Jennifer smiled sweetly. "I sat in the seat next to Eileen Hirsch on the *Thursday* morning flight from JFK to LAX." Jennifer sighed. "Honestly, I wish she were on the Friday flight and not mine. I'm a nervous flyer and prefer to keep to myself when I fly. I tried to read, sleep, listen to music. I even turned on a movie, but Eileen wouldn't take the hint. Eileen complained *non-stop* from take-off to landing about Lissa stranding her in New Mexico. Believe it or not, she still yammered about it when the long-term parking lot bus dropped her off at her van. If she continued to complain about Lissa once we were back in the mart, I'd have to move to another aisle."

Queenie prompted. "Jen, tell her the rest."

Good grief. There's more?

Jennifer continued. "The Monday after Lissa's murder, Eileen came in and asked to borrow a sample crate. Strange, since she bought two new ones maybe a month ago. I told her no problem, but curiosity got the best of me as to what happened to the new ones. She said last Friday one of them got damaged and needed to be replaced. She ordered a new one, but it hadn't been delivered yet. She had an appointment at the Bainbridge buying office, and all the samples wouldn't fit into one crate. Sounded reasonable, so I loaned her the crate."

I croaked deep as a frog. "Anything else?"

Before Jennifer responded, Eileen and Adrian walked past Jennifer's room on the way to theirs, both dressed in stained painters' overalls and old sneakers.

We said our hasty goodbyes to Jennifer and walked past Eileen's on the way to the down escalator. Queenie and I locked eyes as Adrian lifted a metal rack and held it to the wall while Eileen Hirsch grabbed a nail gun and drove five nails on each side, securing the rack perfectly into place. I pulled out my mobile phone and called AJ.

****

The rest of the afternoon passed in a blur. We went

through the motions of doing our jobs, but it seemed like we were swimming in Jell-o. Mario, the owner of Pasta by The Pier, poured two glasses and set a bottle of the house Chianti on the center of the red and white checkerboard tablecloth. We both chugged the wine in one big gulp and held our glasses out for a refill. Mario laughed and jiggled the bottle from side to side. "Donta worries, we gotta lot more." Good thing. We both might need our own bottle.

Queenie took a sip of wine and smiled tightly. "You practically stood on your head, but *finally*, the cop paid attention. Jennifer called and said an hour after we left, your pal the detective arrived and interviewed Adrian and Eileen. Eileen kept the door open to air out the paint fumes, so Jennifer positioned herself at a workstation close to her door and overheard part of the questioning. Eileen offered no proof she flew last Friday."

I hoisted my wineglass in a toast. "I guarantee you that AJ already confirmed Jennifer's story with the airline before she confronted Eileen."

Queenie tapped her finger on the tip of her nose. "That must have cooked Eileen's goose."

I wagged my index finger. "Along with Eileen lying about having a nail gun."

Queenie broke a breadstick in half with a loud snap. "Jennifer said the detective came back an hour later with two uniforms and a search warrant. They took the room apart for over three hours and Jennifer lost count of the amount of stuff they confiscated. It took the uniforms six trips to get it all out. The cops read Eileen and Adrian their rights and hustled them out."

I stared into my wineglass as though the vino held the answer. "How come an *assistant* is willing to put himself in such jeopardy and lie to the police for his boss? Did Eileen have something on Adrian making him more afraid of her than lying to the police?"

I spent a sleepless night pacing the length of Queenie's guestroom trying to make sense of it all. No matter which way I arranged the pieces of the puzzle, none of them fit completely together. Each of the suspects looked both guilty and innocent. Maybe a group effort? Murder by committee? Nah.

Someone messed with my house and my car. Someone tried to kill me. Eileen as the perp wreaking havoc with my life? I wracked my brain for a motive, but I couldn't come up with a single one. It made no sense. It must be somebody else, and I must be close. But who? This must be the way it is for Peso when he's chasing his tail.

I took a legal pad out of my messenger bag and made notes. The revelations from the thirteenth floor certainly made Eileen Hirsch look guilty. But if the motive drove the bus, all roads still led to Bobby Javadi behind the steering wheel. Before dawn broke, I had a game plan. Not a particularly ingenious one, but a plan nonetheless.

A hot shower, a fresh change of clothes, and some strong coffee...Ok. Lots and lots of strong coffee. I called Bobby's cell phone, but it went directly to voicemail. Was he still injured or merely incredibly inept at finding his phone? Or, maybe he recovered and went back to work? I called Garvin Auto and Mason Construction, but both places said Bobby was still out. I called his cell phone a second time, and it still went to voicemail. Was he in the wind or brushing me off? As if I'd allow it to happen. I left Bobby a message, scribbled a note to Queenie, and headed out for another trip to the

San Fernando Valley.

I dropped the top and blasted the last of the remaining cobwebs out by turning the radio to the earsplitting level. I drove north on the 405 to the Ventura Freeway east. The traffic goddess once again smiled down upon me. The pleasant drive took a fraction of the normal time. I exited at Laurel Canyon and headed north to Victory Boulevard. Bobby Javadi lived on a quiet, tree-lined side street off Victory in an old North Hollywood neighborhood adjacent to the Laurel Plaza shopping center. Apartment buildings at each corner anchored the street with pre-war ranch-style houses in between on both sides. Bobby lived in a three-story faded aqua stucco walk-up on the north side at the east end of the block. Since most people worked during the day, I had no problem parking. I slid the convertible into a spot in front of Bobby's building and put the top up.

Before I went to Bobby's apartment, I walked around to the back of the building to the garage. Each apartment was assigned two tandem parking spaces with the apartment numbers painted on the front of each space. Bobby's late-model pickup truck and a battered two-door Japanese compact sat parked one behind the other in his space. Hot diggity dog. Now I'd get some answers. I wasn't leaving without them.

The rusted metal gate to Bobby's building creaked a whiny complaint as I pushed it open. I cut diagonally across the center quad of the rectangular apartment building past a kidney-shaped pool to the back staircase. I hoofed the three flights of stairs and made my way to number three-twenty-six. Bobby lived in the last apartment on the left in the back corner, nearest to the laundry room, and on the other side of the alcove with the ice machine.

I knocked on the door and did a double-take as it swung halfway open. I don't care if your neighborhood is rated the safest in the state. Who leaves a front door open in Los Angeles? North Hollywood might not be the hood, but no one confused it with Beverly Hills either. Maybe he just ran out to get the mail or check the laundry? I leaned over the railing. No one at the mail boxes. Not a soul in the laundry room. No crowd at the ice machine.

I went back to Bobby's unit and stood hesitant at the threshold. I'd been raised better than to barge in without announcing myself. Loud voices came from inside the apartment. Sort of early in the day for a party in my book, but who am I to say? Had he recovered and been celebrating with friends who worked the graveyard shift? If not, why throw a party? I shouted over the din. "Bobby, it's Holly Schlivnik. Can I come in?" Nada. I hesitated a minute more, and then said screw the good manners I'd been raised with. I needed answers and wouldn't get them standing outside. Uninvited, I pushed the door three-quarters of the way open and stepped into the tiny entry. The small apartment smelled musty, as though unoccupied for a while. I called out, "Hey Bobby, it's Holly Schlivnik. Your door was open, so I let myself in." No response. I stood in the center of the entry and scoped the place out.

Bobby furnished the living room modern American guy-style with a faux black leather couch and matching recliner. Two still-life pieces of art the quality of paint-by-the-numbers hung on the wall behind the couch. A particleboard coffee table littered with a stack of week-old newspapers and a greasy takeaway pizza box sat in front of the couch. A monstrously large flat-screen television no doubt more expensive than the entire room of furniture covered three-quarters of the wall facing the couch. The TV was tuned to a cheesy game show blasting on wake the dead volume. Mystery solved. The loud party revelers? None in Bobby's living room. Just a noisy group of yahoos embarrassing themselves while cavorting on a color TV. I found the remote buried under the newspapers and turned off the TV. Oddly, Bobby opted not to shout out his complaint.

A narrow kitchen adjacent to the living room featured Formica counters, old-fashioned appliances, and a week's worth of dirty dishes piled haphazardly in the sink. A small, chipped Formica table and two metal chairs with cracked vinyl seats were set in the corner on a yellowed geometric-patterned linoleum floor. No Bobby in the kitchen fixing himself a snack.

No one confused Bobby's place with Buckingham Palace. I'd already been through most of the small, one-bedroom apartment, and so far, no sign of Bobby anywhere. I opened the closet door in the entry and pawed through the sagging rack stuffed with coats and jackets and a dusty umbrella for the ten days a year we get any measurable rain. I found no Bobby Javadi amongst the detritus.

I called out Bobby's name again, this time a lot louder. Nada. Unless he slept as sound as the dead, no way he couldn't hear me. I gritted my teeth as the pinch of annoyance squeezed my gut. Ignore me? Ha. Not this girl. Hiding in the tub or under the bed? No one was in the bathroom, so I followed a short, dark hallway to the last room left.

I pushed the bedroom door open and stood at the

threshold to check the room out. An unmade twin bed and three-drawer knotty-pine dresser occupied half of the back wall. A closet with two sliding doors took up the wall on the left. Against the narrow wall to the right, a humming printer perched precariously on a rickety TV tray on the right side of a scratched metal desk housing a blinking computer.

Bobby sat slumped over with his head resting on the desk as if he'd pulled an all-nighter and fell asleep while working. But the grip of the twenty-two-caliber pistol clenched in his right hand with the barrel in his mouth and the large pool of blood surrounding his shattered skull and spatter of brains put a damper on the theory. My stomach lurched and I gagged, but I willed my breakfast to stay put.

I crept into the spartanly furnished bedroom for a closer look. Bobby was completely drenched in blood. His wide-open eyes shined with sheer terror. How long was he dead? From the irony smell of fresh-spilled blood, not long.

Guilt punched me in the gut and took my breath away. If only I arrived sooner. Now I'd live with the sting of regret for the rest of my life. The laugh normally bubbling to the surface at the sight of a corpse remained lodged in the back of my throat. The only good news? Avoiding deportation will no longer be a problem for Bobby Javadi.

A blood-splattered piece of paper with a type-written note lay angled backward with its corner resting under the side of Bobby's head. Since moving his head was a ginormous no-no, I twisted myself into a contortionist to read the note sideways. Two of the letters were mistyped on this note same as the threatening letter

I received. A search of the place failed to produce the typewriter. Curious. Maybe the typewriter belonged to either Mason Construction or Garvin Auto and Bobby typed the notes while at work? The answer to the question died with Bobby.

The brevity of the three typed lines chilled me to the bone. The tone of the note was tinged with palpable pain. The words revealed a tragedy too awful for Bobby Javadi to endure. *"I killed Lissa Charney. I can't live with the guilt. God forgive me."*

****

AJ picked up on the third ring. I dispensed with the pleasantries. "Congratulations, Detective Yakamura. You closed the Charney case."

LA traffic has no more respect for the dead than it does for the living. Even with sirens blaring and light bars whirling, it still took AJ forty-five minutes to get to Bobby Javadi's apartment. I led the detective to Bobby's body, and AJ made her cursory examination of the corpse. I left after giving my statement. I combed the beach the rest of the day, searching the foamy surf for salvation.

****

I spent a restless night fighting my demons and prayed for a measure of solace at coffee the next morning with my friends. The Yentas toasted me with their cups, but I declined to share in the celebration. At best, I deserved the benefit of the doubt. Certainly no adulation.

Queenie tapped my saucer with a spoon. "You should be doing a happy dance. What's with that *you lost your best friend-long face?*"

I squirmed in my seat.

Joan gave me an attaboy pat on the shoulder. "You

pegged it right all along. You're our own Miss Marple."

I stared into my coffee looking for absolution. "Yeah, but if I arrived at his apartment sooner, Bobby would be still alive."

Joan snapped. "BS."

Hope pinched her lips into a tight line of disapproval. "You didn't put the gun in his mouth and pull the trigger. He did that all on his own."

I tapped my forehead. "You're right." I covered my heart with my right palm. "Not so much here."

Queenie clucked her tongue. "What in the world is the matter with you? This is an obvious open and shut case." She counted the points with a tap of a teaspoon on the edge of the table. "The cops say he's guilty. Bobby wrote a confession, for crying out loud. The police found the murder weapon in his toolbox, and they traced the anonymous call framing Joan to his cell phone number. Good golly, Miss Holly. How much more proof do you need?"

I smiled tightly. "I agree."

Queenie sighed. "And yet a but is coming."

"Nothing gets past you, Queenster."

The yentas groaned with the agony of an overweighted ship when I refused to throw in the towel. "But my gut says things don't add up."

Sonia tsked. "Take your nana's advice and don't borrow trouble."

I twirled my index fingers in a circular motion next to the sides of my head. "Call me crazy, but a guy working two jobs to save enough money to buy a house all of a sudden decides he doesn't want to live, and blows his brains out? I don't think so. A guy fights deportation tooth and nail and hires a pricey immigration lawyer. He is willing to do *anything* to stay in this country. Even a sham marriage. That's a guy who wants to live. That's not someone who'd murder his one possible savior, and later kill himself over the guilt."

Joan's eyes flashed with excitement. "You been on the swimwear aisle recently?"

So much happened the last few days, I couldn't remember. "Lemme think?" I scrunched my eyes closed to remember. "The day before yesterday. Why?"

Queenie followed Joan's lead as the light of recognition shined in her eyes. "Yesterday, something different on our aisle caught my attention."

Sonia smacked her forehead. "You're right. It caught mine too. And at first, I went nuts trying to figure it out."

It would be a shame if a vendor went out of business. Whenever a competitor shuts its doors, it's bad for the whole industry. "Who closed shop?"

Sonia gave me a funny look. "No one."

The twitch of annoyance you get when people jerk you around flitted around inside my tummy. I talked through clenched teeth. "Enough with the twenty questions. Spit it out."

Hope smiled a Mona Lisa tug of her lips. "The aisle missed a delicious aroma."

I gave her the stink eye before the proverbial light bulb blinked on. Mental head slap. No roses. Holy guacamole. "Either Bobby murdered Lissa, or the killer wants us to think so. And I can't rest until I figure it out."

Chapter Twenty-Six

Sue Ellen Magee made a sour face as she arranged the fabric swatches she'd selected into a neat pile. "If I sewed the garments myself by hand, it would be with fewer complications than this promo program." She put the fabrics in her messenger bag and graced me with a death ray-worthy glare. "With all this trouble, the crap better blow out of the store, or else…"

I deadpanned. "Yep. All it takes is a pesky murder to throw things completely off track."

She handed me a spreadsheet and narrowed her eyes. "If you don't want to be the next murder victim, this program better get delivered without another hitch."

Anyone else, I'd laugh at the joke. With this gem? Never in a million years. No one ever confuses Sue Ellen Magee with Joan Rivers. Sue Ellen aimed her fingers in the shape of a pistol at my head to either drive home a warning or make a promise. She left me to ponder which one. I considered myself lucky. Meeting over. Wrote a big order. Still vertical. Hot diggity dog. It doesn't get any better.

I finished putting the sample line back in order, and then my cell phone rang. Caller ID said The Boat Doctor. My stomach flipped higher than a trampoline. I steeled myself for the prospect of being homeless.

A dead ringer for Popeye, the salty guy's voice sounded sandpapery, as if he had to constantly clear his throat. He growled. "Wanna sleep in your own bed tonight?" Popeye explained everything done to make my houseboat buoyant again, and I went weak in the knees. These guys? Nothing short of miracle workers. My girl was on life support and they brought her back from the dead. My heart skipped several beats as Popeye gave me the bottom line. Double gulp. Thank God for insurance. I'd never made a claim before, but after this costly adventure, I'll need a miracle for the insurance company not to cancel my policy.

I arrived at my dock as the marine tug pushed the houseboat gently into the slip. Muriel came by to welcome us back and asked if any suspects were arrested. Regrettably, I answered no. The Harbor Patrol gave no encouraging news. The detective handling the case said they'd keep investigating, but not to hold my breath for the perp to ever be identified. Muriel said we still had a great reason to celebrate. She went back to her boat, and returned with an expensive bottle of wine she'd been saving for a special occasion. This certainly qualified. We sat on the aft deck and polished off the delicious Merlot with a glorious sunset as the hors d'oeuvres.

Always a party-hardy animal at heart, Mark, the ex-navy seal who owned the boat moored in the slip next to mine, moseyed over and contributed two six-packs of beer to go with the takeaway pizzas I ordered. Three other dock mates wandered aboard, and one of them brought a boom box. The spontaneous welcome back party lasted late into the night. I appreciated the spacious accommodations at the Hotel Queenie Levine, but yes, Dorothy, there really is no place like home.

****

Since life without Rocky Road ice cream and Thai chicken pizza isn't worth living, ensuring they remained my core food groups and my jeans still zipped meant making some lifestyle changes. My New Yorker nana's secret to keeping a girlish figure? Walk. Good enough for Nana? Certainly good enough for me. Daily at the crack of dawn, I walk two warm-up laps around the Porto Paloma Marina. Then I take Palawan Way across Admiralty to Washington Street going west till it dead-ends at the pier. Before the asphalt becomes sand, I always stop at A Jolt of Java. I get two biggie-sized to-go cups of high voltage blend roast coffees: One for me and one for Pop, the old guy I'd become friendly with who has been fishing from the same spot on the pier day in and day out for over a decade.

The following morning, I donned my sweats and sneakers and started out and about long before the sun rose. Gunmetal gray clouds hung low in the overcast sky. A cold wind blew in from the roily ocean, casting a dark gloom over the mostly-deserted pier. I handed Pop his coffee and glanced into the dented plastic bucket nestled between his feet. "Catch much so far this morning?"

Pop pointed a gnarled finger at the four puny fish swimming in the murky salt water and sputtered a gravelly laugh. "I can't make up my mind. Whaddaya think? Appetizers or bait?"

Pop's fish gut-stained jeans sat loosely on his narrow hips and stayed held in place by a bungee cord for a belt. A faded UCLA track team T-shirt covered his barrel chest and fitted tightly enough over his protruding beer belly so the hem curled revealing an "outie" navel. Oily, unlaced tennis shoes with a hole large enough for his big right toe to stick out like a barometer encased his size eleven feet.

The old man glanced at the overcast sky and shivered further into his thin windbreaker. He rested his fishing rod against the battered tackle box under the railing and took a big slurp of coffee.

Pop was a wise man of few words who never wasted his breath on anything trivial. He possessed a sharp, analytical mind, and I valued the old guy's insights and opinions. Pop took a fortifying glug of coffee and listened intently with no interruptions as I told my story. I finished telling the tale and gave him an expectant look.

Pop took off his LA Dodgers ball cap missing the D so it read LA odgers. He scratched the crown under his yellowish-gray hair sun-bleached to the color of sour milk. He narrowed his faded blue eyes and stared into the churning water at high tide. "Mebbe the guy got helped."

My heart sunk with disappointment. "Nah. He did it on his own."

My eyelids sprang wide open to attention as Pop mused out loud. "Not with him killing the gal. I meant Mebbe he got helped to the other side, whether he wanted to go or not."

****

Joan snapped her fingers in front of my face. "Hellooo, Earth to Nancy Drew."

The flush of embarrassment colored the front of my neck a lovely shade of red. I'd been a space cadet ever since my conversation with Pop. His comment stuck in my head. Pop might be right. Say Bobby killed Lissa, but not himself? And if not, who murdered Bobby, and why? Or, he killed Lissa, but he had help? And if yes, who helped him? Is it the reason Bobby was killed? My head spun with a bazillion questions but offered no answers.

I smiled sheepishly. "Sorry. Guess I zoned out for a minute. I'm back now. You were saying?"

Joan shoved the latest edition of *the West Coast Apparel News* in front of me. "You see this morning's paper?"

The boldface headline above the fold screamed, "Swimwear Exec Solves Charney Murder-Suicide Mystery" I gritted my teeth. "Their words, not mine. The reporter called for a quote, and I corrected her, but she didn't change the storyline the way I told her to."

Hope asked, "Which is to what?"

I spat. "The truth."

Sonia re-read the headline aloud. "Swimwear Exec Solves Charney Murder-Suicide Mystery. Yeah, you're right. The truth. That's what the reporter wrote."

I jabbed the word *solves* on the headline with a teaspoon. "Wrong. I didn't *solve* anything. I guessed right on a few things and found the body. The end."

Queenie twitched her nose. "Nah. Waaaay too boring. They're in business to sell papers. They won't sell too many copies listening to you."

Joan peered at me over the top of her eyeglasses. "You majored in journalism in college, right?"

I puffed out my chest with pride. "Yep. Won two major collegiate awards for investigative reporting. Editor-In-Chief of the university newspaper junior and senior years."

Joan batted her eyes. "Refresh my memory. The phrase you editors use to decide the placement of a story on the front page?"

I grinned. "If it bleeds, it leads."

Joan smirked. "Well, the headline proved your point."

Sonia clapped ta-da and laughed. "See? You're famous. Bet you bought all the copies of the paper."

Good grief. Could she be fishing for autographed copies? I made a sour face. "No, and I'm not signing them either, so don't get any ideas about snapping them all up and selling them."

I rolled my eyes as Sonia muttered, "Killjoy."

Queenie studied my face. "Your panties are still in a bunch over this one, aren't they?"

I'd never make a living as a poker player. I twisted my lips into a fatalistic smile. "Yeah. You're right. I've got more questions than answers. I'm not done turning over all of the rocks yet."

Chapter Twenty-Seven

I'd barely settled into the Adirondack when three sharp raps on the forward rail interrupted my first savory sip of a sunset-celebratory glass of Chardonnay. A deep masculine voice called out, "Request permission to come aboard." Is Admiral Halsey on the dock? Is it mandatory to stand and salute? Hardly. Nonetheless, my curiosity peaked as to the identity of my visitor. So, despite feeling foolish, I played along and called out, "Permission to come aboard is granted."

Charlie Hammond's long legs swung over the rail and rocked the boat as he planted his size twelve deck shoes on the outer rim of the forward deck. I patted the seat cushion and the tall, gone to seed, balding Dockmaster grinned a toothy grin as his husky bulk filled the Adirondack chair on my right. I held out the wine glass, but he declined the offer. The fiftyish guy with a burgeoning paunch took off his Captain's hat and joked. "Sorry, I'm not old enough for the hard stuff yet."

I gave him an expectant look. "To what do I owe the honor?"

He smiled. "Following incident procedure."

I pointed to the manila file on his lap. "For me, or do you take work home?"

My internal antenna perked to life as he flicked a wrist. "It's for you, but nothing too important. Strictly routine."

Susie Black

I held out my hand. "Ok, hand it over."

He opened the file with a meaty paw and handed me a typed sheet of paper with the Porto Paloma Marina logo and corporate address on the masthead. "It's a standard release. Strictly routine." He took a ballpoint pen out of a plastic holder in his shirt pocket and clicked it open. He pointed to the bottom of the page. "Now, if you'll sign your John Henry on the line above your name and date it, I'll be on my way, and you can get back to your wine."

I read the document and spat. "I'm not signing anything."

His smile faded. "Why not? It's a standard release."

I waved the release like a flag. "The *incident*, as you called it? Anything *but* standard. My boat was viciously vandalized on *your company's* property. A major portion of my *exorbitant* slip fees go to security, but Porto Paloma Marina failed to protect my property on *your* watch. I'm not releasing you or the marina from anything."

He spoke through clenched teeth. "You'd be wise to sign it, missy, or you might find your lease has been violated. If you're evicted, finding another slip might be a challenge. We're one of the few marinas still renting slips to houseboats." He pointed to the channel. "Pretty rough out on the open water for a little bitty girl such as yourself. A few big waves turn you around and you're floating out to sea."

My hackles backed up faster than a sewer. I gave him my famous death-ray glare. "You threatening me, Mr. Hammond?"

He held out his palms. "Of course not. But sometimes, bad things do happen." He flashed a used car salesman-worthy smarmy smile. "But, of course, if I'm *properly motivated*, this pesky release goes away." He rubbed his hands together. "Your choice, if you get my drift?"

Shake me down to avoid signing my rights away? Let him kiss my grits. "Expect a call from my attorney." I waved the release toward the dock. "Permission to come aboard is revoked." I smiled like a shark. "In case you don't get my drift, Mr. Dockmaster, let me spell it out for you. Get your shyster ass off my boat."

****

I called Uncle Barry the moment Charlie Hammond disembarked. My uncle assured me he'd handle it, and not to worry. Nonetheless, after my run-in with the crooked dockmaster, I expected the arrival of my eviction notice at any moment. Until Uncle Barry called me three days later, I couldn't sleep a wink. "I'll meet you at the Dockmaster's office at five today." He warned. "Wait for me. Don't go inside or talk to anyone in the office until I arrive."

I gulped. "Am I being evicted?"

Uncle Barry laughed out loud. "Trust me, by the end of this meeting, you're gonna be a happy camper."

****

Queenie squealed like the squeak of the tires on a bank robber's getaway car. "Are you for real? Lemme get this straight. The Dockmaster got fired, a new one is hired, and the marina gave you a new lease. Twelve months free rent, they reduced your monthly rental fee by twenty percent, reimbursed you for the repairs to your houseboat, and gave you a hotel and meal allowance for the week the boat was being repaired?" She held out her open palm and joked. "So, this means you'll be forking over the bucks for your stay at the Hotel Levine?"

I gave her a "nice try, but nothing doing" grin. "Not, but dinner is on me Monday nights for the rest of the month." Queenie grinned and toasted me with her scotch. I gave her the big eyes. "Turns out, I wasn't the only one who had a run-in with Charlie Hammond. The owner of the marina received a boatload of complaints lodged against the crooked Dockmaster. The threat of a huge lawsuit they'd never win proved to be the last straw for the marina owners." I grinned. "Uncle Barry is *not* someone you want as an enemy. If Charlie Hammond hadn't strong-armed me with the release, I'd never have threatened to sue the marina." I pursed my lips. "Honestly, it never occurred to me. The new Dockmaster, Audrey Camarillo, is gonna help me find out who owns the diver's boat. Under Charlie Hammond's reign, the marina's reputation got one heck of a black eye, and they've lost a lot of tenants. Audrey's trying to do right by me and help turn their reputation around. With her position as the Dockmaster, she has access to a statewide Marina Association database. It cross-references boat and boat owner information. I asked her if a slip lease can be written with a corporation or if it is required to be in the boat owner's name? Corporations can be the name on the lease. Maybe that's the way the boat got registered and the corporation name is on the lease." I jutted my jaw. "The marina compensated me, but I won't be satisfied until the culprit is found and punished."

Queenie said, "So, Bobby didn't damage your boat?"

I shook my head no. "I confronted him, and he swore he didn't own a boat. In fact, he couldn't swim, and said water terrified him. If his story was true, I don't see him diving into a murky channel for almost a half-hour to damage my boat."

Queenie asked, "And you believed him?"

I smiled tightly. "I didn't believe him at the time, but I'm not sure what I believe anymore. But one thing I am sure of is, whoever tampered with my boat and my car murdered Lissa Charney."

****

AJ was prepared to close the book on Lissa's murder and Bobby's suicide. But I still went round and round as to who killed who. Pop's voice kept running a continuous loop through my head, and it's driving me crazy trying to figure it all out. I'd gone as far as possible on my own. I needed help getting over the finish line. I spun the mental Rolodex. With its vast array of resources, LAPD is the obvious first choice. But since AJ already had her mind made up, I'd get no help from my pal the cop. Imagine the punishment for sticking my nose in her case again? She'd throw my scrawny tush in a jail cell and lose the key. And the Yentas? A well-meaning group, but equally as clueless as me. I donned my big girl panties and called the one person with some answers and who might share them with me.

A professional voice answered on the second ring. "Los Angeles County Coroner's Office. Assistant Coroner Doctor Sophie Cutler speaking. You stab 'em, we slab 'em."

I cackled. "How did you ever survive without caller ID?"

Snip coughed out a laugh. "Intense therapy. Listen, I'd love to stay on the phone and chat, but right now I'm elbows deep in a patient's chest cavity. I need to get back to him before the left ventricle of his heart dries out. In thirty words or less, how may I help you?"

"Did you do the autopsy on Bobby Javadi yet?"

Snip said, "Not yet. Only gunshot residue, tox screen, and stomach contents tests so far. We're waiting for the results before we do the complete autopsy. The results will be back in a day or two." She asked, "Aren't you the one who kept pointing AJ in Mr. Javadi's direction?" She snickered. "You're right for once. Case closed. Why are you still asking questions?"

"But I still…"

She interrupted. "Did I hear a but?" Snip and Queenie must be rehearsing their lines together. I made a mental note. No more girls-nights out with them together.

I whined. "But a couple of things are still bothering me."

Doctor Death indelicately snorted loud as a hungry hog. "Of course they are. Why am I not surprised?" She sighed with the inevitability of answering my questions, or losing all hope of getting back to her patient's chest cavity anytime soon. "Such as?"

I mused aloud. "I've been thinking…"

She quipped. "Gack. Already a bad sign."

I ignored her snide observation and soldiered on. "I've been thinking about the probability of Bobby Javadi committing suicide. The way I found him says he killed himself, but it doesn't pass the sniff test."

Snip said, "Until we get the test results back, nothing is cast in stone. But so far, this is a pretty open and shut case the physical evidence seems to support. He killed her. The guilt consumed him. He killed himself. The end."

Until my conversation with Pop, I couldn't have

agreed more. "I admit it. Bobby always headed the top of my suspect list, but looking at it from his point of view, I agree with him. He had no motive. Dead, Lissa Charney does him no good. Alive, he still has a chance she saves his hide. With his legal marriage to a US citizen, he avoids deportation. Once Lissa turned up dead, his chances of staying in this country went from maybe to slimsky. And don't forget the suicide note."

Snip asked, "What about it?"

I replied. "The typewriter? Not in his apartment."

She countered as though playing a game of tit for tat. "So? Maybe he typed it at work."

Not so fast, sister. "After Bobby got injured on the job, he missed work for several days. So, unless he typed it way before he killed her, it doesn't add up. Besides, the threatening note I received came from the same typewriter. I questioned Bobby about sending the threatening note, and he denied it. He claimed he didn't own a typewriter, and neither place he worked used one."

Doctor Sarcastic replied, "Gee, call me crazy, but did you ever consider maybe the guy lied?"

Undaunted, I kept at it. "No one willing to do *anything*- from hiring a pricey immigration attorney way over his budget or trolling for a trumped-up marriage to fight deportation wants to die. He wanted to live, or he'd never have fought so hard to stay in this country. He worked two jobs to save money to buy a house. No way this guy chose to die. If he wanted to die, getting sent back to Iran granted him his death wish."

Doctor Death sighed. "Anything else?"

I sighed. "Yeah, but it's stuck in the back of my brain, and it's driving me nuts. My gut says it's the one piece missing to solve the puzzle."

Snip lectured. "Science, not speculation will solve this case. Hold your horses for a couple of days until the test results are in. The gunshot residue test will be the telling of the tale."

I muttered. "If Bobby Javadi's hand has no gunshot residue on it, then the only thing he shot is my original theory of him as Lissa Charney's murderer."

****

The Yentas didn't exactly do cartwheels after I gave them their marching orders. "I counted two hundred and twenty-two storage unit locations in the San Fernando Valley. If we each call forty and I take the extra four, it won't take long to find out if Bobby Javadi stored a boat in the valley."

Hope scrunched her nose. "Why keep a boat in the valley and not closer to water?"

I held my hands out and rubbed my fingers together. "To save money. I went online and compared prices. Storage units on the west side go for a third more than in the valley. And the ones near a marina? Almost fifty percent higher."

By lunch, we'd hit another dead end. No Bobby, Robert, Roberto, Reza, or anyone with the surname of Javadi regardless of the first name, rented storage units in the San Fernando Valley. With the monthly fees so much higher near any marina, I doubted he rented one in a storage park adjacent to any water. The following morning, I distributed the coffees and surveyed the table. "I've been doing some more thinking."

Queenie moaned. "Those are the most dangerous words in the English language."

Joan muttered under her breath. "Guaranteed it translates to more work for us."

I ignored the peanut gallery and continued sharing the theory I came up with. "If not Bobby personally, either he hired someone to tamper with my boat, or maybe we don't see the forest for the trees."

Hope squinted as if trying to focus. "I don't see where you're going with this…"

I lead them down the path I'd taken. "We've all been in Annette and Roddy's showroom and seen the items displayed on the credenza in the back…"

At first, they all looked at me as if a set of horns sprouted on my head. A moment later, the proverbial light switched on in the Yentas' eyes and they chorused. "Waterskiing trophies."

Bingo. Bongo. Jackpot. Like a proud professor, I prompted the class. "And a key element to successful waterskiing is…?"

The Yentas chimed. "A ski boat!"

I toasted them with my coffee cup. "Annette's factory is in the San Fernando Valley. You guys call the same storage unit places on your lists and ask if either Annette or Roderick or Roddy Mason rents a storage unit. I'll take the marinas. I'll talk to Audrey Camarillo and see if she's able to access all the marinas' registries. Maybe the Masons have a slip. I'll contact the DMV and see if they show a boat registered in their names."

We reconnoitered in A Jolt of Java after lunch, and the palatable look of defeat on the Yenta's faces sucked the air out of the room. Audrey Camarillo held the last card left to play. Or we'd fold and have to throw in our hand.

Chapter Twenty-Eight

No hello, you doing okay, or wanna get a pizza Saturday night? Snip cut right to the chase. "You hit a grand slam home run, madame super sleuth. Mr. Javadi didn't commit suicide."

My heart jumped to my throat. "So, the gunshot residue test came back negative?"

Snip replied, "No, the test results aren't back yet."

I did a mental double-take. "Hold the phone, Hortense. You said the gunshot residue test is the true telling of the tale."

Doctor Death agreed. "I did. But as it turned out, it doesn't matter. Mr. Javadi didn't die from a gunshot wound. He died of a massive insulin overdose. The death occurred *before* the gunshot wound and was virtually instantaneous."

On which planet does a gun barrel in his mouth and a skull blasted to smithereens *not* matter? "Maybe he injected himself earlier and pulled the trigger later?"

Snip spoke slowly, weighing the possibility. "It's possible... but highly improbable. A massive insulin overdose goes directly into the bloodstream and death is usually instantaneous. Hypoglycemia..."

Having been Snip's friend for so long, I'd become familiar with a lot of medical terms, but not this one. "Hypo who?"

She repeated the term. "Hypoglycemia. In its worst

form, it is insulin shock. Less massive doses aren't normally fatal, but they can be quite destructive. A diabetic might experience seizures, dizziness, behavior changes such as irritability, loss of coordination, difficulty speaking, confusion, blurry vision, shakiness, sweating, extreme hunger, concentration problems, loss of consciousness, a coma, and with a large enough overdose, death."

And so? "Okay, so, he was diabetic. Maybe he didn't pay attention and took too much insulin by mistake. Later he's overcome with remorse for murdering Lissa and blows his brains out."

Her voice rang with surprise. "Our initial diagnosis agreed with you. No question. A diabetic who overdosed. The tox report confirmed a massive insulin overdose, but the odd thing is, that his pancreas functioned normally. And a search of his apartment uncovered no insulin in the refrigerator, and no needles, test sticks, or diabetic paraphernalia of any kind. We found no pinpricks on his fingers or toes from testing his blood sugar. We got the victim on the table and examined him from head to toe for injection marks, and found none. But a dosage as massive as Mr. Javadi's could only be administered by injection. So, we re-examined him and still almost missed it. The injection site was concealed by the victim's hair at the back of his head where the top of the neck meets the base of the skull."

I used my right hand to reach the back of my head to re-create the way the injection had been administered. "So, you're saying he held the syringe in his right hand and reached behind his head and shot the insulin into his neck? Why make it so hard to do when a shot in the arm

187

is a heck of a lot easier? Behind the neck is pretty awkward to do, especially with a long and thin syringe."

Snip said, "You're right. The victim *didn't* inject himself. From the angle of the injection site, someone else left-handed did it. The killer came behind the victim and injected a massive dose of insulin into Mr. Javadi's neck."

Whoa. "So, you're saying Bobby didn't die of a gunshot?"

"Nope. The suicide was staged post mortem."

Eek. "As in someone sneaked up behind him and injected him with a huge dose of insulin. Once he died, someone put the gun barrel inside Bobby's mouth and pulled the trigger? And they placed the handle of the gun in Bobby's hand and put his index finger on the trigger?"

Snip said, "To use your terminology, yep, precisely. No gunshot residue on his hands or arms. You found him with the grip of the gun in his hand and the barrel in his mouth, but someone else put it in there and pulled the trigger, not him. The victim didn't kill himself. He had help."

Holy guacamole.

Maybe Pop ought to quit fishing and start detecting.

Chapter Twenty-Nine

I was still reeling from my conversation with Snip when the cell phone rang. Caller ID announced Audrey Camarillo. I hit the hands-free button and said hello.

"Good morning," Audrey said, "I apologize if I am calling too early, but I didn't want to miss you once you started your day."

I snorted. "Are you kidding? You must be new in town. This is LA. You snooze, you lose. I've been up and about for hours. I walked the perimeter of Porto Paloma Marina twice, made a roundtrip to the Washington Street pier, and back on my houseboat an hour after daybreak. Now, I'm sitting on the freeway with the rest of the commuters getting nowhere fast. Are you calling with the information I need or to say you tried your best, but I'm outta luck?"

Audrey's tone lilted with a smile. "Door number one. I went into the California Association of Marinas database and launched a state-wide search. A large number of slip leases are made out to corporations in all the marinas." My heart rate jumped to warp speed for a minute until she continued. "Unfortunately, for your purposes, almost all of the slip leases made out to corporations are for luxury yachts, not small craft boats. I found over twenty-five thousand listings for slips with *individuals'* names on the leases with power boats."

Cripes. Finding a condom in a convent is easier.

"Wait a minute. You said you had the information I needed. This isn't it."

Audrey laughed. "Hold your horses a minute. I'm getting to it. I narrowed the criteria to powerboats between twelve and twenty-six feet in length with slips leased under a corporation name on the lease in the Los Angeles, Orange, San Diego, and Ventura Counties marinas. I now need much stronger prescription glasses, but after almost an hour of searching, I found two ski boat-sized small craft with corporations on the slip leases."

Two boats? And this is the good news? Merde. My heart sank below my socks. The chance of my recognizing either of them is slimsky to nonesky. But since she'd gone to such trouble, for giggles and squeaks, I gave it a shot. "You have the names of the corporations?"

She said, "Yes, mam. Carousel Toys Incorporated and ANRO Incorporated. Ring any bells?"

Ha! I'm never so lucky. I sighed with disappointment. "No such luck."

Before I thanked her for trying her best, I had one last idea. If this one is a bust, I had no choice but to throw in the towel. "Does it say which marinas the two boats are moored in?"

"Lemme see. Yes, here we go. The Carousel Toys boat is moored in Camino Real Marina in Redondo Beach and the ANRO boat is in the Castaic Marina at Lake Castaic."

I had a hunch and played it. "Can you get the address for ANRO?"

She replied. "Hold on a sec. and let me get to the correct screen." Twenty clicks later on Audrey's keyboard and the pulse roared with the power of a freight train inside my head. She read me the address and asked, "Is this the one?"

I resisted the urge to yell hallelujah, and focused on keeping my raging emotions in check and the car from veering into the eighteen-wheeler in the next lane. "Yep, it sounds right. If it is, I'll give the information to the Harbor Patrol." My voice quavered. "I'll never be able to thank you enough."

She said, "Put the word out to all your boater friends that your marina has a new Dockmaster who does right by her tenants, and we're square."

We rang off and my synapses fired hot on all burners and snapped with the crackle of a live wire in an electrical storm. The pieces of the puzzle fell into place. All the clues stared me right in the face, yet I couldn't put them together. Now I had a score to settle and was itching for a fight. Bring it on. Not the best decision I ever made, but hey, it's not as if it hasn't happened before. I've done my share of zigging instead of zagging. I had too much blood in my eye to see the idiotic choice I'd made. I pushed any rational ideas out of my head and locked them all in the trunk of the car. Only one road led to the truth. I switched freeways, goosed the accelerator, and kept driving. The wheels spinning inside my head turned faster than my car's new set of tires. But as the two-eighty-nine chewed up the freeway, the blood froze in my veins. If the killer had any inkling I'd finally figured any of this out, I'd be the next victim on the hit list. Do the smart thing, I told myself. Turn the convertible around and call AJ. As if. No guts, no glory, no fun. Nosiree, logic be damned. The plane had already been committed to the runway.

Chapter Thirty

The good news is my vintage bubblegum pink convertible sticks out like a sore thumb. So, unless parking attendants channel Hellen Keller, none ever lose my car. The bad news is if you're trying to be under the radar, you're not sneaking in unnoticed with a high-profile set of wheels such as mine. To be on the safe side, I parked the car around the corner from the building and hoofed it back.

I circled the perimeter and went around back to the parking lot to get the lie of the land. Oddly, Annette Mason's white luxury SUV sat alone in the Barely There parking lot. Curious. No cutters? No sewers? No packers? No shipping team? Production people typically start work at six in the morning and clock out at three in the afternoon. Did Annette close up shop for good? Emotions of relief and disappointment duked it out after not seeing Roddy Mason's black crew cab pickup truck parked in his space.

I walked to the side of the building and peeked in a window with a light on. Annette was busy in her office. Either the company was on life support, or a few loose ends were left for Annette to tie up before closing Barely

There for good. One thing's for sure. I'd never get to the truth through osmosis. I went around to the entrance, twisted the handle, and the front door swung open. With no relaxing taped background audio of jungle noises playing in the lobby, the place was quiet as a tomb. The creepy dead silence filled the air with an unmistakable sense of dread. The air conditioner-induced breeze waved the palm tree fronds as though warning of something sinister.

The dimly lit lobby appeared eerily vacant. The ditzy blonde behind the reception desk the last time no longer manned the phones. No one took her place. It didn't matter. I stood rooted to the spot for five minutes at the height of the swimwear season. The room was as silent as a cemetery when the phone should have been ringing off the hook. Curious. Maybe the phone was disconnected?

The air conditioner clicked off, but an involuntary shiver traveled the length of my spine as a sense of foreboding chilled the air. Anyone with a brain runs, not walks, out the front door. But no one ever confused me with Albert Einstein.

I walked the length of the long lobby, opened the door to the factory, and went inside. No one in the semi-dark production area. The large room was dimly illuminated by emergency lights embedded in the floor around the perimeter. Two wooden cutting tables covered with yards of fabric overlaid by pattern pieces from one end to the other anchored the front of the space. The fabric lay stretched tautly across the table and held in place with heavy iron anvils to ironically "relax" the yardage for cutting. The center of the room consisted of a production line with three rows of unmanned industrial sewing machines with ten machines in each row. Fabric laid out ready to cut, partially sewn garments waiting in the unmanned sewing machines to be finished. Yet not a single soul in the place to do any of the work. I consulted my mental calendar. Not a holiday, yet the place is empty.

I stuck my head into the design room adjacent to the sewing floor. Two dozen bolts of printed fabrics were squeezed tightly into the middle shelf of a metal storage rack. A dozen bolts of solid fabrics sat on the bottom shelf. Bags of trims, zippers, and bra pads separated by category lined the top shelf of the storage rack. A half-dozen more bolts of print and solid fabrics lay spread across a metal design table with cardboard swimwear frames laid over them. A dozen swimsuits hung on a grid adjacent to a rack packed with other samples. A mannequin stood next to the grid dressed in a bikini with pins inserted in strategic places for fitting. Weird. Who designs a new line if they're not staying in business?

Empty cartons were piled to the ceiling in the packing and shipping bays, and the bins held no inventory. No goods in stock or being sewn meant no plans to ship more orders. None of this made any sense.

Located on the other side of the room, the door to Roddy's dark office appeared ajar. I scanned the space for Roddy hiding in the shadows. I didn't see him, so I hit the flashlight app on my mobile and crept inside. A computer set in the center and an empty metal in and out basket in the top right corner above the three-line phone were the sole occupants of the chrome and metal desktop. A LaserJet printer connected to the computer sat on a small metal table on the right side of the desk. Behind it was a metal three-drawer file cabinet.

Photos of Roddy and Annette water-skiing behind a powerboat, interspersed with photos of models wearing Barely There swimsuits covered the wall behind his executive-style, modern desk.

The walls on the left side of the desk featured photos of Roddy in a wetsuit with air tanks strapped to his back and holding a couple of trophies. The photo in the center of the wall caught my eye. Roddy and an older man who Roddy resembled in build and around the eyes, presumably his father, were dressed in hunting gear, holding rifles, and standing on either side of the bloody carcass of a buck. Eek.

The right-side wall stopped me in my tracks. Covered from one end to the other, from floor to ceiling, it featured a gallery of photos of Lissa Charney. The various mustaches, devil's horns, and daggers through her heart drawn over the photos, made for a cringe-worthy creepy, but blatant display of Roddy's opinion of Lissa.

Two innocent lives were viciously extinguished decades before their expiration dates. Try revenge as the motive? At first glance, from my perch in the cheap seats, no question about it. But the telling of the tale lay hidden behind the juvenile graffiti on the wall. Klieg lights shined in my head with the realization. Forget about revenge. Think jealousy and unrequited love. Bingo-bongo. Jackpot. Ding-ding. We have a winner, ladies, and gentlemen. Give the girl a Kewpie Doll. Way to go. Test drive this one for a theory. Roddy's head over heels in love with Lissa. She only has eyes for Bobby Javadi and doesn't give Roddy a second look. Dunderhead Roddy's brilliant solution? Eliminate the competition. How? Tip off the INS to Bobby's incorrect paperwork from Mason Construction. Yet nothing Roddy does gets him any closer to Lissa. Daily deliveries of gorgeous roses? A waste of money, since Lissa's convinced the bouquets prove Bobby's love and devotion. And the INS? A lot of help they are. A flurry of interest, a rash of thinly-veiled threats. Bottom line? Lots of talk, not much action. Darn those pesky rules and protective regulations gumming the works. Bobby wasn't deported. At least, not fast enough to suit Roddy Mason.

And if life's not bad enough for Roddy already, Annette hits him with the company's dire financial situation. Her solution? Throw a bucket of bucks she doesn't have to spare and a partnership at Lissa Charney to get her back. If Lissa takes the offer? The girl Roddy loves doesn't love him, and now she's gonna steal his part of the company? Oh yeah, right. The same day donkeys fly. A deadly combo of anger and jealousy extinguishes all other emotions and you can kiss love goodbye.

Roddy goes crazy. He messes with Lissa's car and magically arrives to save her as she's off to the partnership meeting he's also set to attend. He lures Lissa out with an offer for a ride to the meeting. Instead, he kidnaps her, takes her to one of Mason Construction's building sites, kills her, crams her body into a sample crate, sneaks it back into the mart, nails her battered corpse onto the closet wall for good measure, and frames Joan Binder for the murder.

Whoa. I slammed on the brakes to reconsider my theory. Is it possible for a dim-witted clod like Roddy, barely capable of putting a complex sentence together, to plan and successfully execute the crime of the century?

Quite a challenge wrapping my head around the concept, but still, anything is possible. Isn't it?

The evidence against Joan doesn't hold, and she is released from jail. AJ gets an anonymous tip and Annette is questioned. Annette's fingerprints aren't on the bloody crate in the trunk of her car, and her accountant gives her an alibi for the day and timeline of Lissa's murder.

Annette is cleared, but the questions remain. Who put the bloody sample crate in Annette's car trunk? Who's to say it wasn't Annette? Maybe she wore gloves? Am I in the right church but sitting in the wrong pew with the wrong Mason doing the deed?

Maybe Annette lied about Lissa not coming to the meeting or she bought off her accountant? Toss enough money at the guy and he goes along with the lie about the alibi. Say Lissa arrives, listens to the offer, and declines it. The accountant sees no reason to hang around. He says adios and leaves, but Annette begs Lissa to stay, hoping to change her mind about signing the deal. Maybe things get ugly when Lissa isn't swayed. A confrontation between the two women ensues and during the struggle, Annette shoots Lissa with the nail gun.

Say Roddy arrives after the meeting and sees Annette killed Lissa? Maybe I've got it all backward and Annette murdered Lissa and Roddy helped her get away with it? Either the mother or the son looks good for Lissa's murder. But which one did the deed is the question?

But even after I found Bobby with his brains splattered all over his desk, I still pegged him for the crime. And if Bobby figures out Roddy killed Lissa?

Or Bobby figures out Annette was the killer? Or Bobby figures out Annette and Roddy killed Lissa together and Bobby confronts Roddy? Roddy can't risk Bobby blabbing to the cops. The INS wouldn't do his dirty work for him, so Roddy murders Bobby with an overdose of insulin, and once Bobby is dead, Roddy sticks the gun barrel in Bobby's mouth and pulls the trigger. He puts Bobby's finger on the trigger and makes it appear Bobby committed suicide.

Roddy's diabetic? No. Insulin is a prescription drug. How did he get it? Mental head slap. All the water Annette guzzles? Unless you've been aimlessly wandering the desert for days, *no one* is that thirsty. She exhibited the signs of being diabetic the day I questioned her.

Of course. Roddy got the insulin from his mother. Either she gave it to him or he stole it from her. Is Roddy able to administer a fatal dose of insulin? The concept made me laugh. Annette either taught him how to do it, or she went with Roddy to Bobby's place to do the deed. Say Roddy overpowers Bobby and knocks him out. Annette injects Bobby with a massive amount of insulin. One of them puts the barrel of the gun into Bobby's mouth, puts their hand over his, holds his finger on the trigger, and pulls.

But if my original theory proves right and Annette had nothing to do with Lissa's murder, it means Roddy stole the insulin from his mother. With the enormous amount of insulin Roddy pilfered, Annette must have put two and two together. By now, Annette realizes her precious baby boy is a stone-cold killer. Or did she figure it out a lot earlier? If yes, is she complicit in his crimes? Does Annette protect her son? And if yes, at what cost? Does a price too high to pay exist for his mother to protect Roddy? Take the fall for him? Shield him from having to pay for his crimes? Willing to die for him? He'd already committed two brutal murders. Would his mother become his victim number three? From my spot in the bleachers, the concept of Roddy murdering the woman who gave him life is a big no never mind.

A matching chrome and glass credenza in the corner held two dozen large binders lined in a row on each of the top two shelves. The lower shelf housed a single object. An old-fashioned Remington typewriter. No wonder my search for it in Bobby's apartment proved fruitless. Now Annette's flustered reaction to the threatening letter made perfect sense, and yet muddied the waters all the more. My head spun with endless questions but no answers came around. Who sent the threatening letter? Annette or Roddy? Is Annette complicit in Roddy's crimes, or the perpetrator? Whichever one of them did the deed must be held accountable.

With all the possible scenarios, it would be no surprise if I missed something. I turned a visual one-eighty and focused on a plaque on the left-side wall I didn't notice before. "*Lefties do it right*" and in a moment of clarity, it all became crystal clear. The important thing in the back of my brain? It arrived and smacked me in the face. Bobby held the gun with his *right hand*, but he and Roddy were *both left-handed*.

If I'd remembered my first conversation with Bobby, the last piece of the puzzle fit a lot sooner. Southpaw Bobby's right hand? By him, pretty useless, except to balance him out. I'm the same way. No way to hold the gun steady enough in his right hand to aim. Nor did he have the strength in his right hand or the flexibility in his right index finger to pull the trigger and blow his brains out. Lefty Roddy put the gun in Bobby's *right* hand and pulled the trigger. Pop hit the nail on the head. Bobby died, but he had help getting dead. And here I am nosing around in his killer's office. Holy guacamole.

My mother didn't raise stupid children. Better bring in the cavalry and fast. I dialed AJ, but got no answer on either her office phone or mobile. Why is a cop only around when you don't need one? I left two messages and hoped she listened to her voicemails more often than I do mine.

I aimed my cell phone and snapped pictures of all the photos on the walls, the plaque, and the typewriter. Ten minutes later, still no call from the cop. As I E-mailed the last photo to the detective, I prayed AJ reads her E-mails more often than she played her voicemail messages. The message notification icon blinked received as the light went on in Roddy's office, and the cold barrel of a gun poked into the small of my back. Merde.

Roddy's evil taunt made Snidely Whiplash sound sweet as an innocent choir boy. "Looky who's snooping around my office. Miss Busybody herself." He jammed the gun into my back harder in case I missed his point. "You just can't stop snooping."

Nothing gets past you, Snidely.

He said, "Somebody smart pays more attention to all my warnings. But not you." His tone of voice was apologetic, but the blood in my veins still turned into ice. "And now it's gonna cost you a lot more than repairing a boat or a car."

As he put a baseball glove-sized hand on my shoulder and spun me around, I tapped the third key on the cell phone keypad. Did I remember the order of the numbers correctly? Hopefully, I speed-dialed Snip and not the weather forecast. I turned the volume to the maximum and slid the cell phone into the front pocket of my jeans. I gauged my chances of getting past the big goon. With my short legs and him sporting a bazooka? Slimsky to nonesky. I'd been down this road before, and needed no prompting. I had the drill memorized. Dead is forever. Don't do anything stupid. I wisely reached for the sky.

Roddy stood over a foot taller and outweighed me by at least a hundred pounds. I was no match for Roddy Mason physically, but I ran circles around him with my brain. As if. I shoved my fist on my lips so as not to laugh out loud. If Roddy murdered Lissa and Bobby, he fooled me until five minutes ago.

If you can't outrun 'em with fancy footwork, dazzle 'em with a nifty bunch of words. I'd better keep the quiver of fear out of my voice. My life depended on it. I channeled my eighth-grade homeroom teacher Mrs. Sutter's authoritative tone. "Roddy, for God's sake, put the gun away. This isn't the way it looks." Yeah, right. Only if you're blind.

Roddy held the gun steady and sighted it in the middle of my forehead. He arched a brow. "Ok. Why don't you tell me?"

My dad always said if you've got nothing, make trouble. Making trouble while facing a loaded gun? Not a good option. His plan B was if you can't make trouble, punt. So, I punted and hoped for the best. "Your showroom has been closed for a week. Rumors spread fast as a wildfire that your company went out of business. It's bad for the entire industry if any competitor closes its doors. I came to see for myself." I gave myself a mental pat on the back. Pretty good for a girl not usually too fast on her feet.

Unfortunately, Roddy wasn't buying the tall tale I was selling. He growled. "That's a filthy lie. We're doing fine."

Better get out the front loader. A shovel won't do for such a huge load of crap. I ticked off all the points of evidence like a waitress reciting the luncheon specials. "No one at the reception desk answering the phones. Doesn't matter. They're not ringing anyway. Disconnected? So what? You don't need phones if no accounts are left to talk to." I waved towards the empty production floor. "No cutters cutting fabric, no sewers sewing swimsuits, no product in the distribution bins, no cartons packed with goods or anyone shipping orders, or designing the new line, and a dark showroom." I made a ta-da motion with my hands. "If it looks like a duck and quacks like a duck, it's a duck."

Roddy sucked in his cheeks. "I got a sniff INS planned a raid in this area, and we told the crew to stay home."

I batted Betty Boop eyes. "Your company hires illegals?"

He smirked. "And your company doesn't?" He grinned. "And so what if we do? We're helping all those poor people live the American dream."

Good grief. Gag me with a spoon. "And I'm sure you pay them adequately for the work they do."

Roddy clucked his tongue with faux righteous indignation. "No one complains. And for the record, the way we pay our employees is none of your business."

He waved the gun under my nose. "Enough of this crap. All you're doing is avoiding my question." Roddy might be a tad smarter than anyone gave him credit for. "Why are you in my office taking pictures?" He snorted. "Need decorating ideas?"

I batted my eyes once more. "Pictures?"

He said, "The photos you shot from your phone."

I widened my eyes. "Photos?"

Roddy pointed the gun at the pocket I'd covered with my right hand. "You took pictures of the photos on the walls with the camera on your phone."

Dad's reminder that image often trumps facts ran a loop through my head. My knees knocked as loud as an untuned engine, but I struck an indignant pose. "No way."

Roddy waggled his fingers. "Gimme the phone." He pointed to the desk. "Take the phone out of your pocket. Be a good little girl, and put it on the desk nice and easy. Keep your other hand out so I can see it."

Oh sure. I give you the phone and lose any hope of escaping along with it. Not gonna happen. I jutted defiance with my chin. "No."

Roddy's eyes bugged. "Do it!" He snarled. "Or I swear to God, I'll blow your brains out right now."

Roddy planned to shoot me whether I gave him the phone or not. I eyed the desk and got an idea. I held my hands out in surrender. "Ok, Roddy. I give up. No problem. I'll put it on the desk."

He huffed self-righteously. "S' better."

I held my left hand out for him to see I had nothing. I pulled the phone out of my pocket with my right hand and turned around to face the desk. I leaned over to lay the phone on the desk. Instead, I grabbed the in/out basket with my left hand. I pivoted, powered up with my knees, bounced on the balls of my feet like a basketball forward, and lobbed the metal basket at Roddy's bowling ball-sized head. A satisfyingly loud thwack echoed the office as the sharp corner of the metal basket slammed into the bridge of Roddy's nose. Roddy's knees buckled, and he folded as fast as a cheap card table. He dropped the gun, wrapped his sausage-sized fingers around his bleeding schnozz, and screamed loud as a banshee.

A fountain of blood gushed high as the Old Faithful geyser. It sprayed a Rorschach test pattern on the front of my silk shirt and covered the back walls. I swiveled my head around, searching desperately for the gun, but it bounced away somewhere. No time to keep looking for it. Roddy will stop writhing like a snake any minute. I grabbed my phone, hurdled over him, and ran for my life.

Slow him down, I told myself, even if for only a few precious seconds. I slammed his office door shut and raced into the design room. I shoved the mannequin in front of Roddy's office door and pushed the rolling rack packed with samples behind the mannequin. Maybe the blood from his broken nose gets into Roddy's eyes, and he doesn't see the obstacle course. With any luck, he'd trip over the mannequin and rack, fall, and crack his head open on the cement floor.

I found the master switch and killed the lights. The place instantly turned dark as a moonless night. I lurched my way around toward the door leading to the lobby with the same skill level as a blind guy playing hide and go seek.

Annette yelled, "Who's here? Roddy? Roddy! Roderick Mason, you better answer me this minute. Did you turn off the lights? Are you blind? Didn't you see my car parked in the lot? For crying out loud, it's pitch black. Turn on the damned lights before I fall over something and break a leg."

Roddy's screams echoed through the production room like in an arcade funhouse as he crashed into the obstacle course. I looked back to Roddy's office. Roddy jerked around like a marionette on a string trying to untangle himself from the samples strewn all over the place. The swimsuit straps were wrapped around him as tight as a mummy. The more he squirmed, the more he lay trapped beneath the mannequin and rolling rack. He yelled. "You can run but you can't hide. I find you and I won't need a gun. I'll kill you with my bare hands!"

Annette screamed, "Who are you gonna kill now, for crying out loud? Corky and me?"

Roddy yelled back, "Holly Schlivnik," and a shiver tap-danced over my heart.

I debated whether or not to scream and give my location away. Screw the location. I needed help, and I needed it now. I screamed my bloody head off. "Help me, Annette! Call the cops. He's gonna kill me!"

Roddy yelled, "Touch the phone, Big Bird, and you're dead!"

Was Roddy capable of killing his mother? Annette needed no convincing. She slammed her office door closed and went radio silent. Fanfreakingtastic. Schlivnik was all on her own.

Roddy finally freed himself, and an awful crashing sound echoed around the room as the rolling rack smashed into the metal wall. He heaved the mannequin the length of the room as if it were a javelin. It bounced off one of the cutting tables and hit the ground. I dodged it as it rolled on the floor. Roddy's steel-toed work boots stomped loudly against the cement floor. I lost sight of him, but the pounding of his footsteps was closer and closer with every step he took. With his long legs, Roddy's stride was far greater than mine. But my slight, slender frame moved a lot faster than the slow lummox. Like a chicken with its head cut off, I ran a zig-zag pattern diagonally across the production room trying to fake Roddy out. Which direction to go? No clue, but stopping to get my bearings wasn't a good choice. I might go down, but not without a fight. I'd be damned if I'd make it easy for Roddy to snuff out my life.

The lights went on as I got to the door separating the production area from the lobby. Annette opened her office door a crack, but who cares? She'd be no help, so no point in calling out to her and giving Roddy my new position. The crack of the gun rang loud as a cannon. Roddy fired on the run and the shot went wild. For once being a shorty worked in my favor. A half-inch taller, my skull would have shattered instead of the glass on the window of the door.

Roddy ran a few dozen steps behind me as I raced into the lobby. I slammed the door and eyeballed the distance between the door separating the lobby and factory to the building entrance. Was an escape remotely possible? With my short legs? Not a chance. I'd never make it through the long, narrow entry before a bullet pierced my back.

I desperately scanned the lobby for a hiding place. The closet behind the reception counter? Nah, it's the first place he'd look. The choices? Slim pickings, but you must play the cards you're dealt. I scampered behind a large, leafy palm tree adjacent to the reception counter as Roddy entered the lobby. I willed myself to stop shaking or my tremors would rustle the palm tree fronds, and give my position away. The best shot at my seeing tomorrow? If Roddy assumed I escaped and he went back to his office to lick his wounds. As if. I'm not so lucky.

I peeked through a palm tree frond for a lie of the land. Did Roddy give up his search? Of course not. The first place he checked? Inside the storage closet in the back of the reception desk, behind the counter and shelves. Good thing I guessed right.

I held my breath as he stood in front of the palm tree and put a meaty hand on the leaf in front of my nose. By a stroke of a miracle, he moved on.

Drenched in blood, Roddy leaned over the bamboo reception counter and rooted around for something to staunch the fountain of blood still gushing out of his broken nose. He took a handful of tissues from a dispenser on the desk, rolled them into tubes, and stuffed them into his nostrils.

Standing behind the palm tree forever? Not an option. Getting out of this alive on my own seemed less probable with each tick of the clock. I needed help, but I counted on none from Annette. I pulled the cell phone out of my pocket. No messages. Why is a cop only around if you're speeding ten miles over the limit? I dialed the first three digits of AJ's number but disconnected halfway through. I couldn't trust my voice to whisper low enough. I tapped a short text to AJ: SOS and prayed she read it and understood.

A twinge of jealousy pinched my gut as Corky flew onto the palm tree frond right above my head. I'd pay a king's ransom for a set of wings. The parrot screeched, "Don't talk to strangers! Don't talk to strangers!" And I almost dropped the phone.

Roddy swatted a catcher's mitt-sized hand at the

bird. "Get outta my way, Corky. Go back to Annette."

I stood stock-still as the parrot flapped his wings and squawked, "Roddy, danger! Roddy stranger, Roddy danger!"

Roddy narrowed his eyes and peered at the palm leaves. I prayed he didn't look down and see the toes of my neon pink sneakers sticking out at the base of the palm tree. Cripes.

Chapter Thirty-One

The air conditioning kicked on and a stale, cold breeze filled the stuffy room. The vent blew directly over the palm tree, and the air rustled the fronds. My nose twitched as a frond in front of my face brushed back and forth on it. I beat back the urge to sneeze. I fought the good fight, but I lost the war with the overwhelming ache to scratch my itchy snout. I inched my right arm over my body. When I got to my boobs, I bent my arm. I slowly raised my hand to my face and scratched the tip of my nose raw.

I rubbed my hands on the front of my jeans, but my palms kept sweating. The fear of discovery ignited my sweat glands to work overtime. Perspiration slicked my hands as I held the cell out far enough to check for messages. Nada. Zip. Nothing. Of course, only five minutes passed since I'd texted AJ, but who cares? I bit my lip hard enough to draw blood to keep from screaming my frustration.

If I bent my head, I'd rustle the palm fronds. So, I tried putting the cell back in my pocket without moving my arm. Big mistake. I miscalculated the distance, and missed the pocket. The phone slipped out of my sweaty fingers, bounced off my left sneaker onto the cement floor, and landed between my feet. Bending over to retrieve the phone meant disturbing the palm fronds and guaranteed my discovery. I held my breath and manipulated the phone with my toe to push it behind my shoes.

Roddy didn't notice the phone hitting the cement floor, but Corky went crazy. Corky's wingtips flapped frantically against the palm fronds. I froze still as a statue as the parrot dive-bombed the palm tree and squawked at the top of his lungs. "Danger! Danger. Don't talk to strangers!"

Did Roddy not hear my heart pounding with the boom of a bass drum? How could he not? My firecracker pulse exploded inside my head. I chanced a peek through a frond for a look-see. Roddy brushed his big hand on the palm frond in front of my face and my stomach dropped to my toes. Roddy gently held the bird in the palm of his hand, and spoke softly, in a concerned and soothing tone. "Corky, what has your feathers flapping?"

"BRRRRRRRING. BRRRRRRRING!"

Before the parrot could rat me out, AJ Yakamura conveniently chose *that* moment to return my call. I made a mental note. If I lived through this, remember to activate the vibrate feature on my phone.

Roddy grabbed the ringing phone from between my feet and parted the palm fronds. With two purplish-green shiners and his bloody, swollen, cauliflower nose ballooned to the size of a ripe grapefruit, his battered face bore a resemblance to the loser of a destruction derby.

Roddy held the cell close to his ear and deadpanned." You've got a call coming in." He tossed the phone on the floor and ground it into a hundred pieces with the heel of his work boot. Does the warranty cover this? He tapped his fingertips to his cheek and tsked. "Darn. Don't ya just hate it when a cell phone drops an important call?" Another aspiring comedian.

Hey, Stephen Colbert. Roddy Mason's auditioning for your job.

I toed the pieces of the destroyed phone and gave Roddy the stink eye. "Think you solved your problem, wise guy? No way. Better to let me take the call and tell the detective I'd been mistaken. Say no problem, sorry, a false alarm. When she redials and doesn't reach me, she's gonna realize I'm in trouble, and send in the cavalry to rescue me. So, genius, congratulations. I hope you're proud of yourself. All you've accomplished is to get yourself arrested even faster."

He waved the gun in my face and smiled a nasty smile. "This is LA. With our traffic? By the time they get to the valley, you'll be dead and I'll be long gone." He poked me in the ribs with the barrel of the pistol. "We're done playing hide and go seek. No more games. Let's go." He clamped his free hand on my shoulder with the grip of a vise and pulled me out from behind the palm tree. He pushed me in front of him and stuck the pistol in the small of my back. "March."

I planted my feet firmly on the floor. "Nothing doing." My eyes teared as he jammed the business end of the gun into the base of my spine.

He growled. "Move, or I'll shoot."

My goose appeared cooked. I might as well go out swinging. "Go ahead macho man, shoot an unarmed woman half your size in the back like the pathetic coward you are." With nothing left to lose, I went for broke. "The pictures in your office said it all. You were in love with Lissa. You're the one who sent her the daily roses, not Bobby Javadi. No matter what you tried to win her over, she wouldn't give you a second look. She only had eyes for Bobby, and it made you crazy."

I turned around and faced him. He'd have to look me in the eye to shoot me. "So, you came up with a brilliant game plan to eliminate the competition. Getting the INS to do your dirty work for you by deporting Bobby."

He spat. "As if I'd waste any effort on a nothing like him." But the deep blush flaming his neck betrayed his denial.

I pushed him to a place he'd never willingly go. "You intimidated Bobby with the INS. Told him you'd turn him in if he didn't kill Lissa."

Roddy huffed. "You're crazy."

I jutted my jaw. "You wish. First, you tried to get him to do your dirty work. But Bobby refused to kill her, so, you sicced the INS on him and killed Lissa yourself."

Roddy clucked his tongue. "And why would I?"

I gave him the big eyes. "I've seen the contract. If Lissa signed it, your share of the business went to her. So, you disable her car and offer to take her to the meeting with Annette."

His eyes widened to the size of silver dollars. Bingo. Bongo. Ding, ding. Jackpot. We have a winner, ladies, and gentlemen. Hopefully, I'd live long enough to tell the tale to the cops.

"Did you take Lissa to one of your construction sites and kill her or do it here in the factory? Shoot her with one of your nail guns and stuff her in one of your sample crates? Sneak her back into the mart and nail her to the closet wall?"

Roddy's response? A smack of the gun barrel across my mouth. My lips split open wide like a cracked coconut. He bared his teeth and snarled. "Maybe now you'll finally stop your yammering."

Blood gushed from my lips with the arc of a broken fire hydrant with a pain so intense I saw stars. The blood ran down my chin and stained the front of my shirt. I dragged my tongue over my gums and three loose teeth shifted. I licked my sore lips and tasted the metallic tang of blood. As my lips swelled, some of the words mushed off my tongue, as though talking with a mouthful of marbles. "Come on Woddy. Confession is good for the soul. Admit it. You killed her. Bobby confwonted you, so, you killed him too."

Before I could react, Roddy grabbed me around the waist, yanked me off my feet, and tucked me under his arm like a halfback taking the football into the endzone. I tried to punch him in the nuts, but my short arms couldn't reach his crotch. I wriggled squirmier than a worm on Pop's fishing hook, but to no avail. The more I wriggled the tighter Roddy's grip. He squeezed so tight, that taking a deep breath proved impossible. I stopped my wriggling before he squeezed the life out of me.

I turned a visual one-eighty around to get my bearings. Still inside the Quonset hut. Good news, bad news. The good news? Even dunderhead Roddy Mason understood a big lummox holding a gun and carrying a woman under his arm might look conspicuous out in public, so he stayed inside the building. The bad news? He had one other option. And it's one not too good for my long-term health. He headed for the back exit. My only hope to see tomorrow was to stop him. Once he got me out of the building and into his truck, it's all over but the shouting. He'd take me to one of the Mason construction sites, kill me, and stuff me in a crate or bury me in the foundation of a half-finished building. Either way, I'd be dead.

Roddy held the gun in his left hand, grasped me with his right, and found himself lacking a free hand. He stood staring at the door leading into the factory, trying to figure out a way to open it. He looked at me and angled his head at the door. He expected me to open it for him? Oh, sure. On the second Tuesday of next week. I answered by sticking my tongue out at him. He growled his displeasure, lifted his big right foot, kicked his size thirteen work boot into the center of the door, and shattered it. The shards of glass made a snap, crackle, and crunch like the breakfast cereal when Roddy stepped on them as he marched double-time towards the rear exit with me trapped under his armpit.

The red exit sign over the rear door in the far corner loomed ahead. Roddy headed straight to it. I had maybe two minutes at the most to stop him. I wriggled and he tightened his grip. I screamed at the top of my lungs, "Annette! Help me! He's gonna kill me! He's killed two people already. You already have their blood on your hands. Stop him before he makes it three." Dead air. No help from the peanut gallery. My survival was all on me.

I knuckled my left hand free and dug my fingernails into the soft roll of fat around Roddy's thick middle. He flicked my hand away with the barrel of the gun as though I was a pesky gnat. I twisted my torso around to face him. My aching split lips throbbed like a wildly pulsing heart as I reared back and punched him in his bloody nose as hard as I could with my left hand. He screamed like a girl and dropped me. I hit the ground with a thud and landed on my keyster. I sprang up fast as a jack in the box on crack and a mind-bending pain radiated around my midsection. I fought it off and ran for the back door with the speed of an Olympic sprinter. The sound of the gunshot reverberated around the room as deafening as a thunderclap. A searing, white lightning stab of pain in the right shoulder stopped me in my tracks. I fell and hit the side of my head hard on the cement floor with a jaw-rattling crash. And then the world went black.

****

I came to with a splitting headache, trussed the same as a rodeo calf, and tied to one of the cutting tables with a gag in my mouth. Was I out long? Maybe a few minutes. But long enough for Roddy to wrap me tight as a mummy. Remarkably, I appeared still alone, but not for long. Curious to be lashed to a cutting table and not in his truck on my way to certain death by now? Maybe he stopped to get another crate? That must be the reason. I inhaled a deep breath through my nose and a piercing pain encircled my ribcage as the oxygen filled my lungs. My head pounded with the strength of a jackhammer while I tried to wriggle out of my bonds. The wounded shoulder ballooned to the size of a small boulder and stars flashed in front of my eyes from the pain. Roddy wrapped me from my shoulders to my shins and used strips of swimwear fabric to lash me to the cutting table. But swimwear fabric is made of spandex and nylon. It stretches if it's pulled and is easily manipulated. All I needed were two free hands.

A pair of cutting shears lay tantalizingly close, but just out of reach. An experienced boater same as me, Roddy used a reliable bowline knot to lash me to the cutting table. Fortunately, I honed the skills of a master knotter. To live on a houseboat safely and securely, it was a necessity. Roddy's bowline knot was virtually impossible for an amateur to undo, but an easy one to untie, even one-handed, if you knew the trick. Unfortunately, a complication arose that the nautical knotting instruction book failed to cover. The blood oozing from my wound traveled the length of my arm to my hand. My blood-sticky fingers slicked slippery as an oil patch, preventing a good enough grip on the shiny fabric to work the knot out. I stretched my fingers as far as they'd go and wiped them dry on my jeans. I had to work fast before more blood leaked onto my hand.

My head hurt too much to lift high enough to see my progress as I worked the knots. I depended on a sense of touch and memorization of the way the knots formed to untie them. I twisted my wrists inward as far as they turned and worked the knots with my index fingers and thumbs to loosen them from the centers outward. The left hand popped free in thirty seconds. I untied the right hand with my left. I sat up and ignored the pain and the stars flashing behind my eyes. I used the cutting shears to slit the ties binding my torso and pulled the gag out of my mouth.

I craned my neck in an arc to get an updated lie of the land. Loud voices came from the direction of Annette's office. Roddy and Annette. Arguing. Preoccupied and not concerned with me. Good news. But for how long? With some luck, a few minutes tops.

As I slid off the cutting table, I nicked my wound on the sharp corner. The stars flashed again behind my eyes. Drenched in the red stuff and in agony from the pain, the throbbing wound oozed, making me woozy from the loss of blood. I shuddered, remembering Snip's lecture on the impact on the body if it loses too much blood. I needed to staunch the bleeding and fast. I cut three-wide pieces of fabric and wrapped them tightly for maximum pressure and stretched them around the wound. I used the strips Roddy bound me to the table with to secure the bandages. Not exactly the primo first aid, but it would do for the time being. After a few minutes, the throbbing subsided noticeably. I moved without seeing stars, but taking a deep breath? Still out of the question.

Anyone with a brain runs out of the building and ditches this deadly popsicle stand. But a Mensa, I'm not. I grabbed one of the anvils by the handle off the cutting table and crept across the room. I hid behind a metal set of shelves filled with sewing supplies outside of Annette's office.

I leaned around the shelves and peered into her open door. The credenza shelves were empty. The room was packed with cartons stacked halfway to the ceiling. A six-line phone, a dark computer, and Corky's travel cage were the only things on the desk. It didn't take a rocket scientist to see Barely There swam its last race.

Chapter Thirty-Two

I angled my body so I could see them, but they couldn't see me. His back to me, Roddy and his mother faced one another. Annette stood behind her desk with terror etched into her wide blue eyes. Roddy aimed the gun directly at his mother's heart.

I leaned in and eavesdropped on their argument. Annette spat the words out like a chunk of wormy apple. "Forget it. It's over. We have no choice. We must accept it and move on. We're done. The accountant ran our quarterly statement and advised cutting our losses and closing the company." She waved around the packed-up office. "And I took his advice."

Roddy's face contorted with disgust. "And you took the advice of a moron bean counter who has no experience in the swimwear industry?"

Annette jerked her head, and the wild mop of curly bleached -blond hair billowed out as if ruffled by a breeze. "He doesn't need to be an expert in the industry. Numbers are numbers, and they don't lie. We can't expect Mason Construction to carry Barely There on its back forever. We've put a huge financial strain on the construction company. Before long, Barely There destroys it too, and then? It's not fair to your father, or all the employees who depend on the company to feed their families to let our company bleed Mason Construction dry."

Roddy pleaded. "Come on, Big Bird. All I ask is we go through the rest of the season. If the numbers aren't improved by the end of June, ok, we throw in the towel."

Annette dipped her head and the untamable hair whipped around and curtained her eyes. "Forget it. I've already let all the employees go. I refuse to keep throwing good money after bad."

Roddy turned to the side to examine the packed cartons, and his eyes bugged as big as a couple of headlights. "And you decided this without first telling me your plans?" His deep voice rose to a high-pitched screech. "This company is still part mine! Don't I get a vote?"

Annette ignored his question and pointed to the gun aimed at her heart. "Put the gun away. I can't talk to you with a pistol pointed at my chest."

Roddy stomped his foot like a cranky toddler who didn't want to share his toys. "No."

Annette arched a brow. "You gonna shoot me too?"

Roddy jutted his jaw. "If I have to."

Annette held out her hand and begged. "Roddy, please. You need help. Give me the gun and let me help you."

Roddy waved his free hand to the factory floor. "If you want to help me, help me get rid of *her*."

Double gulp. What better motivation is there needed for me to boogie and fast? Yet morbid curiosity kept my tootsies cemented to the spot.

Annette put her hands out like a traffic cop. "No. It stops right here. It stops right now. I already helped you plenty, and look at the great way things worked out. Two people are dead thanks to all my help. I have to live with the guilt for the rest of my life. I'm not gonna help you add one more to the score."

Roddy snorted, "You helped me? That's a joke. This is all *your* fault. You hire lazy Lissa. She quits in the middle of the season and you don't replace her. The business tanks, and your brilliant idea to save Barely There? Give the person who dumped you *my share* of the company."

Annette cocked a brow. "A hundred percent of nothing is still nothing. If you wanted to save the company, you blew it. You killed the one chance to bring it back by murdering Lissa."

Roddy scoffed. "Such a crock. There's nothing special about Lissa Charney. She's not the second coming. Not even close. You should have replaced her, but you didn't. I took action to save what's rightfully *mine*. What *you* chose to give away without my permission, and to who? A two-bit tramp who managed to make a few sales if they fell in her lap."

Annette tried to be gentle, but there was no sugarcoating her words. "You loved her. She didn't love you back. I'm sorry you were hurt so badly."

Roddy yelled. "I didn't love her!" His voice cracked. "I couldn't love someone who picked a nothing like *him* over me."

Annette pinched her lips. "Eliminating the competition didn't work, so, you killed them both. And God forgive me, I helped you get away with it."

And there it was. Means, motive, and opportunity. All neatly wrapped into one tragic package. Two deaths for the price of one.

Roddy's voice quavered with emotion. "Mothers are *supposed* to help their sons."

Annette steepled her fingers. "Yes, you're right.

Mothers help their children. And now I have to get you the help you need." Annette held out the telephone handset. "Turn yourself in. If you cooperate and make a deal now, maybe you won't spend the rest of your life behind bars."

And you, Annette? Will you turn yourself in too, or let your son bear all the blame?

Roddy sighted the gun at Annette's desk. Corky squawked his head off as Roddy blasted the phone base to smithereens. Roddy's grin shone with pure evil. "That's how much your idea of help is worth." Roddy aimed the gun back at Annette's heart.

Corky screeched, "Roddy's a bad boy! Roddy's a bad boy!"

Roddy aimed the gun at Corky's head. "If you don't shut him up, I will."

Annette screamed, "No!" She pulled Corky into her cleavage as Roddy sighted the gun at the bird's chest. Annette kissed Corky's head and cooed to calm the agitated parrot. "Don't worry, sweetie. Mommy won't let Roddy hurt you."

Roddy waved the gun back and forth as though leading an orchestra. "There's something seriously wrong with you in the head. You love the stinking bird more than Dad, more than me, more than anyone."

Annette scowled. "You're jealous of a bird?"

Roddy sneered. "You wanna save your precious bird? Give me a sample crate." My heart jumped to my throat when he said, "I'll need one after I take care of our one last complication."

Annette dipped a shoulder. "They must all be in the showroom. You took the one from the factory, and the police confiscated it."

Venom laced Roddy's voice. "There were six here, not one. They didn't roll out of the factory on their own." He waved the gun around Annette's office. "Did you use them to pack?"

Annette pointed to the stacks of boxes. "Do you see any crates?"

Roddy spoke through clenched teeth. "Where are they, Big Bird?"

Annette answered his question with one of her own. "If they're not in the mart, where were they before?"

Roddy pointed the gun towards the shipping area. "In the storage bin."

Annette protruded her lower lip and rubbed her chin. "They must still be in the same place as last time. I haven't touched them. If they're still not in the storage bin, my guess is as good as yours."

She was too young to be having a senior moment, so Annette must be doing her dumb blonde routine to save my life. Better late than never to re-discover her conscience. Hopefully, it's not too late.

Roddy tsked. "I've already been in the storage bin. It's empty." Roddy pointed the gun out to the factory. "Come on. You're gonna take me to them."

Annette jerked her head and her cascading hair curtained her eyes again. "Not gonna happen." She pointed to the office door. "If you won't turn yourself in, run for your life. Get in your truck, drive to the border, and lose yourself in Mexico."

Roddy spat. "Give. Me. The. Crate. Now."

Annette's eyes glittered. "No."

Roddy aimed the gun at Corky. "Your choice. Say goodbye to Corky."

Annette put her hand over the bird's head and jutted

her jaw. "You're gonna have to shoot me first."

Roddy dared his mother with a devilish smile. "Think I won't? Go ahead and try me."

Roddy's hand trembled as he pulled the hammer back on the gun. Corky squawked, "Roddy's a bad boy! Roddy's a bad boy." The parrot wriggled out of Annette's clutches, flapped his wings, and took flight.

Roddy aimed for the parrot but the shot went wide and obliterated two cartons stacked next to Annette as she screamed, "Nooooo!" Corky flew right into Roddy's face. Roddy swatted wildly as the bird divebombed the big ape's head. Roddy screamed in agony as Corky dug his razor-sharp claws into the hapless giant's face and used his beak to peck at Roddy's eyelids. But despite the painful attack, Roddy still managed to hold onto the gun.

Bits of Roddy's bloody skin hung on Corky's claws as Roddy grabbed the parrot by his wing and swung him around. Corky bit Roddy's hand and flew to the back of Roddy's head and zeroed into Roddy's crown. Corky dug his claws into Roddy's head and pecked the hapless goon's scalp to a bloody pulp.

Roddy twisted his torso around and smacked the side of the bird's head with the butt of the gun. The bird dropped like a rock to the floor at Roddy's feet. Roddy raised his booted foot over the supine bird ready to squash him like a bug. Annette screamed, "Stop! For God's sake, you're gonna kill him!"

Annette's anguished cry momentarily distracted Roddy. He lurched a couple of steps to the right, but kept his balance and aimed the gun back at Annette's heart. Sparks of rage glittered in Roddy's eyes. "The crates, Big Bird. I'll give you to the count of ten to tell me what you've done with them, or I'll shoot you both dead. I've nothing left to lose, so don't test me. I promise. You and Corky will die." Annette stood rooted to the spot as Roddy began the count backward. "Ten-Nine-Eight-Seven-Six-Five-Four..."

Roddy pulled the hammer back with his thumb and sighted the gun at Annette's head, prepared to shoot at the count of three.

He'd already murdered two people and planned to kill me. Now murdering his mother in cold blood proved no big deal. I couldn't let him. I glanced around Annette's office to assess my options. Corky's travel cage would do if it was closer. Nothing else jumped out. I grabbed the anvil off the floor and tiptoed through Annette's office door. With the element of surprise my sole advantage, I prayed Roddy didn't notice Annette's eyes widen as I put my index finger to my lips.

I crept behind Roddy and aimed for his head, but with my lack of height, I couldn't come close. Dang. I lowered the anvil along with my expectations and eyed his middle, but the padding of his thick waist prevented inflicting much damage. I lowered my arm, wound up with the arc of a discus thrower, and let her rip with all my might. The anvil cracked into the backs of his knees, and Roddy never knew what hit him. The weight of the anvil knocked Roddy off his feet, and he folded faster than a poker player with a losing hand.

Roddy got off a wild shot as he fell, and it brought Corky out of his stupor. The bird flew to Annette's side and screeched, "Corky loves mommy! Corky loves mommy!" An apple-shaped red splotch spread over a stunned Annette Mason's chest as she collapsed two feet in front of her son.

I grabbed the gun out of Roddy's hand and leaned

over his crumpled body. I growled into his ear. "Don't move a muscle. Don't even twitch, or I swear, I'll put more holes in you than a slice of Swiss cheese."

I called nine-one-one to report the shooting while Roddy stayed put, but how long would he stay down? Why isn't a cop ever around when you need one? Ask and ye shall receive. Two minutes later, AJ Yakamura and four LAPD uniforms stormed Annette's office. AJ yelled. "Police! Freeze and drop your weapons."

I dropped the gun at my feet and raised my hands in front of my boobs. "It took you long enough," I smirked. "Next time, try blaring the siren."

A moment later, I fainted.

Chapter Thirty-Three

The incessant beeping roused me groggy and disoriented out of fitful sleep.

A familiar voice chirped a waaaay-too cheery greeting. "Good morning, sunshine. Welcome back."

Welcome back from…? I cracked open an eye and groaned. "Marvelous. If you're standing over me, I must be dead."

My favorite medical examiner chortled her reply. "Good to see you haven't lost your sense of humor yet."

I grumbled. "Who's joking?"

It took too much energy for me to keep up my end of the banter, so I closed my eyes.

Snip leaned over and tsk-tsked as she stuck an ice-cold stethoscope between my boobs. Satisfied my heart still beat, she grasped my swollen left wrist between her index and middle finger to check my pulse rate. She shined a blinding beam from a penlight-sized flashlight in my eyes, and I smacked her hand away.

She said, "With the whack against the cement floor your noggin took, it's amazing all you got is a goose egg on the side of your head and a slight concussion." Snip rubbed the side of her head to demonstrate. "It's a good thing you're such a hard head."

I made a sour face and a kaleidoscope of light lit behind my eyes. I snapped. "I realize your other patients don't talk back, so you're obviously out of practice. But no offense, your bedside manner stinks. Your delivery needs some fine-tuning."

She held out her hands. "Hey, I'm just sayin'."

Friends. Go figure. Geesh.

She glanced at a chart hanging on the bedframe and smiled. "You took a licking, but you're still ticking."

Nothing gets past you, Doctor Death.

Her concerned eyes searched mine. "You doing okay?"

I took a few beats to inventory my issues before I replied. My ability to move was hampered by an aching, heavily bandaged right shoulder and right arm strapped to my side. An IV was stuck in my left arm, and it hurt to move my left wrist. With my midsection tightly wrapped, I wiggled my toes and an electric zap of pain raced the length of my spine. I tried taking a deep breath and almost fainted. I raised my head and the stars exploded behind my eyes. The goose egg-sized knot sent pulsating pain to the right side of my head. I ran a finger over my lips swollen as fat as two inner tubes. I opened my achy jaw and it creaked with the scratch of a rusty gate. My sandpapery tongue felt thick as a brick and too big for my mouth. I jiggled my loose teeth with the tip of my tongue. Even my hair hurt. I massaged my temples to ease the jackhammer banging inside my head. Otherwise, doing peachy. "It's a tossup if I have the mother of all hangovers, or I've been run over by a train."

Snip laughed. "Close, but no cigar."

I inventoried my surroundings and realized the bed I occupied wasn't mine. "Where am I?"

She said, "Providence Saint Joseph Hospital in Burbank."

I shuddered as memories of the gruesome events of

the day before came flooding back.

Snip said, "Try not to move around unnecessarily. Your surgery lasted for over four hours. The more you lay still and rest your body, the faster your wounds will heal."

I gulped. "Besides the gunshot wound, there's something else?"

She counted them on the fingers of her left hand. "You also have three cracked ribs. And let's not leave out a concussion, bruises, and contusions."

I smirked. "Another item on my bucket list of things I wanted to experience. Now I can cross it off."

She waggled a finger and tsked. "Sarcasm is such an unbecoming character trait."

Snip's turn arrived in our eye-rolling contest. "Har-har, Miss Smarty Pants. Your arm broke your fall. You've got a sprained wrist from the fall, but that didn't crack those three ribs."

I sighed. "Roddy yanked me off my feet and carried me under his arm. I wiggled trying to get loose, but the more I squirmed, the tighter his grip. He squeezed tight enough to crack three ribs. I'm not surprised. He almost squeezed the life out of me. It's a wonder he didn't break me in half."

She grinned. "Not moving fast enough to suit him?"

It hurt too much to laugh. "Nope. I refused to do as I was told and he got pissed."

The pain in my head clanged loud as a church bell when she laughed out loud. "You seem to elicit the same response from a lot of people."

Another comedian. Doc Death doing stand-up. "Funny as an aneurism."

Doctor Death continued the inventory of my

injuries. "You have three loose teeth, each lip required eight stitches, and your jaw needed re-alignment. You're lucky the jaw wasn't broken, or they'd wire it shut." Snip's smile went all the way to her kind eyes. "You not talking for three weeks? Hard to imagine you quiet for three minutes. And I'd hold off on running any marathons for a few weeks, but otherwise, you're in tip-top shape."

Who says doctors have no sense of humor? "You should see the other guy."

Snip blew the air out of her cheeks. "I have. The other guy is a train wreck." She grinned. "Next time, pick on someone your own size."

I winced, trying not to laugh. "Don't make me laugh. It hurts too much, but it's funny you said it."

She gave me an odd look. "Why?"

"Not long after I started asking questions, I ran into Roddy in the mart parking structure. He warned me to back off and threatened me if I didn't. He came at me and I whacked him in the nuts with my laptop case. While he rolled around on the ground, I told him to pick on someone his own size."

Snip pursed her lips. "You inflicted a lot more damage this time. In addition to his broken nose and two shiners, thanks to your anvil whack on the back of his knees, he'll be walking with a cane and a limp for the foreseeable future." Snip closed her eyes and shuddered. "But nothing compared to the parrot. Mr. Mason's surgery lasted for nine hours. He needed over three hundred stitches to heal the pecks on his face and scalp. And until the bandages are removed, it's iffy whether they saved his right eye."

I asked, "And Annette?"

As someone always tasked to deliver bad news, Snip's sigh came from the depths of her soul. "Mrs. Mason didn't make it."

I struggled to sit up and choked on my words. "What are you talking about? The EMT guys arrived three minutes after I called nine-one-one."

Snip softened her tone, but the gentle delivery didn't make the clinical information any less painful to hear. "Still too late. She'd already bled out. The bullet struck at the junction of the super vena cava and subclavian arteries in the chest cavity. She never had a chance."

My eyes filled as a lightning strike of guilt pierced my heart. "Oh my God, no. She's dead and it's my fault."

Snip puffed out her cheeks. "Mrs. Mason and her son destroyed one another. Their collision course is one they created, not you." Snip pursed her lips. "You didn't pull the trigger. Her son did."

Nice try bucko, but no dice. "No, but I might as well have. The whack with the anvil delivered the bullet all the same."

Snip dipped her head. "The outcome would be the same with you or without you." I pushed her hand away as Snip brushed a stubborn lock of hair out of my eyes.

I snarled. "Don't patronize me."

Snip's eyes widened with alarm. "Take it easy, kiddo or your injuries will not heal correctly."

I pressed my bandaged fingers over my heart. "A wound this deep will never heal."

Chapter Thirty-Four

AJ Yakamura knocked on the door and stuck her head in. "Good morning. Are you strong enough to give your statement now?" And they say cops lack a sense of humor.

Not even close, but the sooner I got this over with, the better. "Good news. I can pencil you in as I don't have any other plans."

Snip put the instruments back in her medical bag and gave AJ a stern lecture. "She's still pretty weak. Don't overdo it. You may need to come back for her to finish it."

Snip patted my cheek with a love tap and slid into her jacket. "I'll be back as soon as my shift is over." She grabbed her purse and waved goodbye. "Try not to get into any more trouble between now and then."

I fired back. "Try to improve your bedside manner between now and then."

She held out her palms. "My patients never complain."

I rolled my eyes and laughed. "Dead men tell no tales."

My favorite coroner grinned and gave me the middle finger salute as she walked out the door.

AJ took a small tape recorder out of her messenger bag and put it on a metal tray table stationed on the left side of the bed. She sat in a visitor's chair between the table and the bed. She studied me over the rims of the eyeglasses perched on the end of her flat nose. "Considering everything you went through, you look pretty good. Are you?"

I winced as I made a so-so sign with a slight flip of my wrist.

An exhausting hour and a half later and all talked out, I finished giving my statement. AJ stowed the recorder back in the messenger bag and smiled. "I appreciate you giving me your statement now. It's important to give it while the incident is still fresh in your mind."

Still fresh in my mind? She must be joking. The faces of those three dead people were indelibly seared into my memory. I'd never wake up from this nightmare.

AJ hefted the messenger bag and stood. "I'll get this transcribed and you can sign the written copy once you're back on your feet." She studied my battered face. "Get some rest and I'll check in on you tomorrow."

Already at half-mast, my eyes snapped wide open at the sound of a knock on the door followed by a familiar male voice. "Are you well enough for a visitor, or is later better?"

Was I dreaming? Only one way to find out. "Now is dandy. Come on in and join the party. We're having a ball." I pressed the button with one of three unbandaged fingers and the mechanized bed whirred into a sitting position. With the bathroom door open, I caught a glimpse of a face in the mirror. Yikes. Look at the scary broad with the two shiners and skin the tone of wet cement. OMG! It's me. Yikes. Perhaps it was a tad premature to invite a guest in, especially this particular one? I jounced my head to clear my addled brain and the pain almost knocked me unconscious. Wait. What? Especially which particular one? Must be the meds messing with my head. Right? Yep. No other explanation. Good grief.

He held a gorgeous bouquet of daisies mixed with babies' breath in the crook of his muscular arm. Who told him daisies are my favorite flowers? Not me. His easy smile filled the room and warmed my soul like snuggling into a warm, comfy cardigan on a rainy day. The wide grin creased the sexy five o'clock shadow already darkening his chiseled face as he closed the door behind him. He had broad shoulders, a narrow waist, and slim hips.

At six-foot-two and all toned muscle, dark-haired and mustachioed LAPD Homicide Detective Miguel Martinez stood out in a crowded room. He took off his suit jacket and his biceps bulged beneath his dress shirt as he loosened his tie. His trousers fit snugly around his hips and hugged his fine tush. Hmm. Maybe I might not be as close to death as I appeared.

The corners of his intelligent obsidian eyes crinkled when he smiled, but they never miss much. The tips of his lips twitched as I patted the bedhead hair sticking out as if I'd put my finger in an electric socket. The wild woman of Borneo decked out in a snazzy hospital gown. Oye.

The cop and I go back a couple of years. Miguel Martinez was the detective in charge of the case when I discovered buying office executive Bunny Frank's corpse in the mart parking structure elevator trussed like a Thanksgiving turkey with a Gotham Swimwear bikini stuffed in her mouth. The detective and I had a rollercoaster-worthy bumpy relationship. For some inexplicable reason, he didn't cotton to my interfering with his investigation or telling him how to do his job. I solved the case and captured the killer, yet the detective still didn't do the happy dance. Go figure. Once the case closed, we lost touch with one another.

He strode across the length of the room and I instinctively pulled the covers to my neck. He stood uncomfortably at the side of the bed with the awkwardness of a gawky teenager and thrust the bouquet into my hands. A spark of electricity sizzled between us as his fingertips brushed my palm. He held my gaze with his honest, open eyes for a few moments. The temperature in the room shot up to scorching until he broke his eyes away and found something fascinating to study on his shoes.

He arced an arm around the room and motioned to the beige walls. "Hospital rooms are way too dreary." He tipped his head to the flowers, and a cute dimple cratered his right cheek when he smiled. "These will brighten the place a bit."

I clutched the bouquet to my chest and managed a tiny smile. "Daisies are my favorite flowers. These are lovely. And they do brighten the dull room." I arched a brow. "Do you make it a habit to bring all your witnesses flowers?"

The blush crept from his neck to his widow's peak. "Only the memorable ones."

I teased. "Do you have many of those?"

He laughed. "A few, but believe me, you're in a class all of your own."

I could take his answer a couple of ways. Better not to ask. I narrowed my eyes. "It's nice to see you again, but all kidding aside detective, to what do I owe the honor? Are you taking over the case from detective Yakamura?"

He shook his head no. "Actually..."

AJ interrupted him. "Actually, it's Captain Martinez now."

I tried to applaud, but the IV got in the way. "Congratulations!" I smiled slyly. "Surely my little contribution helped your career along."

Martinez threw his head back and laughed out loud. "Without a doubt, the determining factor in my promotion."

I narrowed my eyes. "Captain Martinez, you still need to answer my question. What brings you here?"

He pointed to AJ. "Detective Yakamura and I interviewed Mr. Mason earlier."

I blinked my confusion. "You're in two separate precincts, so how are you working together?"

He angled his head at AJ. "We're not in separate precincts anymore. I requested Detective Yakamura be transferred from the Pacific division to Rampart."

Wait. What Transfer? I racked my overwrought brain. Nah. Even in my present condition, I'd remember something so important. But right now, with Martinez standing so close I grew heady just inhaling his manly citrusy-scented cologne? Nosiree. The jury is still out on my addled brain.

AJ detailed her history with Martinez. "Captain Martinez and I went through the academy together. The transfer is a big deal. Rampart is a much bigger division and gets a lot more high-profile cases than the Pacific. If I catch a few of those big cases and close them, it's a fast track to promotion." AJ beamed a hundred-thousand-watt smile at Martinez. "Thanks to Captain Martinez, my career received a big boost."

AJ took the bouquet of daisies out of my hands and grinned like a loon. "Let me find a vase to put these into while you two chat. I'm sure you have lots to catch up on."

Wait. Huh? She said *while we chat*? *Lots to catch up on*? Good grief. AJ Yakamura playing cupid? Whoda thunk? Holy guacamole.

Martinez eyed her strangely. No kidding, Captain. Get in the boat and row.

A touch of panic raised the timbre of his deep voice to a mouse-squeak. "Ok, but don't take all day. We still need to arrange for Mr. Mason's transfer to the jail ward at County General and get back to the cop shop in time for the afternoon staff meeting."

Hmm. Is it possible that a big, brave policeman is afraid to be alone with little me?

AJ snapped a two-finger salute and slipped out the door.

Martinez sat in the chair on the right side of the bed and steepled his long, bony fingers. "Are you feeling okay?"

"As if I've been run over by a train." The cavalier retort danced off my tongue by rote. Since all my family and friends no doubt will be asking the same thing, I ought to record my response.

His eyes searched mine. "Mr. Mason is a big, strong man. You're lucky he didn't kill you with his bare hands."

It sure wasn't from lack of him trying.

I saw stars as I wiggled my brows. "Exactly the reason I snuck up behind him." My swollen lips ached as I smiled sweetly. "My mother didn't raise stupid children."

He scratched the back of his head. "This is what now? Must be your third murder?"

"Might be a few more. But who's counting?" I gave him the big eyes. "I don't go looking for trouble. It seems to find me."

He mused to himself out loud. "Maybe it's a sign."

Which one? Astrological? Neon? Traffic? Blinking? I parroted. "A Sign?"

He tugged on the ends of his mustache. "You're nosy, persistent, and good at figuring things out. You should apply to the academy. A few years on the force, you'd make a good detective."

Me in a uniform? Me packing a gun? Imagine my mother's reaction to the good news. She'd put my boat up for sale in a minute and have me locked in my old room for at least a decade. I slit my eyes. "Are you making fun of me or recruiting me?"

He laughed and waved off the idea with a flick of a wrist. "Neither. Who am I kidding? You'd never last a day."

I wasn't interested in the job, but the nerve of him. I glared with righteous indignation. "Why the hell not?"

He lifted a shoulder. "Following orders doesn't seem to be in your DNA."

He'd get no argument from me.

My heart thudded as he leaned over and brushed a lock of hair out of my eyes. His deep voice went reedy. "You need to quit doing this. You realize dead is forever, right?" He cleared his throat with a few coughs. "Will you be hospitalized long?"

I stretched my lips' stitches to their limits, and it hurt like hell when I grinned. "If you're planning another visit, roses are always a good choice."

He blushed beet red when he answered. "No, but I've got a yen for Chinese food. You recover, and if you want to, we'll go back to the great place you took me to across the street from the mart." He tapped his index fingers to his thumbs up and down a few times to demonstrate. "As I recall, you're a regular whiz with chopsticks. Maybe you'll teach me the trick?" He twisted his fingers into a knot and laughed. "I've tried my best to remember your technique, but so far, my efforts have been an abysmal failure. All I've accomplished is dropping lo mein in my lap. Whaddya say? Any hope for a guy who's all thumbs and as uncoordinated as me?"

Serve the soy sauce with the Sichuan, Shirley. Things are about to get interesting.

Chapter Thirty-Five

I gingerly eased my tush into my regular seat at the Yenta table and let Sonia distribute the coffees. I'd been released from the hospital two weeks ago, but an arthritic tortoise still moved faster than me. With my ribs still tightly wrapped, I found breathing deep rather difficult, especially sitting. Still a bit tender to the touch, but the gunshot wound healed nicely. I can finally bend my right arm and raise it to level with my boobs. But it will be a while before I'll be able to lift it over my head. I won't be hefting any heavy sample crates for the rest of the season.

My mother wanted me to recuperate in Miami, but a five-hour cross-country flight? Out of the question. I begged Uncle Barry to intercede on my behalf with my parents and convince them not to come to LA. I originally declined Queenie's offer to stay at her house while I recovered. Independent me wanted to be in my own bed and let the gentle sway of the houseboat rock me back to health. Thank goodness she insisted. I would never have been able to manage on my own. Until a few days ago, I still needed help getting in and out of the shower and dressing. Queenie will be chauffeuring me around in the immediate future. I won't be driving for at least a month.

Hope gave me the once-over. "Are you doing okay?"

An excellent question. I took a few beats to consider my reply. "Physically, I'm stronger each day." I pointed to my head and heart. "Not so much."

Sonia slit her eyes. "Why?"

I discovered something fascinating in my coffee cup. "Annette."

Joan peered over her glasses, like a professor disappointed with her star pupil's response. "Annette? What about her?"

I hung my head. "If I minded my own business, Annette's blood wouldn't be on my hands."

Joan tsked. "Horse puckey."

Queenie pursed her lips. "The whack on the head must have caused major brain damage."

I barked. "Meaning?"

Queenie smacked the table and half the coffee sloshed out of her cup. "There's no other plausible explanation for you making such an idiotic remark"

Since I still needed her help getting around, I swallowed the sarcastic retort on the tip of my tongue. "Before I stuck my nose into Annette's building, two people already died, two lives ruined, and a business destroyed by one man's jealousy and thirst for revenge. With my contribution, the body count climbed. A third person lost her life and another will spend the rest of his life in prison."

Joan gave me a round of applause. "Wow. Congratulations. Pretty darned impressive. You're a regular one-woman wrecking ball."

Sonia gave me the big eyes. "And *you're* single-handedly responsible for it all?"

I clucked my tongue. "Don't put words in my mouth."

Joan surveyed the table. "I dunno. Whaddya you girls say? Sure sounds like what she said."

Sonia glared at me. "It is *exactly*, and you're freaking *wrong*."

I dipped my head. "Ok. Let me clarify my statement. I'm not responsible for Lissa and Bobby's murders. Those are on Roddy. But Annette? If I didn't go to her building, she'd still be alive."

Queenie twisted her torso, as though trying to work a painful kink out. "And maybe not. You said Annette and Roddy argued over keeping Barely There open. Say things heated up a lot more, and Roddy killed her anyway?"

Hope pursed her lips. "The way you described it, it sounded as if Roddy didn't mean to shoot. The gun went off as he fell."

Bingo. Bongo. Jackpot. Ding-ding. Give the girl a kewpie doll. Finally, one of these dunderheads understood the point. I twirled a ta-da with my hands. "*Exactly*. And the reason he fell?" I jabbed my middle finger into my cleavage. "*I* whacked him in the back of his knees with an anvil."

Joan pursed her lips. "And what's that have to do with the price of tea in Timbuktu? You didn't put the gun in his hand, he did." She pointed her index finger under my nose. "Don't you dare let him off the hook. Roddy Mason is the one responsible for this tragedy, not you."

I sucked in my cheeks. "The jury is still out."

Queenie tapped the tip of her nose with her index finger. "Too many things don't make any sense."

The other Yentas chorused, "Such as?"

Queenie smacked a fist into her palm. "Any guess to Roddy's motive for killing Lissa and Bobby?"

The other yentas shrugged, so I took the baton. "In the beginning? Revenge was the catalyst of unrequited love. But Lissa's murder? No question about it. To prevent her from signing the partnership papers."

Hope crossed her eyes. "Who loved who and which one is the revenge?"

I gave her the big eyes. "No matter what Roddy tried to win Lissa over, she blew him off."

Sonia's expression said the hospital released me prematurely. "Besides constantly insulting her, what else?"

I tapped a spoon on my coffee cup. "For one thing, Roddy sent Lissa the flowers every morning. Not Bobby."

Hope asked, "I can't keep score. Who didn't love who?"

I snickered. "Lissa didn't love either of them."

Joan clucked her tongue. "The only person Lissa Charney *ever* loved? Lissa Charney."

Sonia sighed. "Too bad Roddy never figured it out."

Hope shook her head. "If you're thinking with your heart instead of your brain, you're not thinking straight. If you're in love, nothing makes sense, but you don't care."

I continued my analysis. "After the flowers failed to help him win Lissa's heart, Roddy tried eliminating the competition by siccing the INS on Bobby. Bobby told Roddy he asked Lissa to help him stay in the country by marrying him, but she said no. Roddy used it as leverage to force Bobby to kill Lissa, but Bobby refused. The love triangle on its own is bad enough, but the partnership agreement sent Roddy over the edge."

Sonia held up a finger. "Wait a minute. Now you're

saying money and not love motivated the killer?"

I spouted the reasons as if they were the daily lunch specials on a menu. "No. Think of a combination plate. One. Roddy loved Lissa, but she didn't love Roddy back. Two. She preferred Bobby to Roddy. Three. Lissa stealing Roddy's part of the business. Roddy's solution? Get rid of both Bobby and Lissa. Four. Who pissed off Roddy more? Bobby, refusing to kill Lissa or the INS who didn't work fast enough deporting Bobby? A tossup. Five. Roddy stole Bobby's cell phone and used it to call in the anonymous tips to the cops. Roddy framed Joan for Lissa's murder, but she's cleared. Six. Next, he framed Bobby for the murder. The cops traced the calls back to Bobby's phone. Roddy switched his nail gun for Bobby's."

Joan pointed at herself in surprise. "Whoa. Roddy pointed the police at *me*? Why?"

I bunched my shoulders. "Remember the morning you and Lissa had the run-in here at A Jolt of Java? Roddy and Annette sat at the table behind ours. He heard the argument and pegged you a perfect patsy for Lissa's murder."

Queenie wrinkled her nose. "The police cleared Joan, so, Roddy framed his mother? A thoroughly rotten son."

I shook my head. "Nope. Annette framed herself."

Hope speared me with a look as though my coffee had been spiked with something a lot stronger than sugar. "Why?"

Recognition lit Sonia's eyes. "Mama bear protecting her cub."

I gave her a round of applause. "Bingo. Give the girl a kewpie doll."

Queenie scrunched her eyes. "Why?"

I fluttered a napkin. "The threatening note."

Joan wrinkled her nose. "What's the threatening note have to do with anything?"

I shrugged. "Annette's reaction to the note said it all. She went white as a sheet when I showed it to her. She stumbled and bumbled, but she lied through her teeth, either to protect herself or Roddy. I discovered the typewriter in Roddy's office, and it explained a lot of other things. The reason the police took Annette in for questioning, for example. She set herself up. Say she found the bloody crate in Roddy's office and realized it implicated her baby boy. So, she put it in her car trunk. She used a phone in Roddy's office, which turned out to be Bobby's cell, to call in an anonymous tip on herself. The police later found traces of Lissa's blood in Roddy's office, but not in Annette's. Annette wrongly assumed the crate contained the murder weapon when she framed herself with the police. But Roddy switched his nail gun for Bobby's and put another one in the crate. Roddy removed Bobby's nail gun from his truck and planted his nail gun in its place. But the police didn't discover the real murder weapon until after Bobby's death when they searched his truck. Bobby figured out Roddy killed Lissa and threatened to go to the cops. Roddy freaks out and tells his mother. Annette stood ready to accept the blame for Lissa's murder, but the police released her after the evidence fell apart. So, to protect her son, she helped Roddy kill Bobby. Diabetic Annette came up with the idea to make Bobby's murder look as if he committed suicide. She gave Roddy the insulin and instructed him on the way to dispense it. With the same letters mistyped on both notes, Bobby's suicide note was typed on the same typewriter as my threatening note. But I didn't find the typewriter in Bobby's apartment. I discovered it in Roddy's office. So, either Annette or Roddy typed both notes. Annette lied about the reason Roddy wasn't at the meeting. She said he was busy with a construction problem. But the truth is, she realized Roddy killed Lissa Friday afternoon."

Queenie said, "So, Annette wasn't responsible for Lissa's murder."

I shook my head no. "No. Roddy murdered Lissa all on his own. In one fell swoop, he destroyed his life and Annette's best option to save her company."

Joan asked, "Lissa hated Roddy. How did Roddy get Lissa alone to kill her?"

I held up my index finger. "Remember, Roddy was trained as an auto mechanic. He found Lissa's car in the mart parking structure. He removed the distributor cap from her engine. Roddy magically appeared after Lissa's car wouldn't start. If she waited for the Auto Club, she'd be late for their meeting. Since they were both going to the same meeting, Roddy offered to drive her. But instead of going to the Barely There factory, Roddy took her out to one of the Mason Construction sites and killed her. He stuffed her into a crate, took her back to the mart, and the rest is history." I snapped my fingers. "By the way, in all the excitement, I forgot to tell you guys something big. Snip gave me the lowdown on the wound in Lissa's neck." I widened my eyes. "Snip said she's extracted some strange things from patients in her career, but nothing topped this. I bet you guys never guess in a million years. The tip of Corky's beak."

The Yentas did a double-take. Joan choked out the words. "How could *Corky's beak* get into Lissa's neck?"

Sonia tipped her head. "Now I'm completely confused. So, then Annette and Roddy *did* kill Lissa together?"

I shook my head no. "Nope. Corky was with Roddy when he murdered Lissa."

Hope blinked rapidly as if something was in her eyes. "I read African Gray parrots are one-master pets. It seems kind of odd he'd go with Roddy."

I nodded my agreement. "Normally it's true. But Roddy and Corky grew up together as brothers. Anyway, to answer your question, Annette made a dental appointment in the morning and forgot Corky's vet appointment was at the same time. So, Annette asked Roddy to take Corky to the vet for her. This complicated things considerably for Roddy. He can't say gee whiz, Annette, sorry. I'll be too busy murdering Lissa Charney to take Corky to the vet. "

Sonia looked at me oddly. "Are you saying Roddy took the bird with him?"

I shook my head yes. "Yeah. He couldn't leave the parrot at the mart or take him back to Annette early. So, he took the bird with him to the construction site."

Joan rubbed her chin. "Ok, but it still doesn't explain the bird's beak getting into Lissa's neck. Don't they keep the parrot in a cage?"

I dipped my head. "This stumped me too until I remembered what Annette said the day I went out to question her. Annette said Corky doesn't fancy being in his cage and normally squawks a storm until he's let out. I'm guessing he squawked enough and Roddy took him out of his travel cage and let him loose after Roddy parked the truck. Corky followed Roddy to the murder site. Lissa and Corky hated one another. Maybe Lissa put up a fight when Roddy threatened her with the nail gun, and Corky attacked her trying to protect Roddy."

Sonia said, "Well, it explains Corky's chipped beak and the reason he kept saying Roddy's a bad boy. Roddy's a bad boy."

Hope tapped her cheeks. "What happened to Corky with Annette gone?"

Joan arched a brow. "Need a roommate?"

Sonia said, "Wouldn't Annette's husband take Corky?"

I pursed my lips. "Nope. Corky is at an exotic bird sanctuary not far from the San Diego Wild Animal Park."

Joan snorted. "Pity the attendant stuck taking care of such a nasty bird."

Hope said, "The poor bird must be heartsick. I'm sure he doesn't understand why he's not home with Annette. I read his breed is extremely sensitive to change. My guess is he won't last too long. "Hope shook her head. "Annette was my pick as Lissa's killer. After the police released her, I almost fainted." Hope looked at me and grinned. "Glad you're the sleuth of the group and not me. I'm not too good at this sniffing around."

Sonia shook her head no. "Not true. Annette is not exactly an innocent bystander. She gave Roddy the motive for Lissa's murder *and* played a major role in Bobby's death."

Hope shook her head. "Maybe so, but I ended up getting it completely wrong. Twice no less."

Sonia dipped her head. "Twice?"

Hope said, "Yeah. Twice. Remember, I also kept Eileen in the running." Hope patted herself on the back and laughed. "Who wins a medal for being as wrong as the cops?"

Joan batted her eyes. "Boy, talk about a shocker. Eileen and Adrian are mother and son!"

Queenie clucked her tongue. "How did I manage to miss this one? Adrian is her spitting image. Same brown hair, hazel eyes, rangy build." She smacked her palm against her forehead. "He even has the same hitch in his walk like her." Queenie tapped her nose with her fingertip. "Bet Adrian is the reason for the falling out with Eileen's family and her moving west."

Sonia said, "Well, this explains Adrian's willingness to lie for Eileen. But why would either of them lie in the first place?"

I bunched my shoulders. "Given her threatening calls to Lissa, I don't blame her for lying. The truth about the day of her flight put Eileen on the top of my suspect list."

Sonia said, "I was stumped by who vandalized your boat. I swore it was Bobby."

I widened my eyes. "He was my prime pick. But boy oh boy, I figured it all wrong. I confronted Bobby about my car and boat being vandalized, and he denied having anything to do with either one. His injury occurred before my car problem. I accused him of damaging my boat, and he said he couldn't swim and that water terrified him. He said he only showered, never bathed in a tub. He didn't scuba dive and had never stepped foot on a boat, let alone owned one. At the time, I didn't believe a word he said. Turns out, he told the truth. If I'd believed his story, things could have ended differently. I guess my nana is right. Things happen for a reason, even if we don't always understand why. If not for my boat being vandalized, and Audrey Camarillo getting me the information on the Mason's boat registration, Roddy gets away with everything Scot free."

Hope smiled sweetly. "Cut yourself some slack. With virtually nothing to go on, you kept at it until you solved the case and captured the killer."

Queenie treated me to a salute with her coffee cup. "The murder magnet of the mart has solved another one."

I grinned. "This time I went to Cleveland by way of Cairo, but I finally figured it all out."

Joan smirked. "You sure you don't wanna make a career change and join the force? A rumor's going around the swimwear aisle that a cute police Captain recently recruited you."

No way. "So far, nothing's convinced me to swap my swimwear samples and crates for a nightstick and a gun." I grinned. "But the cute police Captain and I are meeting for lunch at Blue China Moon Tuesday. Stay tuned for later developments. I'll report back if his recruiting skills are any better than the way he handles chopsticks."

A word about the author...

Born in the Big Apple, award-winning cozy mystery author Susie Black now calls sunny Southern California home. Like the protagonist in her Holly Swimsuit Mystery Series, Susie is a successful apparel sales executive. Susie began telling stories as soon as she learned to talk. Now she's telling all the stories from her garment industry experiences in humorous mysteries.

She reads, writes, and speaks Spanish, albeit with an accent that sounds like Mildred from Michigan went on a Mexican vacation and is trying to fit in with the locals. Since life without pizza and ice cream as her core food groups wouldn't be worth living, she's a dedicated walker to keep her girlish figure. A voracious reader, she's also an avid stamp collector. Susie lives with a highly intelligent man and has one incredibly brainy but smart-aleck adult son who inexplicably blames his sarcasm on an inherited genetic defect.

Looking for more? Visit her website: http://www.authorsusieblack.com Sign up for her reader list and receive a free swimwear fit guide. Or reach her at mysteries_@authorsusieblack.com

Thank you for purchasing
this publication of The Wild Rose Press, Inc.

For questions or more information
contact us at
info@thewildrosepress.com.

The Wild Rose Press, Inc.
www.thewildrosepress.com